More praise for
ROBIN PAIGE'S
Victorian Mysteries

"I read it with enjoyment . . . I found myself burning for the injustices of it, and caring what happened to the people."
—Anne Perry

"I could ... ... urder & Mayhem

"An intriguing mystery . . . Skillfully unraveled."
—Jean Hager, author of *Blooming Murder*

"Absolutely riveting . . . An extremely articulate, genuine mystery, with well-drawn, compelling characters."
—Meritorious Mysteries

"An absolutely charming book . . . An adventure well worth your time . . . You're sure to enjoy it."   —*Romantic Times*

DEATH
AT
DAISY'S FOLLY

Robin Paige

BERKLEY PRIME CRIME, NEW YORK

DEATH AT DAISY'S FOLLY

A Berkley Prime Crime Book / published by arrangement with the author

PRINTING HISTORY
Berkley Prime Crime edition / February 1997

The Penguin Putnam Inc. World Wide Web site address is
http://www.penguinputnam.com

ISBN: 0-425-15671-0

Berkley Prime Crime Books are published
by The Berkley Publishing Group,
a division of Penguin Putnam Inc.,
375 Hudson Street, New York, New York 10014.
The name BERKLEY PRIME CRIME and the
BERKLEY PRIME CRIME design are trademarks
belonging to Penguin Putnam Inc.

PRINTED IN THE UNITED STATES OF AMERICA

ACKNOWLEDGMENTS

Our thanks once again to Ruby Hild of the village of Dedham, in Essex, whose generous loan of bed, board, and library card makes our research trips infinitely more comfortable and productive. Thanks also to Prime Crime editor Natalee Rosenstein, for believing in us, and to our agent Deborah Schneider, for her support and encouragement.

Susan and Bill Albert
AKA Robin Paige

CAST OF CHARACTERS

PRINCIPAL CHARACTERS

Albert Edward (Bertie), *Prince of Wales (later King Edward VII)*

Lady Frances (Daisy) Brooke, *Countess of Warwick*

Lord Francis Greville Brooke, *Earl of Warwick*

Sir Charles Sheridan

Miss Kathryn Ardleigh, *aka Beryl Bardwell*

GUESTS AT EASTON LODGE

Lord Bradford Marsden

Lady Verena Rochdale

Lord Malcolm Rochdale

Lady Celia Rochdale

Lord Reginald Wallace

Lady Felicia Metcalf

Lady Lillian Forsythe

Sir Friedrich Temple

Sir Thomas Cobb

Mrs. Milford Knightly

Mr. Milford Knightly

Mr. Samuel Isaacson

Mrs. Eleanor (Ellie) Marsden Farley

Lieutenant Andrew Kirk-Smythe

SERVANTS

Harry Gordon, *groom to the Prince of Wales*

Lawrence Quibbley, *valet and mechanic to Lord Bradford Marsden*

Amelia, *lady's maid to Miss Kathryn Ardleigh*

Richards, *valet to Lord Reginald Wallace*

Winnie Wospottle, *chief laundress*

Wickett, *Easton Lodge coachman*

Marsh, *Easton Lodge footman*

Meg, *Easton Lodge laundry maid*

DEATH
AT
DAISY'S FOLLY

1

Death surprises us in the midst of our hopes.

—THOMAS FULLER
Gnomologia, 1732

A cock was crowing in the coop at the foot of the dark orchard when Harry Gordon, groom to His Highness the Prince of Wales, entered the stable. Inside, the air was warm after the early morning chill, scented with the earthy fragrance of horse and hay, and in the gloom Harry could hear the delicate music of pigeons cooing and the gentle *whuffle* of a horse. In all of his fifteen years, Harry had found no better place on a frosty morning than the inside of a grand stable.

The stables here at Easton Lodge were not as large or as modern as those at Sandringham, where His Highness's three great sires stood to stud, servicing something like a hundred mares a year in addition to the Prince's own brood stock. But the Easton Lodge stables were not inconsiderable. The Countess of Warwick, whose family home this was, kept her own horses here, together with the tall chestnut hunter left by the Prince for his frequent visits. This morning, the stable was full of horses brought in for any of the weekend guests who might choose to ride.

Harry walked down the aisle between the shoulder-high wooden stalls, admiring the handsome horses and still marveling at the amazing fortune that had brought him here, so far from home. Until a month ago, he had been one of the dozen or so Sandringham stableboys, assigned to curry and

feed His Royal Highness's horses and muck out the stalls.
He had never been farther from the estate than the village
school two miles away, and that for only the few obligatory
years required to spell his tedious way through the *Royal
Reader*. Having emerged from his education nearly unlet-
tered, he had gone to service in the Sandringham stables, and
had yet to earn sufficient holiday to make the half-day walk
to the nearby market town.

But all that was changed, and now the whole world lay
at Harry's feet. A few weeks ago, he had saved the Princess
of Wales from a nasty fall by grasping at the reins of her
rearing horse, frightened by a stable cat. The Prince and Princess, known for their loyalty toward those who served them
well, had thanked Harry graciously. The next day, Princess
Alexandra had sent his mother, an undercook in the Sandringham kitchens, a basket of jellies and sweets, with a
handwritten note of praise for her son's courage. The day
after that, the chief steward of the stables had summoned the
fifteen-year-old boy, bestowed on him a smart new livery,
and instructed him to make himself ready to join the Royal
entourage. Harry was to travel with the Prince and attend His
Highness's horses, wherever they might be stabled.

Harry's remarkable elevation in rank had been the proud-
est moment of his young life, and that of his mother, as well.
Her son's unexpected distinction gave her something to boast
of over tea in the servants' hall.

"So 'andsome in 'is livery, my 'Arry is," she was heard
to tell her gossips in the kitchen, "that 'e's bound to catch
th' eye o' th' Queen when th' Prince goes next t' Balmoral.
Then 'e'll be raised to 'is proper station as a Royal footman,
'e will, and 'e'll powder 'is 'air an' wear pink poplin knee
breeches an' shiny silver 'paulettes th' size o' pot lids.''

With or without epaulettes, Harry was proud to be num-
bered among the Prince's traveling household. At Sandringham, the stableboys were at the bottom of the servants'
hierarchy, "grubbin' i' the muck an' mire," as his mother
said, far below the elevation of the senior staff—the Upper
Ten, or the Uppers, as they were called. Life on the lowest
rung of this social ladder often entailed cold food, scanty
victuals, and meager holidays. But on tour with the Prince,

Harry had discovered to his delight, his life was quite different. Here at Easton, for instance, where distinctions of rank were observed belowstairs as carefully as they were above, Harry, a mere groom, outranked not only the Countess's stableboys and grooms, but her ladyship's chief groom as well—or so it seemed to Harry. At meals and between, he was awarded all the honors befitting his status, such as slices of grouse and pheasant left from the table abovestairs, and magnificent sweets, and even a glass of the estate's best home-brewed beer, served by a solicitous kitchen maid with a seductive smile. For Harry, life had suddenly become very sweet.

The Royal stall which housed Paradox, the Prince's hunter, was marked with the Prince's insignia. Harry stopped before it, set down the wooden bucket filled with oats, and cocked his head, frowning slightly. In the dimness, Paradox was moving about, stamping a nervous forefoot, flicking an anxious tail. Something had disturbed him. It was none of the Easton grooms or stableboys, Harry knew. They were a lazy lot and had arrived at the servants' breakfast late, accepting their reprimand with sleepy-eyed equanimity. It was none of the gentlemen, either, for although one or another might rise for a dawn canter across the Essex hills, last night's entertainment—parlor games, Harry had understood from the footmen's sly comments at breakfast—had been late and boisterous. Breakfast was already laid upstairs for the earliest risers, but Harry would have wagered a tanner that none were yet out and about.

He'd have lost his money. While the young groom was still pondering the horse's nervousness, a nearby door opened with a creak. A man—a gentleman wearing Norfolk tweeds and a shooting cap, a stick under his arm—was briefly silhouetted against the light, then slipped inside and closed the door. He moved furtively, and Harry's frown became a knowing grin. Surreptitious assignations were commonplace at country house parties, according to the footmen who had reported on last night's frolic. While Harry personally felt that such a rendezvous was more appropriate to a lady's chamber, behind a discreetly closed door and between scented sheets, he could also imagine that a more daring lady, or one whose husband had a jealous turn, might prefer to carry on her amorous intrigues somewhere else—in the straw, even. Harry grew warm, recalling the brazen allure of the kitchen maid who had placed her hand on his—

But now was not the moment for such thoughts, pleasant as they were. Silently, he raised the wooden bar and slipped into the Royal stall, ducking under Paradox's warm belly. If a lady were expected, she would no doubt soon appear, and it would not be prudent of Harry to make his presence known. Best wait in the stall until the business were over. But Harry had as much curiosity as the next man, and he wanted to see which of the ladies had consented to a tryst in the stable. Was it the red-haired one he'd glimpsed sweeping across the croquet lawn yesterday afternoon, her hair like flaming embers? He had heard that red-haired women were looser in their morals than other women, and she was said to be an American. Perhaps—

The door creaked again, and Harry stood up to peer over the side of the stall. He saw a cloaked woman enter, close the door, and stand still for a moment, as if getting her bearings.

"Over here," came the husky voice of the waiting man, and the cloaked woman turned swiftly. The light was poor, but Harry did not think it was the red-haired lady. It might even have been a slender man. Unfortunately, the answering voice offered no clue. It was low and husky and had a certain sweetness, but it could have been that of either a woman or a man.

"Where is your colleague?" the cloaked figure asked. "I assumed that he would be here as well."

"Momentarily," the other replied. His voice was eager. "Then you have decided to join us?"

"Quite the contrary. I wish no part of this sordid business, and I've come to tell you so. I am a loyal subject of the Crown. Some of the things you have proposed would be deeply embarrassing, and might even tend toward treason."

Treason! Harry thought, all idea of a tryst flying out of his head. A plot against the Prince! What were they scheming? An accident to the Royal person? A plan to blow up the Royal train? He had better listen closely, so that he could report the conversation to the proper authorities—to the Prince himself! His reward would certainly be that pair of silver epaulettes his mother was so anxious for him to win.

"Oh, but I say!" the first man protested. "You have it wrong. All we mean to do is—"

Beside Harry, Paradox moved restlessly, pawing the straw with a shod hoof. Harry tensed, catching out of the corner of his eye a fleeting movement in the shadows behind him. He turned and saw a pale face looming over the side of the stall, a hand upraised, wielding a heavy object, about to strike.

It was the last thing Harry saw.

2

At the end of November [1895] the Glasgow magistrates had refused the permission sought by a local umbrella manufacturer to run a [petrol-powered] delivery van in the streets. This anonymous tradesman reacted with gusto: "Those in authority in our city," he declared, "might as well try to beat back the waves of the sea with a broom as try to stem the tide of horseless carriages that are looming in the distance."

—T. R. Nicholson
The Birth of the British Motor Car

"I have a poser for you, old man," said the Honorable Bradford Marsden, clutching the steering tiller in both hands.

Sir Charles Sheridan smiled at his friend, who was maneuvering his Daimler along the narrow road, trailing clouds of suffocating dust. Having suffered a mechanical breakdown beside the road the previous afternoon (to the manifest amusement of two laborers clearing a drain), Charles and Bradford had rolled up their sleeves and effected temporary repairs, then dispatched Lawrence, Marsden's man, to London for the proper part. They had slept the night at the Cock and Thorn in Braintree, breakfasted, then togged themselves in goggles, motoring caps, and poplin dusters, and resumed their journey to Easton Lodge, which lay on the further side of Great Dunmow, only a few miles away.

"Your question would not concern His Highness's sup-

port for the Locomotives on Highways Bill, would it?''
Charles asked lightly.

Bradford grunted. ''Dash it all, man. Am I that obvious?''

''Only to someone who knows your passions,'' Charles
replied. ''Since you've come back from that automobile ex-
hibit at Tunbridge Wells, you've spoken of nothing else but
promoting the motorcar.'' While he and Bradford pursued
quite different interests and did not see one another as often
as they once had, they had been at Eton together and still
remained close friends.

''Passion be damned,'' Bradford growled. ''This is
bloody serious.'' The Daimler had overtaken a cyclist, a village parson garbed in collar and long wool coat, who, ges-
ticulating wildly, pedaled his safety bicycle off the road and
upended it in the hawthorn hedgerow. Bradford hardly noticed, he was concentrating so intently on the steering. ''You
know as well as I do that if this country doesn't get off its
arse and regain its prestige in industry, we're finished. Germany will see to that. The Kaiser is not above causing us
mischief wherever he can—even if he is the Queen's grand-
son. The Prince is crucial in this matter. He *must* be brought
to understand that the motorcar represents the Future of England.'' He coughed. ''Let's make a stop, old man. This
confounded dust is choking me. I need a drink of water.''

The Future of England struggled noisily to the top of the
rise, hiccuped, and lurched to a halt. As Bradford pulled a
jug of water from beneath the seat and swigged at it, Charles
raised his goggles and looked out across the gentle slopes of
west Essex. The fields were painted in pleasing harvest hues
of browns and grays and golds, brightened by swathes of
early morning sunlight. A group of village women, hempen
sacks over their shoulders, were gleaning among the yellow
stubble, while a placid herd of stocky Ayrshires and black-
and-white Freesians grazed on the other side of the hedgerow, watched over by a herdsboy and his collie dog. Beyond
lay the market town of Great Dunmow, its citizens going
about their daily business in the narrow streets overhung with
buildings built in the century of Henry VIII and Elizabeth.
No alarms—other than a noisy flight of rooks rising from a
nearby tree—stirred the pastoral peace of this rustic scene;

no motorcars—other than the one in which he sat—broke the resonant silence. Since the advent of the railway in the earlier part of the century, heavier traffic had gone by train, leaving the roads to bicycles, horses, and foot travelers. Not even the whuffle and clank of an ox team intruded upon the quiet. The prosperous heart of England seemed to beat in these idyllic hills, just as it had for centuries past.

But Charles knew that at present, the heart of England beat somewhere else. To the south and west lay London, the seat of international commerce. To the north rose the great, grimy cities of Manchester, Birmingham, and Sheffield, built on iron and coal. The fields and meadows, villages and towns, that had once been England's chief treasure no longer earned its livelihood. The cities were now the country's promise, its future. It was as an industrial society that the nation would stand or fall, and the motorcar would certainly play its part.

"You don't believe me, eh?" Bradford asked, misunderstanding Charles's silence. "You scientists have been too busy looking at beetles to see how fast Germany's star is rising, how fast ours is sinking."

"On the contrary," Charles replied. "I spent several days at the Krupps' Works in Essen this summer, studying the latest innovations in munitions. The Germans have moved far ahead of everyone else since the Franco-Prussian War. Their technological proficiency is quite amazing, actually. It makes one suspect that they are about to realize Jules Verne's fantasy of shooting a man to the moon." He paused, then added, "Of course, there's the horrendous problem of acceleration, which Verne did not consider. No human being could withstand the forces involved in attaining the velocity necessary to escape—"

"Ah," Bradford said hastily, with the air of a man bottling a genie. "You *do* see. And didn't I hear you were down to Sandringham for the Princess's birthday a fortnight ago? Perhaps I can prevail on you to put in a word with HRH about the bill, which has gotten lost in the melee of Rosebery's defeat. Salisbury and the Conservatives oppose it, of course—they are against anything that smacks of progress. But since the motorcar exposition at Tunbridge Wells, popular interest has risen dramatically. A word from you and the Prince might be persuaded to support—"

"But I was at Sandringham on a photographic mission," Charles protested. Princess Alexandra had asked him to take pictures of the family gathering, and although he thought such assignments a waste of his time, he could hardly refuse what amounted to a Royal command. He had, after all, been awarded a knighthood (to him a matter of minor importance) for his photograph of the Queen upon the occasion of her Jubilee in '87. "In any event, I don't have the ear of the Prince," he added. "For that, Marsden, you shall have to approach our hostess. That is the Countess's special privilege."

The quiet was shattered as Bradford pushed the throttle and the Daimler launched itself down the hill toward Great Dunmow. Hearing the racket, the gleaners looked up with frightened faces and the pied cows raised their tails and galloped frantically to the far hedgerow. Charles pulled down his goggles, clung to the seat, and braced his feet against the bone-rattling plunge, thinking that something must be done to cushion the shock, or England's future would be too bumpy to endure.

"The Countess, you say?" Bradford shouted, above the clatter. "But Daisy has her own mission with the Prince, I understand. Isn't that why you've brought along that photographic arsenal?"

Charles waited until they had descended the hill and the clatter had somewhat subsided. "Lady Warwick—Daisy—told you her intention, then?"

"No, she was very mysterious. She said only that she had arranged an excursion to Chelmsford for HRH and that a motorcar was wanted, which I am delighted to provide. She mentioned that you were coming along to take photographs. Knowing how little you fancy country-house weekends, even the informal one she promised, I thought that might be the chief reason you agreed to come—that, and the fact that Miss Ardleigh has been invited, as well."

In the distance, a horse was approaching, pulling a dog-cart. Bradford steered the Daimler well onto the grassy verge and turned off the motor. Horses, as yet unaccustomed to motorcars, were apt to be skittish in their neighborhood.

In the sudden silence, Charles shifted uncomfortably. He had indeed looked forward to seeing Miss Ardleigh—Kate, she had asked him to call her. They had been acquainted now for over a year, an eventful year, as it had turned out. Kate's circumstances had much changed since she arrived from America to work as secretary to her aunt at Bishop's Keep, near the Marsdens' country home in East Essex. Beautiful if a bit headstrong and willful, Kate had succeeded her aunt, now deceased, as mistress of the family manor. Charles had it in mind to marry her, if she would have him. He had determined to lay the question before her this very weekend—a momentous determination for Charles, a man of rational intellect who found his scientific pursuits quite engrossing enough and had never before yielded to love for a woman.

But Charles's romantic scheme had been turned upside down the day before yesterday, when he received the letter from his mother, the Dowager Baroness of Somersworth. Her news had filled him with personal sorrow and the bleak realization that his life was about to change—not, in his opinion, for the better. He was summoned to do his duty. He could not now, after all, ask Kate for her hand. Loving her as deeply as he did, and wishing nothing more than her complete happiness, he would not ask her to join him in a life he knew she would despise.

The thought of it filled Charles with a great sorrow.

3

To get into the best society nowadays, one has either to feed people, amuse people, or shock people.

—OSCAR WILDE
A Woman of No Importance

"I'm sorry you're feeling so unwell, Ellie. Please, let me—"

Kathryn Ardleigh reached for the silver teapot to pour her friend Eleanor Farley a cup of tea, but an immaculately gloved hand and green-sleeved arm suddenly appeared over her right shoulder. A reproachfully respectful male voice murmured, "Permit me, please, miss," and both Ellie's and her own cups were refilled.

Kate sighed. She had done it again—forgotten that instead of reaching for what she wanted, she was supposed to sit and wait until she was waited upon. At Easton, of course, one didn't have to wait very long. The Countess of Warwick had trained the footmen and maids to anticipate her guests' unspoken requests and barely imagined desires. Kate did not as a rule attend house parties, and she had arrived only yesterday afternoon. She hadn't yet gotten used to the servants reading her mind.

Eleanor Marsden Farley accepted two cubes of sugar, stirred her tea, and sipped it. "Mornings are the worst," she said with a deep sigh. "Five more months. I will be so glad when this is over. Oh, if only it would be a boy!" Ellie's lovely face was drawn and her spritely voice thin and peevish. "You are not to tell anyone of my condition, Kate. This will be my last house party for some time, and I intend to enjoy it!"

Kate nodded, thinking that Ellie did not seem to welcome her impending motherhood with any special joy. To cheer her friend, she changed the subject.

"Well, you ought to find enough enjoyment here," she said. "I understand that the Countess has invited twenty guests for the weekend, including His Highness." Kate had been presented to the Prince the night before, and had dropped her obligatory curtsy with a disgraceful clumsiness. But his avuncular charm had put her at ease immediately, and before the evening was out, she had even danced with him. "Speaking of the other guests," she added, "I wonder where they are. Will the Prince come down to breakfast?"

Ellie shook her head. "The men usually breakfast early at these weekend affairs, then go out to tour the estate or shoot or fish—some such masculine entertainment. The women breakfast whenever they choose." She looked around at the sunny breakfast room, with its butter-yellow walls, glazed chintz draperies, and silver, crystal, and china arranged in gleaming richness on the mahogany sideboard, and brightened perceptibly. "Easton Lodge is a delightful place, isn't it? You must see my room, Kate. The bed is trimmed in yellow velvet. And I shall show you my new tea gowns, too. They are from Paris—really quite nice."

Kate nodded, although she didn't share Ellie's enthusiasm for personal decoration. It was trial enough to submit to having her abundant auburn hair twisted and braided on top of her head; she drew the line at being laced into a corset, and disliked the elaborate dresses designed to show off a wasp waist. She favored more rational garments: tailored blouses, plain bodices, and simple skirts. Villagers near Bishop's Keep had become accustomed to seeing her bicycling down the lanes in a divided skirt—and occasionally even in knickerbockers.

Ellie gave Kate a scrutinizing look. "I hope you have brought the gowns we purchased when you were last in London, Kate. Especially the green silk, which suits your coloring so well. In the company of Royalty," she added pointedly, "one must not dress carelessly. The Prince may act like a dear old uncle, but when he sees something he does not like, he can be a bear. And remember, he prefers women to wear some sort of headdress at dinner—a tiara, jewels, at the least, a ribbon. You will have an opportunity to put on all your favorite finery."

"I would admit this to no one but you, Ellie," Kate said in a low voice, "but I have precious little favorite finery, and less patience for putting it on. Assembling a wardrobe for this party was a challenge, and I am finding that dressing for the various events takes an inordinate amount of time—not to mention the business of unpacking and sponging and pressing." Women guests were expected to change into fresh gowns for breakfast, luncheon, tea, and dinner, Kate had learned. Even an informal party like this one required almost a dozen different gowns, each appropriate to a particular time of day and degree of formality. Already, she had worn three of the ten costumes she had brought.

"But what else have we to do while the men are amusing themselves out-of-doors?" Ellie asked reasonably. "Anyway, that's what maids are for." She buttered a half slice of toast. "Did you bring Amelia? If not, the Countess will provide you with someone—no doubt better trained." Without waiting for Kate's response, she added, "That little maid of yours is sweet, Kate, but she's only a country lass. I do wish you would find a maid who is *au courant* with the latest styles of dress and coiffure. If you intend to join the Marlborough set—"

"But I don't," Kate said emphatically. "That kind of social life is not for me. I am much more at home in the village than I am in London."

An American of Irish descent who had lived in England for only a year, Kate was uncomfortable with the social hierarchies of British life and had little admiration for the fast Marlborough crowd that flocked around the Prince and Princess of Wales. But if she cared little for Society's glitter and even viewed Royalty with the wry humor of an American outsider, she was deeply intrigued by her hostess, the Countess of Warwick.

Kate had met the Countess at a garden party and several

times since, and had read about her in *The Times* and *The Lady's Realm*. A stunningly wealthy heiress of aristocratic descent who had married Lord Francis Brooke, the handsome heir to the earldom of Warwick, Lady Warwick was a leading beauty of the Prince's circle. With her extravagant costumes and priceless jewels and heedless, spendthrift ways, the Countess was often portrayed in the press as the epitome of wastefulness and questionable morality. Knowing as much, Kate had not been shocked to learn from Ellie that Lady Warwick and the Prince were carrying on one of those clandestine love affairs with which the Marlborough set, having little else to do, amused themselves.

But there was more to the Countess of Warwick than met the eye. Since their first meeting, Kate had suspected that the cool, elegant Lady Warwick, called Daisy by her friends, had another, quite contradictory side. While the women of the Marlborough set cared for little other than balls and race-meetings, Daisy Warwick had a passion for philanthropies. The Countess had mentioned the needlework school she had established in a wing of the main hall at Easton Lodge, and seeing Kate's interest, had invited her to visit, spend the weekend, and be presented to the Prince.

Yesterday, Kate had toured the small school. The thirty or so students were local girls, taught the sought-after skill of fine embroidery by two French instructresses. They earned two and sixpence a week during their preliminary training, and ten shillings after—a quite respectable wage. Their work was sold in a Bond Street shop under the name "Lady Warwick's Depot for the Easton School of Needlework," and the proceeds went to support the school. The project, however, did not meet with overwhelming approval, according to the newspapers. Lady Warwick's friends professed to be shocked by her excursion into trade and whispered that they had seen the Countess herself serving customers behind the counter, while local gentry in the villages around Easton complained that M'lady's scheme robbed them of potential servants and gave the unfortunate girls ideas above their lowly station. "Not fit fer kitchen nor nurs'ry when she's through wit 'em," one country wife had proclaimed, "nor good husband, neither."

But Kate, who had known poverty firsthand, was deeply intrigued by the Countess's attempt to provide training and employment for women. Orphaned as a small child, Kate had been taken in by an uncle who earned his livelihood as a policeman in New York City, with a wage that provided scant food and clothing for the six children in the family. To support herself, she had become a governess. At the same time, seeing the rapidly growing market in sensational fictions, particularly stories of crime and passion, she had assumed a pseudonym and taken up her pen. To date, she had written—

Kate's thoughts were interrupted by the entrance of two women. "Good morning, Ellie," the first said pleasantly. "And good morning to you, Miss Ardleigh."

The woman who had interrupted the wandering train of Kate's thoughts was Lady Warwick herself, a slim, handsome woman in her early thirties with a flawless complexion, dark blue eyes, and hair the color of golden-brown leaves. She was dressed in a pale pink morning dress with a lacy collar and sleeves that puffed at the upper arms and fitted tightly from elbow to wrist. A step behind the Countess was Lady Verena Rochdale, short and round, with graying hair pulled back into a chignon and dressed in a fussy gray silk. Lady Rochdale's bright black eyes snapped with avid curiosity, and she seemed to be peering at everything.

"Good morning," Ellie said, and Kate echoed her. "I wonder, Daisy," Ellie added, "whether you have heard from my brother Bradford? He was expected for dinner last night, and I have been worried about him. He is motoring, you know."

Lady Verena made a face. "Those motorcars," she said. "Someone soon will be killed in one of them."

"Actually, I *have* heard from your brother, Ellie," Lady Warwick said. "He was delayed in Braintree when his motorcar suffered a breakdown. He and Sir Charles expect to arrive this morning."

"Charles Sheridan?" Kate asked, surprised.

"You're acquainted with Sir Charles, then?" Lady Warwick asked with a smile. "I have asked him to photograph an excursion His Highness and I are planning tomorrow."

"An excursion?" Lady Verena asked eagerly. "Wonderful! Where will we be going?"

Lady Warwick turned toward the mahogany sideboard on which breakfast was displayed. "It is a short side trip I have arranged for His Highness's entertainment," she said carelessly. "Other diversions are planned for any who do not prefer the usual riding and shooting." She pointed to a silver dish and the footman lifted its lid. "I particularly recommend the pheasant, Verena."

As one of the two servants filled the women's plates with pheasant, deviled kidneys, coddled eggs, and fruit from the well-stocked sideboard, Kate sat back, feeling that the weekend had suddenly brightened. She had a deep respect for Sir Charles—and more. She would not acknowledge it to anyone, not even to Ellie, but she had grown to love him. What was more, she thought he cared for her, as well. He hadn't yet spoken of his feelings, but when they were together, as they had been often of late, there was a look in his eye and a tender tone in his voice that revealed a great deal.

She felt a sudden warmth. Perhaps this would be the weekend when Sir Charles would declare himself. Perhaps he would sweep her into his arms, declare his love, and—

Kate caught her breath and picked up her teacup. That was a lovely romantic dream, but it was a fantasy that could not be allowed to become real. Sir Charles's declaration would only open a painfully embarrassing exchange, for she could not accept him. Care for him though she might, marriage was out of the question. For one thing, she was an American of Irish extraction, and she had already felt some of the suspicions that many of the British upper class felt toward Americans and Irish. For another—

"Are you enjoying yourself, Miss Ardleigh?" Lady Warwick asked. She and Lady Verena sat down on the other side of the table while the other footman—a dark, pocked-faced young man with heavy black eyebrows and a brooding face—stepped forward to pour their tea.

Collecting herself with difficulty, Kate managed a smile. "Very much, Lady Warwick. I was quite impressed by the needlework students to whom you introduced me yesterday.

Perhaps one or two will someday establish their own dress-making businesses.''

''Spoken like an American,'' Lady Verena remarked. Her dark eyes considered Kate and dismissed her. ''As a people, you are so *irrepressibly* entrepreneurial. So interested in money.'' She spoke the word as if it tasted like a spoiled egg.

''And so down-to-earth,'' Lady Warwick said. ''I did appreciate hearing your ideas and suggestions yesterday, Miss Ardleigh.'' She glanced pointedly at Lady Verena, who was avidly forking up deviled kidneys. ''There is much to be done, and few who are genuinely concerned about the rural poor.''

Lady Verena's eyes narrowed. She appeared to have felt the barb, but she made no reply.

''Kate is quite active in poor relief in her parish,'' Ellie said, sipping her tea.

''Is that so, Miss Ardleigh?'' Lady Warwick asked, interested.

Kate nodded. ''But please,'' she said, ''call me Kate.''

Lady Warwick looked pleased. ''Then you must call me Daisy. My given name is Frances,'' she added, ''but my stepfather, Lord Rosslyn, always called me his fresh little daisy. The name has stayed with me.''

''Thank you, Daisy,'' Kate said. ''My aunt supported several local charities before her death. I am merely carrying on her work.''

''But you have done much more than that, Kate,'' Ellie protested. ''You provide blankets and food to the workhouse and sponsor prizes at the local school and—''

Lady Verena rattled her spoon noisily. ''As I was saying when we came down to breakfast, my dear Daisy, I rose early this morning, thinking to write a few letters. But I opened the latest issue of *Blackwell's Monthly* and chanced on a fiction so engrossing I forgot all about my correspondence. I fear the post has gone without it.''

''I wonder, Verena,'' Daisy said, ''whether you're speaking of 'The Duchess's Dilemma.' My sister Blanche recommended the story to me, and I deeply enjoyed it. The author writes with such frank intimacy that I almost feel I know her characters.''

Lady Verena was slathering butter on a roll. "Oh, indeed," she said. "In fact, the authoress—the name Beryl Bardwell is quite obviously a pseudonym—appears to be writing about people we *do* know." The dark-browed footman put a spoonful of strawberry jam on her plate, and she transferred it to her roll. "Some of the details of the story lead me to suspect, Daisy, that she is one of our class. If this is true, we *must* learn her identity. It is shocking to think that one among us might retail our most intimate secrets. Not that I have anything to hide," she added. "Or you, my dear. *Especially* you." The barb had been returned.

Kate lowered her glance, her cheeks staining. She longed to leave the room, but she could think of no excuse.

"One of us?" Daisy asked, ignoring Lady Verena's scarcely disguised jab. "Perhaps. But no one of my acquaintance is possessed of Miss Bardwell's enviable talent. Surely, if she were one of us, some hint of her skill would have surfaced before this."

Lady Verena agreed, lifting her cup. "As it happens, my husband's former secretary has some position or another in the publishing house that produces *Blackwell's*. I plan to telegraph him this morning. Perhaps he can tell us the real identity of Beryl Bardwell."

"That's a splendid idea, Verena," Daisy replied. "When you find out, I really must know, too." She looked across the table. "And you, Kate? Or you, Ellie? Have either of you read the story we have been speaking of?"

"I fear not," Ellie said, "but if you will lend me the magazine, I shall do so this very afternoon."

Kate made no answer, for she was thrown into an internal chaos. She had no need to wait for a telegram to learn the mysterious writer's identity. *She* was Beryl Bardwell, and one of the reasons she could not accept Sir Charles's offer of marriage—if indeed he intended to make it—was her secret occupation as a writer of detective fictions. It was not an occupation he would wish his wife to pursue. Nor would she give it up, for her writing was a part of her, and she could not imagine her life without it.

"Good," Daisy said. "Perhaps when you have read it, Ellie, you may have an idea as to the identity of the writer.

And you, too, Kate.'' She clapped her pretty hands. "We shall make it a project, shall we? We shall discover the authoress in our midst and unmask her!"

Kate desperately hoped Ellie would not read the story, because it was based on an incident that had happened some months before at the home of Ellie's parents. She would be sure to recognize the setting and characters. Now, when it was far too late to do anything about it, Kate began to wish that she had not drawn her characters quite so true to life, nor portrayed actual events quite so faithfully. She should have realized how dangerous it was to blend fiction and reality.

Before Kate could gather her wits to make an answer, she heard a loud sputtering and metallic clanking outside the window of the breakfast room. Startled by the sound and realizing its meaning, she rose from her chair to go to the window.

Lady Verena waved her hand carelessly. "Oh, don't be alarmed, Miss Ardleigh. It is only one of those wretchedly noisy motors that the men are so keen on these days. I daresay Lord Marsden has arrived."

And with him, Kate thought, filled with confusion, was Sir Charles Sheridan.

4

Our duty is to be useful, not according to our desires but according to our powers.

—HENRI FREDERIC AMIEL
Journal, 1856

"Well, here we are," Bradford said to Charles. He guided the Daimler off the main park lane and onto the graveled drive that circled Easton Lodge.

Charles took his watch out of his pocket and glanced at it. "The men have no doubt already gone out," he said, "but we are in time to join the ladies at breakfast."

Bradford was gratified by their early arrival. They had made the ten-mile run from Braintree to the Lodge in one hour and fifteen minutes, at almost twice the legal maximum speed of four miles an hour and sans the obligatory man with a red flag that—ridiculously—was still supposed to precede them by twenty yards. He had expected to be stopped by a constable and would have welcomed the chance to make a court case of it. But no constable had appeared. The Daimler had ruled the road.

Charles grunted as he looked at the ivy-clad, gray stone building that loomed ahead of them. "Damned impressive place," he said. "But I for one wouldn't want the burden of responsibility for it. Can you imagine what it costs to maintain an estate like this?"

"Too much," Bradford said. "These huge estates are a curse on the heads of those who inherit them."

The Lodge was approached by a two-mile-long drive through twelve hundred acres of park scattered with giant oaks and grazed by deer—three times the size of Marsden Park, which Bradford stood to inherit upon his father's death. The three-story, multi-winged mock-Tudor house had hundreds of rooms and must cost a king's ransom to staff and maintain—a white elephant, in this modern day and age, when the cost of fuel was rising and the new death duties bid fair to impoverish the great estates. In fact, Bradford had heard that falling revenues had forced the Warwicks to close off the main wing of the Easton Lodge—the Countess's family home—except for weekend house parties, and were preparing to sell off sections of the park. But her financial woes didn't seem to affect her lavish spending, or her husband's, either. Bradford had also heard that the Countess had recently constructed a private railway to the Lodge so that the Prince, a frequent guest and her acknowledged lover, could come and go without depending on rail schedules, and that the Earl of Warwick had just lost a substantial sum of money in an ill-fated Mexican mining venture.

Bradford steered the automobile around the looping drive. He and Charles were a day late, to be sure, but Bradford was relieved that they had actually arrived. He was a devout believer in the future of the motorcar, but its present was often trying. It was ten to one against getting anywhere without some accident, such as losing the main drive belt, which mischance had happened late yesterday afternoon. It had been a bit of bad luck, too, for he had not thought to carry a replacement. Exhaustive inquiries in the nearest village had revealed that there was no harness maker who might mend or replace the leather belt, and it wasn't until Charles suggested that they try the cobbler that they began to make progress. By the time the cobbler was located and put to work, however, the sun was setting. After several hours of lantern-lit effort, the man had effected a serviceable repair. But lighting his work had nearly exhausted their supply of the calcium carbide that powered the Daimler's acetylene headlamps, so Bradford had been forced to agree to staying the night in Braintree. Before they left that morning, he had dispatched his man Lawrence to London by train to acquire another replacement belt, a spare tire, an extra cask of petrol, and a canister of calcium carbide. He did not intend to be caught short again.

They turned the corner behind the Lodge, and Bradford braced himself for the excited crowd that always welcomed the arrival of a motorcar. In a moment, servants and stable-boys would be swarming around the vehicle, touching its tires, marveling at the gleaming brass fittings, rubbing the mud off the headlamps with their sleeves. Bradford had owned the car for three months, but the moment of arrival was one he still savored. It came as something of a surprise, then, that when he piloted the automobile onto the gravel apron at the rear of the house, everyone seemed to be running *away* from them, in the direction of the stables.

"Something seems amiss," Charles said.

Bradford sounded his electric bell, ostensibly installed to warn pedestrians and horses but really designed to attract attention. But the electric jangle had no effect on the scurrying and shouting. He brought the Daimler to a stop, stepped out of the vehicle, and raised his goggles.

"I say," he called to one of several servants hurrying toward the stable. "What's happened?"

" 'Is Highness's groom 'as bin kicked in th' 'ead," the young man replied.

At that moment, two men emerged from the stable door, a limp form sagging between them like sacked meal.

"Hold on, there!" Charles cried, jumping down from the automobile and running toward the stable, Bradford at his heels. "He shouldn't be handled that way, with a head injury. On the ground with him, now!"

The two men, startled, deposited their liveried burden on the ground with a thump. The boy, for that's what he was, lay unmoving. Charles knelt down beside the inert form.

"I'll go for a doctor," Bradford said, pulling his goggles back on and turning toward the motorcar.

"Beggin' Yer Lordship's pardon," one of the men said gruffly, "but th' doctor's needed in a *'urry*. Th' boys is sad-dlin' Fiver now, an' Tom'll ride over t' Little Easton by way o' th' woods. 'E'll be there an' back wi' th' doctor afore you can git that contraption turned around an' 'eaded th' right way."

The double stable doors opened and a black, high-stepping hunter was led out of the gloom. Seeing the unfamiliar automobile, the horse reared and whinnied shrilly. Tom, a lanky young man, hoisted himself into the saddle and was off in a headlong dash down the drive, flying hoofs sending a spray of loose gravel clanging against the Daimler's metal fender.

Charles stood. "Somebody ride after Tom and fetch him back," he said soberly. "It's of no use bringing the doctor. The lad's dead."

"Too bad," Bradford said, looking down at the pale young face. The boy looked scarcely fifteen. "How did it happen?"

"Kicked i' th' 'ead, like," the gruff man said. "Found 'im i' th' stall wi' Paradox, th' Prince's 'unter." He shook his shaggy head somberly. " 'E's a mean 'un, that 'orse. 'Ad trouble wi' 'im meself a time er twa."

"What's all this?" The question was asked in a deep, guttural voice with a German accent. "Trouble with Paradox?"

Bradford turned. The portly, bearded man in a Norfolk suit and polished boots was His Royal Highness Albert Edward, Prince of Wales, playboy heir to the throne of his seventy-six-year-old mother, Queen Victoria. He was accompanied by a dark, handsomely mustached man and trailed by a group of seven or eight men.

The gruff man whipped his cap off his shaggy head. "Sad to say, sir," he said respectfully, "but th' lad was kicked. 'E was found i' th' Royal stall."

His Highness bent over the still form. "Has someone gone for the doctor?"

Charles spoke. "A doctor would be of no use, Your Highness. The boy's dead."

"Ah, Charles." The Prince straightened and exhaled windily. "Good to see you, good to see you. Of course, you are acquainted with Lord Warwick." He indicated the erect, mustached man standing at his elbow.

"Good morning, Brooke," Charles said. He motioned at

Bradford. "And you know Bradford Marsden, I'm sure."

"Oh, indeed," said the Prince, nodding. "Good you could come, Marsden." He turned to look at the automobile behind them. "And that is your newly imported Daimler, is it? I trust your delay was not caused by a serious mechanical mischance."

"No, sir," Bradford said, wishing there had been no delay. He particularly wanted to impress HRH with the reliability of his machine. "Just a slight problem, easily repaired," he added offhandedly. "I am looking forward to having you as a passenger tomorrow."

"Oh?" asked one of the men standing behind the Prince. "Where are you going, sir?"

"All in good time," the Prince said jovially. "All in good time." He looked down at the body at his feet. "A sad business, this. The boy was one Princess Alexandra singled out for reward, and she will be sorry to learn that he has died. But it was not Paradox that killed him," he added with a stern emphasis, "and I don't want it bruited about that it was."

"Oh, but it was, Yer 'Ighness, sir!" the gruff man protested. "Th' boy was in th' stall, y'see, an'—"

"Alfred," Lord Warwick cautioned, "remember to whom you are speaking."

Alfred licked his lips nervously, twisted his cap in his hands, and amended his tone. "Beg pardon, Yer Royal 'Ighness, sir. But it 'ad t've bin th' 'orse wot kicked 'im. We found th' lad shut i' th' stall, wi' a spilled bucket o' oats—wot was left, anyway, th' 'orse 'avin' cleaned up most."

The Prince gestured with a gloved hand. "I understand what you're saying," he said impatiently. "But I've hunted with Paradox for going on seven years, and a gentler horse never lived. He wouldn't bring a man down, nor would he put a hoof on him when he was down."

"Then what?" asked a tall man with sandy hair, beard, and a gold pince-nez. Bradford recognized him as Sir Friedrich Temple, a well-known Conservative and nephew of the Archbishop of Canterbury, by the same name. "Accident, d'you suppose? Maybe the lad fell out of the loft."

"Or fell into an argument with one of his fellows," another man said, tapping the polished toe of his boot with an ebony stick. "My stableboys are always rowing. Anyway, what does it matter? The lad is dead." Bradford turned, recognizing the speaker, a burly and heavyset graybeard with steely eyes under thick black eyebrows that jutted out like horns, giving him a look of wily rakishness. Sir Thomas Cobb, retired, of the Royal Grenadiers.

"That's all well and good, Thomas," the Prince said. "But unfortunately, however the fellow died, Alix will feel it her duty to tell his family the truth of the matter. So, unless I am willing to give up a fortnight's peace to Alix's poking at me for details, the truth must be dug out, and shortly." He glanced at Charles. "That's up your line, isn't it, Charles? Don't I seem to recall your mucking about in a recent crime or two?"

"I've had one or two minor successes in forensic investigation," Charles admitted, somewhat reluctantly, Bradford thought.

"That's a fine chap," the Prince said, clapping Charles on the shoulder. "Be so good as to look into this matter, then. You will give me your report this evening after dinner, and I will pass it along to Alix when I write in the morning."

Charles agreed readily enough, but Bradford saw him wince. He knew that his friend had planned to pursue other game this weekend—the fair Kate Ardleigh, no doubt, whom Bradford himself would not have hesitated to woo if his mother hadn't raised a row about it. Poor Charles. In addition to Daisy Warwick's request that he spend tomorrow photographing the mysterious expedition, the Prince had commanded him to spend the afternoon investigating an accident. What rotten luck. But Charles was a man of duty, Bradford reflected. He would resign himself to doing what he must.

Bradford didn't guess the half of it.

5

No one who stayed at Easton ever forgot their hostess, and most of the men fell hopelessly in love with her. In my long life, spent in so many different countries, and during which I have seen most of the beautiful and famous women of the world, from film-stars to Queens, I have never seen one who was so completely fascinating as Daisy Warwick.

—ELINOR GLYN (The "It" Girl)
Romantic Adventure, 1936

It was a warm, bright afternoon, and luncheon was to be served on the terrace behind Stone Hall, Lady Warwick's Elizabethan folly. The two-story cottage—called Daisy's Folly by everyone who visited there—was a pleasant stroll from the Lodge, in a shady corner of the Park. It was an old stone-fronted house with a slate roof that the Countess had rebuilt as a two-story Tudor cottage and furnished with valuable antique chairs and tables, tapestried beds, and quaint books. Behind the Folly was a landscaped terrace and a coppice of young trees, each one planted by her special friends—the Prince's beech trees foremost among them. There, too, was Daisy's Garden of Friendship, planted with flowers given to her by acquaintances, each identified by the name of the donor.

Following Ellie's suggestion, Kate had dressed in her blue wool costume with the gored skirt and matching puff-sleeved velvet jacket—a compromise between style and comfort.

Amelia had wound her heavy auburn hair high on her head and perched on it a blue velvet toque decorated with three peacock feathers. Glancing in the mirror before she left her room, Kate had felt a glow of satisfaction at her appearance—and nervous anticipation at the thought of seeing Sir Charles at luncheon.

Kate and Ellie walked to the Folly together, Kate holding her breath for a mention of "The Duchess's Dilemma." If Ellie had read the story, she would immediately deduce that it was about her mother and that Kate was its likely author. Beryl Bardwell had—quite foolishly, Kate now admitted—used the autocratic Lady Marsden as her model for the imperious Duchess, and the Duchess's home was clearly recognizable as Marsden Manor. Even the plot of the story, which involved some missing jewels, would be familiar to Ellie, for she herself had been involved, as had her brother. True, Beryl had substituted sapphires for Lady Marsden's emeralds and altered some of the most important circumstances, but the remaining similarities would surely catch Ellie's eye. Uncomfortably, Kate wondered whether she should confess what she had done and beg for Ellie's forgiveness. But Ellie gave no evidence that she had yet read the story, and she chattered so much that Kate finally gave up trying to insert anything of importance into the conversation.

Luncheon was to be served under a large yellow tent on the veranda behind Daisy's Folly. The guests took their seats at five tables, each covered by a snowy white cloth, decorated with a crystal vase of hothouse flowers, and attended by its own footman. To Kate's right sat Sir Reginald Wallace, her dinner partner of the previous evening. He was a slender man with a high forehead, pink skin, and a tight-lipped mouth that did not seem to know how to smile. Occupying the opposite seat was Lady Felicia Metcalf, an angular, bony woman in her late thirties with pinched cheeks, improbable blond curls, and a practiced smile, whose conversation seemed to consist primarily of trifling complaints. To Kate's left, much to her consternation, sat Sir Charles Sheridan.

After greetings (did it seem that Sir Charles's glance lingered on her face rather longer and more questioningly than

usual?), the table talk turned to the fatal accident that had
befallen the Royal groom in the stable.

"Bit of bad luck, that," Sir Reginald said, as the footman
removed their empty soup plates and served quail in aspic.
From Sir Reginald's conversation last night, Kate had gathered that he was a staunch member of the squirearchy whose
chief passions were hunting and shooting. "But these things
happen," he added. "My wife, of course, was killed in a
riding accident." Lady Felicia made a consoling noise. "And
last year I lost my best loader. Rose up just as Lord Rib-
blesdale swung the butt of his gun and was caught square in
the temple. Chap turned up his toes and died without a word.
Poor Ribby felt dreadful. Spoiled the morning's shooting for
everyone."

"Especially for the loader," Sir Charles remarked wryly,
but Sir Reginald had already bent his head to hear Lady
Felicia's animated story about someone—Kate didn't catch
the name—who had accidentally shot a beater, causing him
to lose a leg.

Kate turned to Sir Charles. "I saw the commotion from
the breakfast room window this morning," she said in a low
voice, "although I couldn't hear what was going on. Amelia
told me that the Prince has asked you to look into the affair
so he can report back to the Princess." Kate hadn't been
surprised that Amelia knew so much about what had happened. There was no keeping secrets from the servants, especially when one of them was involved. Kate had asked as
many questions as she could without seeming overly curious.

"He did," Sir Charles said somberly, "but there is little
to be learned. From the look of it, I would say that the horse
is not at fault. The blow was struck at an angle, and the
wound is more consistent with that of a blunt—" He stopped
as the footman replenished his wine. "Forgive me, Kate,"
he said with a small smile. "The description is hardly appropriate to the luncheon table."

"Oh, no," Kate said hastily. "I want to hear." The death
of the young groom had given Beryl Bardwell a new idea
for the plot of *The Loves of Lady Lenore* (the tentative title
of her current novel) and she was anxious to fill in Amelia's
sketch with Sir Charles's observations. Identifiable elements

would have to be radically changed, of course; Beryl Bardwell had learned her lesson. "Please," Kate said, more se-
dately, "do continue."

"I fear there is not much else to tell," Sir Charles said,
and went on to say that it appeared that the boy had struck
or been struck by something heavy, and had died of a brain
injury. The accident had taken place at an early hour of the
morning, likely just after sunrise, when the boy had left his
sleeping quarters. Sir Charles had searched the Royal stall,
the adjoining stalls, and the loft overhead and questioned the
stableboys, grooms, and coachmen. But there had been the
usual gaiety in the servants' hall the previous night (servants
traditionally contrived their own entertainment at a country
house weekend), and the men and boys of the stable staff
had risen rather later than usual. No one admitted to hearing
or seeing anything suspicious.

"Is it possible that he fell from the loft into the stall?"
Kate asked.

"It's possible," Sir Charles admitted, "but I found no
evidence in the loft to suggest that he had been there."

Kate watched him, surreptitiously, while he talked. Sir
Charles, a man of medium build, wore comfortable-looking
tweeds that were disreputable enough to earn a glance of arch
dismay from Lady Felicia and their wearer the distinction of
being the worst-dressed guest at luncheon. Convenient to his
interests (Sir Charles had a passion for all sorts of odd scientific pursuits), the pockets of his jackets bulged with such
things as calipers and measuring rules and magnifying lens.
His dusty breeches were tucked into scuffed leather boots,
and when he sat down, he had removed a broad-brimmed
felt hat with a shapeless crown. His overlong brown hair was
curly, but his beard, under prominent cheekbones, was neatly
clipped and his quick, sherry-colored eyes were disconcert-
ingly attentive—at least, Kate found them so.

"And that is the sum of it," he concluded ruefully. "The
lad seems to have been struck while he was attending the
horse. By whom or with what motive, it is impossible to say.
And lacking physical evidence, there is nothing on which to
form even a guess."

"Will there be a coroner's inquest?" Kate asked.

"In all probability," Sir Charles said. "I assume that Lord Warwick has notified the authorities." He sat back to allow the footman to take his empty plate and to place before him a serving of fruit-crowned trifle studded with almonds.

In the lull, Kate's ear caught a shred of their companions' conversation. The remark, Lady Metcalf's, concerned their hostess, seated two tables away. Suddenly intrigued, Kate picked up her fork and began to eat her dessert, listening avidly.

"—and then she got herself elected to the Warwick Workhouse Board," Lady Metcalf was saying *sotto voce* to Lord Reginald. She made clicking noises with her tongue. "Utter folly, the Countess of Warwick presenting herself as a candidate for Poor Law Guardian! Really, I don't know which is worse, her soiling herself with the workhouse or meddling in politics. Why, I have even heard that she has considered standing for Parliament, and that she plans to campaign for Mrs. Pankhurst's Woman-Suffrage Society. Such utter foolishness! And you know, don't you, that she has recently begun taking regular luncheons with both Stead and Blatchford?"

The Workhouse Board? The Woman-Suffrage Society? Kate listened open-mouthed. There was more to Daisy than she had guessed.

"Stead and Blatchford?" Sir Reginald replied with what seemed like genuine concern. "I am sorry to hear it. Those are dangerous men, those two. Daisy should steer clear of them, or she'll find herself in serious trouble."

Sir Charles raised his head. "Willie Stead is a crusader, perhaps," he said mildly, "and righteous indignation may sometimes carry his pen to extremes. But I'd scarcely consider him dangerous."

"On the contrary, Sheridan," Sir Reginald snapped. "An irresponsible journalist like Stead is damned dangerous. The man publicly agitates for reform of the House of Lords, and that Socialist nonsense of his about international disarmament—"

"I have seen the Krupp munitions factories," Sir Charles said grimly, "and watched the Kaiser's armed divisions pass in review. Stead is right. If nations do not renounce violence, the coming conflagration will engulf us all. Even if by some miracle we avoid war, the cost of armaments will soon become utterly ruinous.''

Sir Reginald pursed disapproving lips. ''And Robert Blatchford is an outright Socialist,'' he said, as if Sir Charles had not spoken. ''Advocates an eight-hour day, old-age pensions, trade unions, even a Labor Party. Men like Blatchford and Stead will destroy the future of England as we know her.'' His clean-shaven pink cheeks were suffused with red and his voice was rising. ''Everything we believe in, all decency, all distinction, will go by the board. It is dangerous for Daisy to meddle in such hazardous affairs.''

''Dear Reggie,'' a light voice said sweetly. ''In whose affairs is it dangerous for me to meddle? The Duchess of Devonshire's, perhaps?''

Kate looked up, startled. She had been so intent on the conversation that she had not noticed that coffee and cordials were being served and that guests were beginning to move from table to table. At her shoulder stood their hostess, a crystal glass in her hand, a gay smile on her alluring lips.

''The Duchess's affairs might have distinction, but they can hardly be thought hazardous or indecent,'' Daisy added with a laugh. ''She assures me that they are all *entirely* platonic.''

Sir Reginald scraped back his chair and stood, his thin neck reddening. ''Ah, Daisy,'' he said shortly. He glanced at her and swiftly away, a glance that to Kate revealed a very great deal. ''I was just saying—''

''That you consider the editor of the *Clarion* to be a dangerous man.'' Lady Warwick's trill of amused laughter was colored by sarcasm. ''Really, Reggie, don't you think you are overstating the case?''

Lady Metcalf's smile was lazy, but the pulse beating in her throat gave her away. ''Reggie was speaking out of concern for your welfare, Daisy. After all, a known Socialist like Blatchford— Well, one never wishes to endanger one's position, does one?'' Her eyes flicked briefly to Kate and Sir Charles, and her lips curved upward in an artificial smile. ''But perhaps we could continue this discussion at another time. Our table companions must find us tedious.''

Kate had not found the discussion tedious at all—fascinating, rather. Obviously, there were strong tensions here, both personal and political. She wondered, fleetingly, whether it was possible, under the circumstances, to separate the two.

"Of course," Lady Warwick agreed smoothly. "Kate, Charles, I hope you will forgive our boring chatter. But I must say—dear Reggie, *darling* Felicia—that my choice of luncheon partners is hardly likely to endanger my position or imperil the future of England."

Lady Felicia's eyes went to the Prince of Wales, who was chatting companionably with Lord Warwick at a nearby table. "Of course," she said softly, "you are right. You are always right. My dear Daisy, you are so exceedingly clever."

Sir Reginald had glanced at the Prince, too, and seemed suddenly agitated. He flung down his napkin. "Don't you see, Daisy? It is precisely your position that puts you in jeopardy! It is utterly foolish to—"

"Daisy," Sir Charles said mildly, "may I offer my compliments to your chef?" He had stood as well. "The luncheon was excellent, particularly the trifle. But I wonder—might we have a word or two about your plans for tomorrow's excursion?" And in an instant he had taken Lady Warwick's arm and guided her away from the table.

With flushed face and lowering brow, Sir Reginald stood staring after them. Then he muttered something, stuffed his hands in his pockets, and stalked in the other direction.

Lady Felicia turned to watch him go, her face hardening in a telltale expression. A moment later she turned back, struggling to regain her composure, and gave Kate a vinegary smile. "I fear our little conversation must have been totally baffling to you, my dear. You Americans are so democratic, so refreshingly unimpressed by our distinctions of rank, and our emphasis on one's duty to one's class."

Kate felt the anger rise up in her at the woman's patronizing tone. "Unimpressed, perhaps," she said, "but hardly baffled—although it would be difficult for any American to imagine why Lady Warwick should not lunch with whom she pleases, Socialist or no. And I don't imagine that your conversation entirely concerned duty and distinctions of rank—or even politics.''

No, she realized, it had not. Beneath his anger, Sir Reginald was passionately in love with Daisy Warwick. And Lady Felicia was passionately jealous.

Lady Felicia might have answered, but she was interrupted by the arrival at the table of Lady Lillian Forsythe, a stunningly beautiful woman only a few years older than Kate, with curly black hair, plucked black brows, and a full, pouting mouth. She was wearing mauve with a touch of black lace in honor of her dead husband, for whom she was in the last months of mourning.

Acknowledging Kate with a brief smile, Lady Lillian sat down in Sir Charles's vacated chair. ''Felicia,'' she said, leaning forward urgently, ''who in the world *is* he?''

''Who is who, Lillian?''

''That unkempt man who was sitting in this chair a moment ago. The one wearing the unspeakable jacket.''

Lady Metcalf laughed merrily. ''Oh, yes,'' she said. ''All those bulges in his pockets. Lillian, my dear, you have always fancied the strange ones. Whatever happened to that young man you made such a pet of in Paris—an artist, wasn't he?'' She paused. ''This one's name is Charles Sheridan. *Sir* Charles.''

''M-m-m.'' Lady Lillian arched her eyebrows. ''He is quite attractive, rather, in a rustic way. I wonder I have not seen him before. Is he a sportsman?''

''I fancy not,'' Lady Felicia replied. ''But perhaps our American friend can tell us more. I believe they are acquainted. This is Miss Ardleigh, Lillian. Miss Ardleigh, I present Lady Lillian Forsythe.''

Lady Lillian turned to Kate, held out her hand, and said in a charmingly delicate flutter of run-on sentences, ''Miss Ardleigh? So good to meet you, and do please forgive my inquisitiveness, but you really must tell *all*! Who are Sir Charles's family? Where are their estates?''

Feeling half a traitor, Kate said, ''He comes from Suffolk, near Ipswich. His elder brother is the Baron of Somersworth.''

Lady Felicia sat back, smiling lazily. "Ah, he is a detrimental, Lillian."

Kate frowned, not liking the sound of the word, not liking, even more, Lillian Forsythe's interest in Sir Charles. "What is a detrimental?" she asked.

"A man who is an imminently eligible suitor in every way but circumstance," Lady Felicia said. "A younger son who will not inherit, with no settled income." She gave Lady Lillian a pointed glance. "Detrimentals are suitable chiefly for married women—or wealthy widows."

"Oh, Felicia, you are so *shocking*," Lady Lillian said, examining the tips of her black gloves. "And what are Sir Charles's chief interests, Miss Ardleigh?"

Kate felt a sharp twinge of jealousy. The woman was remarkably beautiful, and although she seemed rather too brittle and calculating to appeal to Sir Charles, she was of his social class. If she were aggressive enough . . .

"His chief interests?" Kate murmured. "Bats, I believe." The remark was true, if disingenuous. Sir Charles had made an extensive study of the habitats of various bat species in the east and south of England.

"Bats!" Lady Felicia's laugh was a mocking tinkle. "What did I tell you, Lillian? You always manage to fall into love with the strange ones."

Lady Lillian arched her plucked brows. "One does quite relish a challenge, doesn't one?"

Charles, leading Lady Warwick from the veranda, was conscious of the curious eyes on them—and of Daisy's gloved hand, light on his sleeve, her lovely face turned up to him. It was a face he knew, for their families were acquainted. His father and Daisy's stepfather, Lord Rosslyn, had both been interested in horses and had been friends, on and off the turf. He remembered his parents commenting, when he was quite young, that since he and Daisy were of the same age and class, she would be a suitable daughter-in-law.

But the magnitude of the fortune Daisy had inherited from her grandfather, Viscount Maynard, destined her for a husband of greater stature. It had been thought for a time that she would wed Leopold, the youngest of Victoria's sons, for the Queen herself was intent on a match between them. The Royal matchmaker was disappointed, however, when Daisy preferred Lord Warwick, one of Leopold's equerries and heir to the Earl of Warwick, whose ancestral home was Warwick Castle. Since then, Her Majesty had not been favorably inclined toward Daisy, and after rumors of her affair with the Prince of Wales reached the Queen's ears, she was forbidden to appear at Court. This was only a minor misfortune, of course, for the Prince and Princess held their own court at Marlborough House, where Daisy was in frequent attendance.

Charles did not know Daisy well, but the woman intrigued him. She was, he felt, far more complex than the silly spendthrift the press portrayed. She had an intelligent interest in politics and government that, Charles suspected, was partly responsible for the Prince's attraction to her, and she had an unfashionable concern for the less fortunate that was at odds with her fashionably lighthearted facade. Her political interests were not likely to endear her to those who worried that the Prince might mix State secrets with his pillow talk. But it was her tendency toward impulsiveness that worried Charles. The Countess of Warwick could easily find herself in trouble.

"This isn't just about the excursion, is it, Charles?" she asked when they were out of earshot of the luncheon gathering.

"No," he said. "I felt that Wallace was becoming altogether too—"

Daisy's face closed. "I no longer find Reggie amusing. He should not have been invited if Sir Friedrich had not insisted."

Charles raised his eyebrows. Daisy had not always disliked Reginald Wallace. The two of them had been the talk of the town one season while Lord Warwick was in Mexico, exploiting a gold-mining franchise. The affair had been most unfortunate, ending when Wallace's wife threatened to sue for divorce. But divorce was impossible, of course, utterly unimaginable. It meant scandal, and scandal meant absolute ruin. Even the innocent parties would have been completely ostracized, their only recourse to go abroad to live. The un-imaginable was averted when Lady Wallace was killed in a riding accident. But that had been five years or so ago. Daisy Warwick's affairs had taken quite a different turn since. Everyone knew that she and the Prince were lovers.

But Charles felt it would be presumptuous for him to re-mark on either relationship. He simply said, "Well, then, shall we talk about tomorrow's excursion?"

"What about it?"

"HRH has agreed to go to Chelmsford?"

Daisy made a pretty mouth. "He has agreed, although I am quite sure he's doing it to humor me. That's why I ar-ranged for Bradford to drive that new automobile of his. I thought the novelty of the ride might make the destination more palatable. Bertie says he is looking forward to it."

Charles understood. Albert Edward, Bertie to his closest friends, was a pleasure-loving man who was usually at great pains to avoid anything ugly or repulsive. Charles could think of no place more abhorrent—and least likely to please His Highness—than the one to which Daisy proposed to take him. To agree, the Prince would have to be deeply infatuated, and even then, Daisy was taking a risk.

"Well, then," he asked, "what do you want of me, Daisy? What is to be my role in your expedition?"

She dropped his arm and turned toward him, her lovely eyes wide. "Why, to document our visit, of course. Your photographs might be used to illustrate a magazine article."

Hearing that, he felt even more uneasy. "What magazine article?" he persisted.

"Don't you see?" she asked. She half turned away from him. "If His Highness shows concern about the appalling conditions of the poor, those in power in the government will find it in their own interest to support a reform of the Poor Law. As Mr. Blatchford says, the Prince himself does not have to *do* anything. He can shape the course of events simply by paying attention to the right issues at the right moment."

"Mr. Blatchford? This excursion was his idea?"

"No," she said. And then, grudgingly, "Well, I suppose he did suggest it." She turned, her blue eyes dark. "What's wrong with that, Charles? If the idea is a good one, what does it matter whose it was?'' And if I have influence over any man, great or small, is it not my obligation to use it to the good?''

Charles eyed her soberly. Reginald Wallace had spoken more accurately than he knew. ''It matters because Blatchford is an acknowledged Socialist,'' he said. ''There are many in high places who fear Socialism more than they fear plague. Even the Queen herself is afraid of the power of the people.''

It was true. The press tended to portray Victoria as a benevolent monarch, universally loved by her people, but in actuality, she was extraordinarily unpopular. The common people resented her obsessive grief for the Prince Consort and her decades-long seclusion at Balmoral, and said openly that she was derelict in her duty. For the last ten years, radical MPs had pressed for the elimination of the monarchy and the establishment of a republic. Not long ago, a writer in the *East London Observer* had noted that ''men and their families are hovering on the brink of starvation, and there is grave reason to fear that a social revolution is impending.'' And Victoria herself was haunted by the specter of what she called ''a new French Revolution in England'' that would rise up and overthrow the monarchy, a fear that was fueled by every new report of labor unrest or Anarchist violence. To many, these were desperate times.

Daisy's mouth tightened and she raised her chin. ''Really, now, Charles, *you* are becoming tedious.''

Charles could not tell whether Daisy knew what he was hinting at and refused to acknowledge it, or was so charmed by the idea of shaping the Prince's character, and hence the social policies of the Crown, that she was blind to others' views of her ambitions. But in either case, he would get no farther with her.

''Then I shall hold my tongue and ready my cameras,'' he replied lightly. ''And you, my dear Countess, will have your photographs, unlovely though they may be.''

''Thank you,'' she said with dignity, and nothing more was said about tomorrow's excursion. But Charles felt, apprehensively, that Daisy was playing with fire. There were those at Buckingham Palace who would be desperately alarmed if they believed she had inflamed the Heir Apparent with such incendiary Socialist ideals as the reform of the Poor Law.

And that was exactly what some would think when they heard that the Countess of Warwick had taken the Prince of Wales to the Chelmsford Workhouse.

6

When lovely woman stoops to folly
And finds too late that men betray
What charm can soothe her melancholy,
What art can wash her guilt away?

—OLIVER GOLDSMITH
The Vicar of Wakefield

"Th' work'ouse?" Lawrence asked incredulously. He held up his cup for another pouring of strong black tea. "Th' Countess is aimin' to drag 'Is Royal 'Ighness t' th' Chelmsford *Work'ouse*?"

"That's as they say," said Amelia, lady's maid to Miss Kathryn Ardleigh and Lawrence's sweetheart. Lawrence, who was Lord Marsden's manservant, knew that if she had her way, the two of them would be married tomorrow. But he'd insisted that the grand day be postponed until their meager savings were enlarged and his goal was within reach, which surely would not be long off now. Lord Marsden, who was a motorcar fiend, was initiating him into the mysteries of driving and automobile maintenance and had generously promised to make him into a motor mechanic and chauffeur. Lawrence was even hoping to be sent on a six-week apprenticeship to the automobile manufactory in Paris, where he could learn everything there was to be known about motorcars. And a few years hence, when there were many vehicles needing repair, he could open his own mechanic's shop.

" 'Tis a puzzle t' me," Amelia said with great sadness,

"why anybody 'ud want t' go t' such a place as the Work-'ouse on a pleasure trip. Fair full o' 'eartache, 'tis."

Lawrence patted Amelia's hand. Her sister had died in the workhouse, and he knew the depth of her sorrow. "Them wot's respons'ble fer Jenny's dyin' got their reward, right enough," he said consolingly.

It was teatime in the large, windowless servants' hall at Easton Lodge, and the trestle benches were crowded with the estate servants and the servants of guests—the rowdier lower echelon servants, that is. The Uppers had gathered in the housekeeper's parlor, reportedly supping on Madeira cake, several sorts of jam, and glasses of claret. Fairy-food, Lawrence thought disdainfully, slathering butter on a slab of bread and forking a slice of cold mutton from the platter in front of him. Give him a proper tea with thick slices of brown bread, a bit of cold joint, and a cup of the strongest, hottest tea that could be had. So fortified, he'd work until bedtime.

"Th' work'ouse," murmured Amelia again. "It don't seem right, some'ow."

"'Ard to credit," agreed Wickett, a dapper, bandy-legged coachman in the green-and-gold livery of Easton Lodge, seated opposite. "I 'eard they're leavin' arter breakfast i' that newfangled motor wot b'longs t'—" He broke off, squinting suspiciously at Lawrence across the wooden table. "Say, now. Ain't ye Sir Marsden's man, wot mekkanics motors?"

Lawrence nodded. "Aye, that's me." He had but an hour ago arrived on the mail train from London, laden with the spare tire, the extra drive belt, the cask of petrol, and the calcium carbide that were wanted to ensure that Mr. Marsden's Daimler was in tip-top form for His Highness's trip on the morrow. And now to learn that the Prince was to go to the poorhouse!

"Whoops!" The bandy-legged Wickett threw back his head and guffawed, showing stained and broken teeth. "Well, then, yer fer it, laddie. Ye'll be wanted t' go 'long, no doubt—an' so will me lady's brougham an' pair. I saw that wunnerful motor when Lord Marsden drove in this mornin', clinkety-clanketty. It'll never git t' Chelmsford. Why, it's all o' thirteen mile there 'n' another thirteen back!"

"Lit'le enough you know," Lawrence retorted warmly.

"That motorcar flew from Colchester in less'n three hours, an' that's twenty-five miles." He omitted to mention the breakdown the motorcar had suffered, which would not have cost them so much time if it had not occurred near nightfall. "Why, that Daimler 'ud make it t' Lunnon in 'alf a day, easy."

Wickett snorted. "Ses 'oo?"

"Ses 'e," Amelia shot back proudly. "An' 'e knows wot 'e's talkin' about, 'e do!" She bestowed a fond glance and a caress on Lawrence. "Nobody knows motors like Lawrence Quibbley."

Lawrence grinned, his heart warming at Amelia's ready defense. "Ses me," he agreed mildly. "Wanter lay a bob on't?"

"Yer on." Wickett slapped the flat of his hand on the table. "Chelmsford an' back i' three hours er less."

"Not countin' th' time spent i' the work'ouse," Lawrence amended. He would have to have a word with Lord Marsden about the wager in order to ensure that there was no dallying. But he knew his employer well, having served at Marsden Manor in various posts—footman, manservant, and now mechanic—for going on eight years. Lord Marsden came of sporting stock and enjoyed a wager better than some. He would rally. And Lawrence himself would see to the automobile's readiness. The bob was as good as in his pocket.

"I'm sure I don't know why the Countess would want to take His Royal Highness to the workhouse," sniffed Richards. He was valet to a visiting gentleman named Wallace and obviously felt that he was not among his betters. He laid mutton on his buttered bread with a judicious hand. " 'Tis not a fit place for His Highness, nor for her ladyship neither, however good-hearted she may be." He pursed his pale lips censoriously. "I wonder Lord Warwick doesn't set her to rights."

"Lord Warwick!" grunted the sullen-faced young footman on the other side of Wickett. "Wot makes ye think he kin tell her ladyship wot t' do?" He hunched his shoulders. "A law to herself, that woman is. Anyway, she *ought* t' go t' th' poor'ouse. She needs t' see it fer 'erself. At th' rate she's spendin', she may git there on 'er own."

"That'll do, Marsh," Wickett warned. "You wudn't speak that way 'bout 'er ladyship where Buffle cud 'ear ye." Buffle was the Easton Lodge house steward, who in addition to his other duties was responsible for the good behavior of the footmen and under-footmen, who were sometimes spirited and inclined to youthful hijinks.

Lawrence understood Wickett's caution, for it was a servant's responsibility, and the better part of discretion, to speak well of his employers, whatever private opinion he might hold. And servants *did* hold strong private opinions, of course, for they were witness to all sorts of secret and immoral behaviors—drunkenness, violence, rage, lechery, adulterous intrigues. But as it happened, Lawrence agreed with Marsh's opinion. The Countess of Warwick was widely known as a woman of questionable judgment. Well-meaning and full of the milk of human kindness, perhaps, but a bit short when it came to knowing how to do things. In a word, foolish.

"Buffle can't hear me, now, can 'e?" growled Marsh, who was hardly more than eighteen. He had a brooding mouth, badly pocked cheeks, and heavy black eyebrows over eyes that were dull as lead. "I'm sick o' ever'one sayin' as 'ow th' Countess is so gen'rous an' kind an' good-doin' an' this an' that."

"But she is, i'n't she?" asked Amelia wonderingly. "Jes' yestidday, when we got 'ere, she'd gone out takin' jellies an' port t' th' sick."

"Jellies an' port, when it's a better livin' we need?" Marsh raised his voice ringingly, and his dull eyes showed a spark. "Let 'er go t' th' work'ouse, I say! Let 'er see wot ends pore people're fetched to, when they got no other way t' live."

Amelia shrank back against Lawrence, startled by the young man's passion. Wickett looked uneasily over his shoulder to make sure there were none in the room who might carry tales. "You an' yer fam'ly 'ave a 'ard cross t' bear, boy," he said in a low voice. "But all of us 'ave our share o' grief i' this miser'ble world. Yer father may be laid low, but 'e's a man o' pluck an'—"

"A'n't ye 'eard?" the boy growled into his mug of tea.

"Me father died a fortnight ago. She *killed* 'im, sure as she'd blowed off 'is 'ead instead o' 'is leg!"

With a sympathetic shake of his head, Wickett put down his fork. "Ooh, I'm that sorry t'ear it, young Marsh. Yer father was a proud man, fallen on bad times." He frowned. "But 'is shootin' was a accident, pure an' simple. Beaters is allus i' danger. She may've shot 'im but she pensioned 'im, too, di'n't she?"

"Killed 'im wi' kindness, she did," the boy said mockingly. "Bein' under-gamekeeper were 'is 'ole life. Yer a proud man, Mr. Wickett. 'Ud ye take a quid a week fer *yer* leg? 'Ud ye let a 'oman try t' wash away 'er guilt wi' money?"

Put this way, the coachman had to reconsider. "A pension's cert'nly no recompense fer a leg lost through a 'oman's folly," he admitted. "An' 'er ladyship's a unsteady shot, t' be sure. She ought niver t'uv bin on th' line, is wot th' loaders say."

"But 'tis not just 'er, an' not just me dad," Marsh said, leaning forward and dropping his voice. "It's all o' 'em abovestairs, th' wemmin wearin' jew'ls an' fine dresses, th' men boastin' 'bout their 'orses an' their yachts. An' not one o' 'em give a thought t' th' rags an' th' 'ovels an' th' sickness 'round 'em." His voice was almost a whisper, his dull eyes suddenly brilliant, mesmerizing. "But their time is comin', fer th' people can't bear it much longer. 'Twill be as 'twas 'cross th' Channel, when th' Frenchies rose up an'—"

"Quibbley!" boomed a woman's loud, rough voice. "Lor' be blessed, it's Quibbley 'isself!"

Lawrence, who had found himself drawn into Marsh's hypnotic polemic, was suddenly shocked to full attention, and something very close to fear. He fancied himself a strong man, but no strength was equal to that of the woman who stationed herself close behind him and wound substantial arms around his neck, pulling him backward against the soft pillow of her bosom. Furthermore, Lawrence felt within himself the stern consciousness of guilt. Inwardly, he quailed.

"Winnie," he cried weakly, grasping her arms in an attempt to extricate himself. "Winnie Wospottle, 'erself! I'm glad t' see yer."

"Glad t' see me indeed!" Winnie bent her cheek to his and wound her arms more tightly around his neck, as though she would choke him. "I ought t've sued yer fer breach o' promise, ye scalawag! Makin' sport wi' a pore foolish young girl wi' a babe in 'er arms, whose 'eart was that set on yer. Ye done a bunk an' left me waitin' at th' altar, ye did!"

The men opposite had decently averted their eyes from this embarrassing spectacle, but Amelia had gone rigid. Lawrence hazarded a glance and saw that her delicate face was white as a winding sheet.

"Amelia," he began desperately, "this is someone 'oo I knew back in Brighton when I was jes' a young—"

But Amelia had clambered over the bench and gone in a flash, leaving her tea unfinished on the table. Winnie, seizing the opportunity to occupy the vacated space, loosened her grip on Lawrence and lowered her ample self into it.

"Well, now, Lawrence Quibbley," she demanded, "wot 'ave yer bin doin' wi' yerself since yer deserted me back in Brighton?"

"I di'n't desert yer," Lawrence growled, beginning to recover his breath. He would have gone after Amelia, but he could see that it was of no use. He would have to explain to her later—if he could. "Like I tol' yer back then, Win, I di'n't want t' be married, an' that was th' long an' th' short o' it. Ye don't need t' make me out a rotter 'oo'd betray a girl when she was countin' on 'im."

"That's as may be." Winnie leaned forward and tweaked his nose familiarly. "But we've met agin, Quibbley, an' I'm that glad t' see yer."

Lawrence pulled away, eyeing her. The years—eight, nine, was it?—had been reasonably kind. Winnie was as charmingly buxom as ever, her brown hair as tightly furled, her cheeks as rosy, her lips as full and welcoming. "Wot're ye doin' i' th' country, lass?" he asked, not unkindly. Winnie had always loved Brighton, with its beaches and bathing machines and gay dancing. "Ain't it a bit out o' th' way fer yer? An' where's yer babe?"

Winnie pulled herself up. "I'm th' laundress," she said

proudly, and even Lawrence was impressed. The position of laundress, while not quite equivalent to that of the other Uppers—cook, housekeeper, steward—was nonetheless an important one, with a fair amount of independence. "Me babe is 'alf-grown now and livin' wi' 'er father. An' as fer bein' out o' th' way—" Giggling, she leaned forward and took his cheek between her thumb and forefinger and shook it. "There's compensations, wudn't yer say, luv?"

Lawrence brushed her hand aside, knowing exactly what she meant. "Oh, er, Win," he began uncomfortably. "I say, ol' girl, I've got other—" He broke off and cast an appealing eye at the bandy-legged coachman. "Wickett," he said, " 'ave ye met Winnie Wospottle?"

Across the table, Wickett was taken with a fit of coughing and had to leave. With a disgusted look, Richards rose from the bench, too, followed by surly young Marsh. Lawrence had been abandoned.

Winnie leaned seductively toward him. "Don't tell me ye don't know wot goes on at these country 'ouse parties, Quibbley."

"Wot d'ye mean?" Lawrence managed, trying to maintain the appearance of innocence.

"I see th' sheets when they come down t' th' laundry," she said in a conspiratorial tone. "There's foolishness afoot abovestairs. Ev'ry lady's got 'er gent, ev'ry gent's got 'is lady."

"But o' course," Lawrence said, making a last effort. "The ladies an' gents 're married, ain't they?"

Winnie boxed Lawrence's ear smartly. "Lor' bless th' man!" she exclaimed. "Did ye jes' ride in on th' hay wagon, Quibbley? Th' lords an' ladies don't tumble wi' th' ones they're wed to, not a bit of it!" She grinned suggestively, showing a gold-capped tooth. "Why don't ye meet me i' th' ironin' room t'night, luv? There's a corner by th' 'ot water boiler that's private an' not too uncomfort'ble."

The sight of Amelia's white face rose before him, and Lawrence knew he had to resist Winnie's wiles. He shook his head determinedly. "I got t' admit, yer beaut'ful as ever, ol' girl, but—"

She stroked his arm. "We don't 'ave t' do nothin', if ye

don't feel like it, Quibbley,'' she murmured. ''Jes' come along an' 'ave a bit o' tipple wi' me, fer ol' times' sake.'' She looked up at him. ''Pleeze?''

And Lawrence, who had once been brave enough to jump onto a runaway motorcar and bring it to a halt, found that he lacked the courage to say no to Winnie Wospottle.

7

When lovely woman stoops to folly
  And finds too late her heart's betrayed,
She'll learn to practice stratagems
  And wield her power undismayed.

—BERYL BARDWELL
The Loves of Lady Lenore

Amelia had no way of knowing the extent of Lawrence's perfidy, but she could guess. Imagining the worst—Lawrence reunited with a love he had once jilted—she stumbled out of the servants' hall. Halfway up the back stairs, she could go no further. She sank down, sobbing, brokenhearted.

After a few moments, she felt a hand on her shoulder. "Amelia?" a voice asked. "Wot's wrong, dear? Is there anythin' I kin do?"

Amelia looked up into the face of the young girl—one of the laundry maids—whose room she had shared last night. Hearing the comforting voice, she broke into a fresh fit of weeping.

The girl, whose name was Meg, sat down beside her on the step and put an arm around her shoulders. "Whatever 'tis," she said practically, " 'tain't bad 'nough t' carry on that way."

"Yes, 'tis," Amelia insisted, sniffling. "It's *worse*."

"It's yer sweet'eart, I bet," Meg said, patting her arm. "Ye ought t' do what th' upstairs ladies do, Amelia. 'Ave more'n one sweet'eart. That way, when one betrays yer, there's another one waitin'."

Meg's advice was sensible enough, but Amelia's gentle heart almost gave way at the thought of dealing with more than one treacherous man at a time. "I cudn't do that, Meg," she said, and dropped her forehead on her knees. "I'm too true."

Meg sighed. "I know," she said forlornly. "I cudn't, neither. First one, then another—I doan't see 'ow th' ladies do 't. I was allus taught t' love one fer life, good er bad, wotever 'e does t'yer."

Amelia wiped her eyes with the back of her hand. "But wot d'ye do when 'e's not true?"

Meg stood up slowly, shaking her head. "Suffer, I reckon." She stood for a minute, looking down. "I'll see yer t'night," she said, and was gone.

Amelia sat on the stairs for a few moments more, then wiped her eyes and settled her cap. Lawrence might be a faithless traitor and her heart might be broken, but it would soon be time for the dressing bell and there was work to be done. She climbed the stairs and went down the long hallway to Miss Ardleigh's room, where she tapped on the door and opened it.

Wearing her dressing gown, Miss Ardleigh sat at the writing desk in front of the velvet-draped window. When Amelia came in, she hastily stacked the pages on which she had been writing and stuffed them into the leather portfolio that she took with her wherever she went. Usually Amelia smiled at this little effort at concealment, because all the servants at Bishop's Keep knew exactly what Miss Ardleigh—or Beryl Bardwell, for that was the name under which she wrote her sensational fictions—was up to. But it was part of the game to make believe that they saw nothing, so when Amelia happened on Beryl Bardwell engaged in the labor of authorship, she smiled and pretended not to notice. This evening, though, she could not summon even a flicker of a smile in response to her mistress's cheery greeting.

Miss Ardleigh grew concerned. "You look as if you've been crying, Amelia. Is something wrong?"

Mutely, Amelia shook her head.

Miss Ardleigh held out her hand. "Oh, come now," she said. "You're not one to cry without a reason. What's happened?"

Prompted by this sympathy, Amelia said, "It's Lawrence, miss," and burst into a flood of tears. In a moment, she had told the little she knew and the more she imagined, and Miss Ardleigh was holding her and patting her back while she wept.

"I am sure," Miss Ardleigh said gently, when the tears had somewhat subsided, "that it is not as bad as it seems. This Winnie person—is she as lovely as you?"

Amelia frowned, wanting to be accurate. "She's . . . much larger."

"Larger, but not lovelier, then. And her age?"

"Oh, *much* older, miss," Amelia replied, from the youthful perspective of seventeen. "All of twenty-five, I should reckon. An' she's quite brazen."

"Well, then," Miss Ardleigh (who was twenty-seven herself, and a spinster) said briskly. "What are we crying for? You have the advantage of beauty and youth. All you need is a little more courage, and perhaps a bit of brazenness on your own account. Let Lawrence know that you care for him, Amelia. His heart is with you, I'm sure of it."

Amelia felt herself blushing furiously. "It's not 'is 'eart I'm worried about, miss," she said in a low voice. "It's th' . . . other thing." She felt quite brave in bringing the subject up, but of course she would not have spoken so openly if Miss Ardleigh had not encouraged her, or if she were not an American. American women, as she knew from her clandestine reading of Beryl Bardwell's fictions, were much more open about physical intimacies than were English women.

A smile tweaked at Miss Ardleigh's lips. "Yes, well," she said, and cleared her throat. " 'The other thing' is a bit of a problem, to be sure, and I am not suggesting that you violate your principles. But where Lawrence is concerned, you might want to practice a stratagem or two."

"A stratagem, miss?" Amelia was puzzled.

"It might not hurt to let him see that you have the power to attract other men. Is there a party belowstairs this evening?"

"Yes, miss," Amelia said. Although house party weekends meant a great deal more work for the servants, they also presented opportunities for socializing. The kitchen maids would still be doing up the pots and pans after tonight's dinner and the house steward would be supervising the washing up of the gold plate in the pantry, but those who could would steal away to dance and trade gossip and play cards around the fire in the servants' hall.

The dressing bell clanged loudly, reminding them both that it was time to change for dinner. "Well, a party should be a fine opportunity to let Lawrence see that other men find you attractive," Miss Ardleigh said, and began to unfasten her dressing gown. "You must take a ribbon from the drawer to dress your hair, Amelia, and some of my scent, if you like. I shall dispense with your services at bedtime, so go and enjoy yourself."

A ribbon, and scent! Well, that put an entirely different face on things. Winnie Wospottle was indeed quite brazen, and Amelia was not so blinded by love that she imagined Lawrence braver than he was. If she were to rescue him from that woman's clutches, she would have to resort to strategy. She straightened her shoulders, determined.

"Yes, thank you, miss," she said. "I shall." She went to the wardrobe where her mistress's gowns were hung. "You wanted t' wear th' gray tonight?"

Miss Ardleigh had stripped to her chemise. "No, Amelia, I've changed my mind. I shall wear the green silk with the matching gloves, and Aunt Sabrina's emerald pendant. And I have taken the peacock feathers from my hat—I shall want them in my hair."

Amelia's eyebrows went up. The green silk was cut low and more daring than the dresses Miss Ardleigh usually wore; she had purchased it chiefly because Mrs. Farley thought she ought to have at least one such gown. And she had never worn her aunt's emerald pendant, which was quite a lovely jewel, the richest Amelia had ever seen.

Taking the green gown from the wardrobe, she changed the subject. "Wud ye know, miss, why 'er ladyship wud be takin' 'Is Royal 'Ighness t' th' work'ouse termorrer?"

Miss Ardleigh had just sat down before the mirror. She

glanced up, startled, the hairbrush in her hand. "To the *work-house*?"

"Yes," Amelia said. She laid the gown on the bed, smoothing the skirts. "T' th' very place where my dear Jenny died," she added sadly. Jenny had been wayward, and when she was discovered to be pregnant, had been turned out of her place at Bishop's Keep (this was in the days before the young miss, of course) and ended up in the Chelmsford Workhouse, where both she and the babe had died. It was a common enough story, but no less sad for that, and sadly unfair. The man who betrayed Jenny had most certainly not suffered as she had. But that was the way of it, Amelia thought, and her sadness became colored by anger. Men used women, and then abandoned them. She must be sure that such a thing never happened to her.

"The workhouse," Miss Ardleigh repeated thoughtfully. "Well, well. It appears that her ladyship has a stratagem or two up her sleeve."

8

I slept, and dreamed that life was Beauty;
I woke, and found that life was Duty.

—ELLEN STURGIS HOOPER
"Beauty and Duty," 1840

I cannot charge myself with neglecting any of the duties that rightly fall to an English country gentleman, as those duties were carried out and taught to me by my own father. If a new standard or conception of duty has sprung up since my day, I can only say that I know nothing of it, and have not seen or heard of its advantages.

—FRANCIS GREVILLE BROOKE, LORD WARWICK
Memories of Sixty Years

It was the hour after tea, when the guests had retired for a rest before dinner and the evening's entertainment. Sir Charles sat at the writing table in his bedroom, staring at his mother's letter. He did not need to read it again, for every word was engraved on his heart.

My Dearest Son,

I am most dreadfully sorry Alas! to tell you that the doctors now offer *no hope* at all for your beloved Brother. Robert is dying and they say will be gone from us in body (tho' not in spirit) by Eastertide. He suffers much, and is obliged to be carried up and down stairs and lifted in and out of bed, and we are all very low in our minds and suffer his Distress as our own. Dear Alice bears up bravely and is most touchingly devoted. She is a noble Wife.

I need not tell you how this sad event, when it comes, will alter your Circumstance. Although you have always been determined to pursue your own ventures, I know the family can rely upon you in the moment of your grief to take up Dear Robert's staff and march on. While your desires may lay elsewhere, your Duty is here at Somersworth, and I have every confidence & trust that you My Darling Boy will do as is right and fitting, when the Day comes that Robert is with us no more.

Your Loving Mother

The dressing bell rang as Charles refolded the letter. He pitied his poor brother (whom he did not know well) and his brother's wife Alice (whom he knew even less well), and pitied himself because Robert and Alice had no children. That his brother would die childless meant that he was about to inherit the title of Lord Sheridan, the fifth Baron of Somersworth. He would also inherit the management of the estates and the family's seat in the House of Lords, and would have to give thought to producing an heir who would in his turn be chained to his feudal obligations.

Charles placed the letter in his writing case and closed it. As a younger son with a modest but adequate income of his own, he had enjoyed the freedom to pursue his interests as he wished, while his elder brother Robert did the work of maintaining the family's estates and social obligations. When Robert died, he would no longer be free to do as he chose, or to marry as he chose. Since it was now a question of the furtherance of the line, his mother would insist on having some say in his choice and would urge him to choose a wife whose family she knew. Independent and unconventional, Kate was not a woman who would appeal to his mother, or whom the Dowager Baroness would consider a suitable wife for her son. And for her part, Kate preferred to live removed from Society. The kind of life the barons of Somersworth had always led would be distasteful to her.

And to Charles. At thirty-four, his interests were many and far-flung. At Eton and later at Oxford (where he had prepared for a career in the Foreign Service), he had acquainted himself with archaeology, paleontology, botany, geology, zoology. In the interval between Eton and Oxford, during a brief posting with Her Majesty's forces, he had pursued technical studies. Having avoided a diplomatic career by fortuitously inheriting his maternal grandmother's small fortune, he was able to follow his diverse interests as they presented themselves, without regard to profit or outcome. In the tradition of the English gentleman scientist, he had conducted a study of Cenozoic invertebrates in the fossil record of West Essex and investigated several rare species of bats. But he was also intrigued by many of the new branches of technology and science—photography, toxicology, serology, dactyloscopy, anthropometry—and their application to the study of criminal activity. He had even enjoyed several successes in the solution of crimes—two, with Kate's help.

But his current inquiry, unfortunately, did not look like being a success. It was his considered opinion that the Prince's horse had nothing to do with the death of the young groom, and that the boy had been the victim of foul play. But the only evidence lay in the circumstances, and unless someone had caught a glimpse of the killer and came forward to offer evidence, a solution was not likely to be found. While Charles was confident that the new sciences would one day make it possible to identify a perpetrator whether or not he had been observed in the commission of his crime, eyewitness testimony was still the only testimony most jurors would accept, and even the police were trained only to deal with the most obvious kinds of physical evidence.

Hence, Charles was left with the awkward task of reporting to His Royal Highness that the matter remained in question. The report would not be well received, for HRH did not easily tolerate ambiguities, relativities, or approximations. But Charles knew his duty and would satisfy the Prince as well as he could.

There was a discreet knock at the door. Charles opened it and told the inquiring valet (a loan from Daisy) that his services were not required. He could perfectly well dress himself. He opened the wardrobe, found his evening clothes where some servant had hung them, and began to put on his shirt, turning his thoughts to other matters. Daisy's plan to take HRH to the Chelmsford Workhouse, for one. Members of the Prince's circle were happy to amuse themselves with such minor naughtiness as adultery and could accept a minor scandal if it did not attract too much attention in the press. They could not bring themselves to tolerate Socialist leanings, however frivolously expressed. Daisy's interests—her needlework school, her campaign for Poor Law Guardian, her interest in Poor Law reform—smacked of Socialism, and were no doubt already seen as supporting the unrest that periodically flared among the people.

Not that Charles himself did not applaud such efforts. He had cheered Keir Hardie, the Scottish miner elected to Parliament three years ago, who had arrived at the House of Commons wearing a cloth cap and accompanied by a brass band. He admired Robert Blatchford's Socialist journal, *The Clarion*, which had advanced a number of progressive (and, in Charles's view, necessary) reforms. But if Daisy intended to influence the Prince in the direction of Socialism, she should prepare herself for trouble, because trouble was what she would get.

After some searching, Charles found cuff links and studs in the tray on top of the dresser, donned his white waistcoat, and slipped his tie around his rigid chimney pot collar, which he hated fiercely, for it chafed his neck. Glancing in the mirror, he combed back his unruly brown hair and surveyed his reflection with a resigned sigh. He was prepared for dinner and the evening's entertainment, although he did not expect to enjoy it. And at all costs, he should have to avoid the attentions of Lillian Forsythe, who had accosted him at tea with some sort of unintelligible remarks about bats. Not even Duty required that he endure such women.

But as he stared at himself in the mirror, his reflection

seemed to speak to him. What *did* Duty require, after all? Did it demand that the fifth Baron of Somersworth live and marry as the first four barons had lived and married, always in the front rank and the public eye of Society?

Could he not perform his duty to the title, the estate, and the family—*and* to himself?

And if that were true for him, might it not be true for Kate, if she loved him? Perhaps he should open the subject with her tonight, sound her out on her feelings about himself and about the change in his situation. He might even raise the subject of marriage. He wasn't entirely sure how he might do this, for he had done nothing of the sort before, but perhaps during dinner he could think of a logical way to open the topic.

Charles nodded at his reflection and ran his finger around the inside of the infernal collar. And as he left the room and walked down the hall toward the stairs, he felt more cheerful than he had since the letter arrived.

9

The chief folly of those who belonged to the Marlborough House set was to imagine that pleasure and happiness were identical.

—FRANCES (DAISY) BROOKE, LADY WARWICK
Discretions

Think, too, how to beauty
They oft owe their fall,
And what may through vice
Be the fate of you all.
—*Anonymous nineteenth-century ballad*

Kate had been introduced to most of the guests the night before, and she had taken a few minutes before dinner to study the guest list, trying to match names and faces. But as she assumed her place in the line to go in to dinner, she still had to make a deliberate effort to remember which names belonged to which individuals.

There was no mistaking the Prince, of course, with those exophthalmic eyes that Victoria had passed on to her children, and that clipped graying beard and portly profile. He was about to lead the Countess into the dining hall.

There was no mistaking the Countess, either. Lady Warwick was dressed in a creamy tulle with ivory velvet ribbons and a froth of lace that gave her a young girl's air of innocence. It seemed to Kate, however, that beneath Daisy's lighthearted gaiety was a certain apprehension. Perhaps, she thought, watching the Countess glance from the attentive Prince to her debonair husband, chatting animatedly with Lady Forsythe, it had to do with the awkward situation in which she found herself. It must not be easy to manage both a princely lover and a husband under the same roof, even if the husband obligingly turned the other way when the occasion called for tolerance. But did he always? Or did Lord Warwick sometimes object to his wife's affairs?

Lord Warwick himself escorted Lady Lillian, brilliant in sapphire taffeta that rustled richly as she moved. Kate saw her catch Sir Charles's eye and speak to him in a low voice, with a smile that promised intimacies. They had obviously made an acquaintance, at tea, perhaps. Kate couldn't help wondering, with a distinct uneasiness, whether Lady Lillian had brought up the subject of bats, and whether Sir Charles had found her remarks interesting.

As for Sir Charles, unusually elegant but stiff and uncomfortable-looking in his evening wear, Kate found herself torn. She had been hoping that they were to be table partners and was disappointed when he was asked to escort Celia, the coyly self-conscious daughter of Lord and Lady Rochdale, who had only recently come out. On the other hand, she thought it might be better if she and Sir Charles did not have easy opportunities for conversation this weekend. Perhaps she could postpone the day when he might bring up the subject of marriage and she would have to tell him . . . Tell him what? That she was not interested? It was a lie, but it was better than the truth: that he would not be interested in her if he knew everything about her.

Behind Lord Warwick and Lady Lillian, third in the procession, came Celia's parents, Lord and Lady Rochdale. Lord Malcolm was tall and stooped, with a perpetual frown between his too-small eyes, a long nose with a droop at the end, and pale, thin lips. Lady Verena's low corsage outlined her bosom in layers of lace, emphasizing her plumpness, and she wore a false black chignon with a bunch of fat black curls that dangled coquettishly over her left shoulder, several shades darker than her graying hair. Kate studied her uneasily, but if Lady Verena had received a telegram that gave away Beryl Bardwell's identity, it was not apparent from her demeanor. Her glance slid past Kate as if she were invisible.

Nor did Ellie Farley seem to have found her out. Ellie gave her a warm smile and touched her arm. "You're beautiful tonight, Kate," she whispered, as she stepped into line behind the Rochdales, on the arm of a handsome young Scots Guards lieutenant whose name, Kate had learned the night before, was Andrew Kirk-Smythe. "But do relax, dear. You look as if you're afraid someone will bite you."

Kate tried to smile, but without much success. In spite of the bare-shouldered elegance of the green silk gown that had seemed so grand in the privacy of her bedroom, she felt herself just plain, ordinary Kate, an American—a redheaded Irish American, at that—and decidedly out of place in the midst of such a splendid company.

The feeling was heightened by the joking, gossipy banter exchanged by the two pairs of couples that followed Ellie and Kirk-Smythe in the line: Lady Felicia Metcalf, escorted by a sandy-haired man of erect military bearing with a gold pince-nez, Sir Friedrich Temple; and Mr. and Mrs. Milford Knightly. Mr. Knightly, a turf friend of the Prince, was a sardonic man with one glass eye, wreathed in an aura of cheap cigars; his wife, several years older than her husband, was dressed in an olive green gown that made her skin look sallow. Behind them came Lord Reginald Wallace, Bradford Marsden, and the financier Samuel Isaacson, engrossed in a conversation about motorcars. Then, after some confusion about the order of the guests, came Kate, on the arm of a retired army officer with surly black eyebrows who glared at her and snorted "American, eh? Too many of you gels over here, looking for husbands."

The feeling of alienation persisted all through dinner, where Kate was sandwiched between the gray-bearded ex-officer with surly eyebrows (whose name, she discovered, was Sir Thomas Cobb) and Lord Malcolm Rochdale, who carried on a conversation with each other over her head. Lord Malcolm owned a country estate named Alwyne, not far from Chelmsford, and was building a grand new house there. That work, and the construction of his stables, occupied all his thoughts, Kate concluded, for he talked of little else. By the time dinner was over, she had learned that the newly constructed house had three wings and a clock tower and that the grounds were enclosed by a wall the height of his wife's head. The whole affair was constructed of locally produced brick (making it sound to Kate remarkably like a prison), and Lord Malcolm commented several times on the extraordinary amount of money he had saved by this expedient. "One pays attention to such mundane business as construction savings these days," he said, leaning forward to speak to Sir Thomas.

"Ah, yes," Sir Thomas answered glumly. "Now that these ruinous death duties have been laid on us, we may all be constrained to build with cheap brick," which remark put an end to the conversation for several moments.

If Lord Malcolm was obsessed with bricks, Sir Thomas was preoccupied with shooting. So far this season, he confided to Lord Rochdale when they were speaking again, guests at the three shooting weekends he had hosted at his Warwickshire estate had bagged two hundred partridges, three thousand pheasants, and nearly four hundred hares—bloody statistics which left Kate pitying the ptarmigan on her plate (a favorite of the Prince) and feeling a trifle ill. But at least Sir Thomas had left off glaring at Kate and muttering about American gels; now his scowl was directed across the table at Sir Reginald, Kate's luncheon partner, who had gotten into the tiff with Lady Warwick. Kate decided that Sir Thomas must have some kind of grudge against Sir Reginald, for he spent the dinner hour bristling his brows and grimacing at him, these quite remarkable facial gestures accompanied by shoulder hunches and audible snorts and hisses.

During the interval between the ptarmigan and the peas and asparagus in aspic, Kate glanced up and down the table. The guests—ten to a side, with Lady Warwick on one end and Lord Warwick on the other—were decorative in their glittering jewels and gleaming shirtfronts. They were attended by liveried footmen moving soundlessly in and out of the shadows while the myriad candles glinted off the crystal goblets and rich gold plate. A tableau of social perfection. The picture of elegant and unceasing pleasure, of well-bred sophistication, of happiness.

But glancing from face to face, Kate suddenly saw the scene as if it were a still life. The guests, frozen in various postures of eating and drinking, seemed to wear their countenances like smiling masks that covered the avaricious expressions of unhappy pleasure-seekers with nothing to do but indulge their insatiable appetites for fine food, fine houses, fine horses, and each other. And as Kate looked up and caught sight of Daisy Warwick, her face decorated with a strained, set smile, there suddenly seemed something quite false and entirely sinister about the scene, and she shivered.

At the head of the table, Daisy caught Bertie's lovingly proprietary glance and returned it. But her accustomed smile covered a surge of cold panic. How was she to tell him that she had mislaid one of his letters—one of his foolish, fatuous, extraordinarily indiscreet love letters? Would he accuse her to her face of carelessness? Would he—?

No. Bertie, whatever else he might be, was the perfect courtly gentleman. Even if he considered her to be careless and irresponsible, he would not tell her so. He might, however, decide that she was not to be trusted. He might never tell her anything important ever again. Worse, he might—

And then another thought struck her, and the panic became a tidal wave. What if she had not mislaid the letter, but it had been stolen? She did not deceive herself: her personal maids, like everyone else, could be bought. And on the blackmail market, such an indiscreet document would be worth thousands of pounds. The panic closed over her head like a dark wave, leaving her gasping for air. Who could have done such a thing?

Her glance went down the table to one face, sullen and jealous, and she felt a sudden cold surge of anger. Reginald Wallace would not have stolen the letter himself, but he was not above arranging its theft. And if that were true, if *he* had it, she might persuade him to give it back. Of course, she had no money to give him. She already owed him thousands of pounds, exactly how much, she had forgotten. But he wanted something else from her, something that would cost her nothing. She took a deep breath, raised her chin, and smiled at him.

But now the Prince was speaking to her, and she had to retrieve her smile, silence her thoughts, and answer him with a witty charm. As the Royal mistresses before her had learned to their cost, His Highness must never become bored.

Midway down the table, Sir Reginald Wallace caught Daisy's smile. What was it the woman wanted now? His forgiveness for her fickleness? His acceptance of a situation over which, at bottom, neither of them had had any control? It was damned late for either the one or the other now, though. She wanted something more tangible, money, most likely. Her estates, her income—they were nothing compared with the fortune that went for clothing and jewelry and entertainment. Yes, by God, he recognized that glance! Later tonight, he'd receive a note from her, asking him to meet her at the Folly, where she would plead with him for another loan.

The idea of it—of being with her again privately, of perhaps even touching her face, her hair—raised a sudden heat within him, and he lowered his head lest his hunger show in his face. For all his disapproval of her actions and her dangerous affiliations, those were external matters, and not the woman herself. His feelings for her had never changed, not even in those dreadful months after Margaret had died and everyone was whispering that he had killed her. He looked up and saw Sir Thomas glowering at him around the fruit-filled epergne, flushed deeply, and looked away, forcing his thoughts back to Daisy.

She was going down a perilous road. Her Socialist fellow travelers were scoundrels, or worse, plotting England's demise and the destruction of the monarchy. He might be willing to make her a loan, but to get any money from him, she'd have to listen first, and he would warn her in terms she could not ignore or laugh away. He would tell her that there were persons close to the Crown who saw what she was doing, feared she might succeed, and would do anything to ensure that she would not. His affair with Daisy may have cost him all his pleasure, destroyed his every happiness, but he loved her still. If it was in his power to keep her from making a ruinous mistake, he would.

He looked up, caught Felicia Metcalf's mooning gaze, and scowled. Blast the woman, couldn't she see that she was making fools of both of them? The business in the upstairs hallway after tea had been uglier than he intended, and he wished that scalawag Knightly had not heard so much of what passed between them. But he and Felicia were finished, that was all there was to it. He was a gentleman and hated public scenes, but was sick to death of her and the sooner she understood, the better. And as for Knightly . . .

Wallace's eyes narrowed. It was just about time for accounts to be settled. Knightly might think he could use that embarrassing business in the upper hall to get out from under his debt. But he was wrong. What Wallace had learned that morning completely eliminated Knightly's advantage. All he had to do now was collect.

With a half smile, Felicia Metcalf released Sir Reginald's glance and allowed the footman to refill her champagne glass. As she did so, she felt Mr. Knightly's boldly amused gaze on her. Her smile faded and she looked haughtily away, feeling the hot flush rise to her cheeks. It was intolerable that Milford Knightly—that wretched man with his glass eye and sardonic mouth—had overheard her little *contretemps* with Reggie in the upstairs hallway. He was such a reprobate, quite common, with nothing to recommend him except his horse-racing friendship with the Prince. And that wife of his—well, really!

She glanced again at Reggie. Of course, he hadn't meant that angry little outburst in the hallway upstairs. During the after-dinner entertainment, she would let him know that her bedroom door would be open to him tonight. Or perhaps they could meet at the Folly, where Daisy saw to it that the bedroom fires were lit so that trysting couples could take their pleasure there.

At the thought of Daisy Brooke, Felicia's lips compressed and her jealous resolve hardened. Daisy was a selfish, manipulative woman who had used poor Reggie dreadfully, used him still, no doubt, whenever she could. And if sweet, foolish Reggie imagined himself still in love with that shallow schemer—well, as Lillian Forsythe had remarked at luncheon, one did quite relish a challenge, didn't one?

Milford Knightly sat back, enjoying the consternation that he read in Felicity Metcalf's face. The woman was a fool, and not even a particularly attractive one, at that. Fancied Wallace in love with her, did she? That was a laugh. Wallace may have tumbled her a time or two when he had nothing better at hand, but he was still mad for Daisy. He'd do anything to have her, although he disapproved of almost everything she did. The folly of some men was quite remarkable.

Knightly looked up to the end of the table, where the Countess, her bare shoulders emerging angelically out of a cloud of creamy tulle, was carrying on a laughing conversation with Bertie. Daisy Warwick's ability to command foolish hearts was remarkable, too. That was precisely what made her such a problem—that, and her ability to hide her real purposes. Who could guess that behind that lovely face was a damned dangerous woman?

Still, he thought he might somehow be able to use her to get Reggie to forgive that annoying debt of his. To be sure, after this morning, things had become more complicated. But since Wallace himself was involved, his advantage was limited. Knightly was sure he could turn the situation to his benefit. After all, that was his special talent, his unique gift—capitalizing on others' mistakes in judgment, on the track and off. Still, one had to be careful. People could only be pushed so far.

His gaze moved across the table and he caught the chilly eye of the dignified, austere Sir Friedrich Temple, sitting opposite, and smiled. He knew exactly how far to push Freddy.

Sir Friedrich—a tall man with sandy hair and beard and a stern eye that passed judgment on all he witnessed—looked coldly away from Milford Knightly's self-congratulatory smile. Sir Friedrich found the man vulgar, inferior, and unworthy, and he regretted the necessity of any sort of association with him. Why Bertie so foolishly cultivated his friendship was beyond Sir Friedrich's understanding. Surely there were plenty of discreet men of good family who shared Bertie's passion for the turf, pugilism, fast women, and immoral revels. But even as a young man, HRH's most attractive personal characteristic had been his capacity for comradeship. His friends were legion. And, because he was almost completely indiscriminate, they were of all sorts, even (Sir Friedrich glanced at Samuel Isaacson) Jews. Bertie called them his "wicked boys." The press referred to the "Marlborough banditti." The Queen called them "The Prince's downfall."

There was a great deal more that Sir Friedrich had never been able to understand or accept where Albert Edward was concerned. A man in his position, who might any day find himself on the throne of England, ought to be circumspect in all matters—or, if he could not restrain his baser instincts, at least be discreet. Moreover, he ought to be involved in issues of state, so he could take up the reins of government when the time came. And here even Sir Friedrich, a devoted friend and fervent supporter of Queen Victoria who had helped the Royal family out of several tight places already, had to admit that Bertie's mother was seriously at fault.

Over three decades ago, when the Prince was still in his twenties, the Queen had decided that her son's unprincely escapades—some of them less than savory, to be sure—rendered him unfit to represent the Crown. She had excluded him from every significant duty, with a sadly predictable consequence: the future King, at bottom a well-meaning if intellectually limited man, had grown into a middle-aged *bon vivant* who filled his days and nights with senseless, perilous frivolities. The Queen felt, and Sir Friedrich and others of her inner circle agreed, that Bertie's gambling, drinking, and womanizing endangered the dignity and stature of the Crown. In fact, Lord Salisbury argued that, in these days of rumored uprisings among the lower classes, fanned by the Socialists and Anarchists, Bertie's notoriously uncontrollable behavior threatened the very existence of the monarchy. Unfortunately, Crown Prince Eddy, Bertie and Alix's oldest son and heir, appeared to have been cut of the same cloth as his father, or very nearly. For over a decade, he had fallen into first one disgrace and then another. It was over now, thank

God, ended with Eddy's funeral three years ago.

But the unfortunate Eddy's vices and inadequacies had been trivial in comparison to the business upon which Sir Friedrich was currently engaged. The Queen was deeply distressed over the recent Tranby Croft gambling scandal, which linked the Prince and Daisy Warwick and provoked *The Times* to pontificate upon the Heir Apparent's "distressing" fondness for wild house parties where money was won and lost on baccarat and men jumped from one woman's bed to another. Sir Friedrich had promised the distraught Queen to do what he could to persuade HRH to drop those of his friends whose influence was most dangerous. To that end, he had managed to obtain—

But no matter. One would see how it all came out. A footman stepped forward to refill his glass with champagne, and he looked up to find the American woman watching him curiously. The Americans—quite charming, they were, and much more free and natural than British women. Randy Churchill's widow, Jenny, for instance, a beautiful lady, amazingly accomplished. Randy had married better than he deserved.

Sir Friedrich smiled at Miss Ardleigh—undeniably attractive, at least as pretty as Jenny, and fifteen or so years younger—and lifted his glass in cordial salute. During the evening's entertainment, he would make her acquaintance. A friendly American woman might be just the breath of fresh air he needed to clear out his stale head. There was certainly nothing wrong with taking a bit of pleasure with one's work, and she might prove very useful.

10

Did ye not hear it?—No; 'twas but the wind
Or the carriage rattling o'er the stony street;
On with the dance! let joy be unconfined;
No sleep till morn, when Youth and Pleasure meet
To chase the glowing Hours with flying feet.

—LORD BYRON
Destruction of Sennacherib

The kitchen and scullery maids had just gotten started with the washing up, and the butler and several footmen were serving after-dinner wines and cordials in the drawing room while the evening's entertainment was under way. Lawrence had laid out Mr. Marsden's clothes and tended to his before-dinner needs (he had, after all, been a valet for some years before he added mechanicing to his bag of tricks), then made his way to the servants' hall, where he joined the general revelry. Some were playing cards on up-turned boxes, others were telling tales in the chimney corner, and several had pushed the table against the wall to make room for dancing. In accompaniment, one of the gardeners was fingering a reel on a wheezy concertina, while a coach-man sawed away on a fiddle and a porter kept time with a spoon on a battered kettle.

"I still say 'twas a kick in th' 'ead," maintained Benton, the shaggy Easton groom who had that morning discovered the body of the ill-fated lad in the Royal stall.

"Belike they'll niver find out 'ow 't 'appened," Winnie

Wospottle said from her stool in front of the fire, a disheveled rose, her face reflecting the firelight and a gaudy red shawl wrapped around her shoulders.

"Too bad," said a pretty brown-haired maid named Meg. "Th' boy were a likely lad, an' 'andsome." She shook her head and her red ribbon fluttered. "Marsh says they doan't want t' find out 'ow 't 'appened. 'E says they doan't care 'bout a dead servant any more'n they cared 'bout a livin' one wi' 'is leg shot off." The disgruntled Marsh, Lawrence had been given to understand, was upstairs tending to his duties as a footman.

"They'll find out," Lawrence said with assurance. He was smoking a cigarette, one elbow propped against the mantel. "Sir Charles is a great detective, 'e is."

Benton shrugged. "Well, yer detective's been detectin' all day an' 'e doan't seem t've learned noffin' yit. So I doan't reckon as how 'e's so great."

Meg got up and went to the other side of the room. Foster, a good-looking youngster who worked as a maintenance man on the estate, stretched out his hands to the fire. "If th' copper wants t' learn somfin', 'e ought t' talk t' Deaf John."

" 'E's no copper," Lawrence said defensively.

"Then why's 'e doin' a copper's work?"

" 'Cause 'e likes it." Lawrence leaned forward. " 'Oo's Deaf John?"

"Th' farrier," Foster said. "Meg's father."

"Why should Sir Charles talk to th' farrier?"

" 'Cause 'e saw somebody comin' out o' th' barn. 'E thinks it cud'uv bin th' one 'oo killed th' Prince's groom."

"Somebody?" Lawrence asked. "A servant?"

Foster shook his head. "No servant. Somebody wrapped in a cloak."

"A woman, then?" Lawrence asked, sensing that he had learned something of potential importance. "I'll tell Sir Charles."

" 'Ullo, Lawrence."

Lawrence looked up to see Amelia standing close beside him. She was wearing the blue frock he fancied, and her hair was tied back with a blue ribbon that matched her eyes. She looked young and demure and lovely, and the sight and scent of her, delicate as lilacs in spring, caught at his throat.

" 'Ullo, Amelia," he said, feeling his heart thump in his chest like a wounded bird.

Amelia's smile was shyly bold, and she held out her hand. " 'Ud ye like t' dance wi' me, Lawrence?"

Lawrence was about to say that it was his dearest wish, but Winnie stood up from her stool and crowded against him.

"Acquaintance o' yers, Quibbley?" She smiled generously at Amelia, flashing a bright gold tooth. "Any friend o' Quibbley's is a friend o' mine."

Lawrence shifted his weight in the opposite direction. "Amelia," he said, "this is Winn, 'oo manages th' laundry. Winn, this is Amelia. Her an' me, we—" His tongue seemed to trip. The room had become fiercely hot.

Amelia held out her hand. " 'Ow 'bout that dance?" she asked sweetly.

As he lifted his arm, Winnie took it and clung. "Jes' what I was goin' t' suggest," she said. She beamed up at Lawrence. " 'Member those nights on th' West Pier, Quibbley? We used t' dance 'til daybreak, we did. An' afterwards—"

Lawrence cleared his throat, beginning to feel desperate. "Amelia," he began, but she interrupted him.

"Oh, that's alright, Lawrence," she said, lifting her chin. "I kin see yer otherwise 'ngaged." She turned to Foster, who hadn't taken his eyes off her since she came in. "Ye look th' sort 'oo likes t' dance, luv," she said gaily. "Shall we?"

And Lawrence, feeling the Saharan winds of jealousy blowing through his soul, was forced to yield to the iron grip of Winnie Wospottle, while Amelia and Foster whirled around the floor on flying feet.

Upstairs, dinner was over in an hour, as it always was when the Prince was a table guest. The women having adjourned to the drawing room, the men pushed back their chairs and settled down to their customary port and cigars. They had broken into two groups, those at Lord Warwick's end of the table and those around the Prince. After his glass had been filled and then filled again, the Prince caught Charles's eye and beckoned. Guessing what was wanted, Charles stepped behind the Prince's chair and quietly reported the outcome of his investigation.

His Highness grunted, obviously displeased. "What am I to tell Alix, then?" He puffed his cigar. "Come now, Charles. You're bound to have found a clue or two."

Charles sighed. The Prince had a reputation for refusing to let go an idea he fancied. "Unfortunately, the boy's body was relocated prior to my arrival, sir. The stall from which it was taken had been so thoroughly disturbed that I could learn nothing there. As I said, the lad's injury might have been caused by a horse—but it could also have been inflicted by a fall from the loft above, or by a blow from a blunt instrument. I doubt that even a surgeon's examination would tell us more."

The Prince puffed on his cigar. "Have you questioned all the servants?"

"I've spoken to the grooms and stableboys. No one admits to seeing anything."

"Well, then, question them again, damnit. Someone is hiding something, I'm convinced of it. If you don't learn anything from the stable staff, question the others."

"All eighty of them?" Charles asked, carefully showing no expression. "As well as the servants of the guests?"

"How else are you going to find out what happened?" The Prince thrust his cigar back into his mouth and spoke around it. "Daisy has given me to understand that you're going along on tomorrow morning's little expedition."

"She has asked me to photograph the occasion, yes," Charles said. "Of course," he added disingenuously, "if Your Highness would prefer me to stay at Easton and question the servants—"

"Question the servants in the afternoon," the Prince said with a wave of his hand. "By all means, come with us. The more the merrier." He sighed ruefully. "I must say, I don't know why Daisy wants to inflict on me the ugly sight of a mass of wretched souls in a workhouse. But she has a generous heart, easily moved. One credits her with benevolent intentions." He glanced down the table at Bradford, who was talking to Kirk-Smythe, the young Guards lieutenant. "And I am to ride in your Daimler, Marsden?"

Bradford looked up. "Oh, yes, sir," he said eagerly.

"You know how to pilot the blasted thing, I trust. It is in good working condition?"

"Oh, right, sir. Tip-top." Bradford cleared his throat. "Of course you know, sir, the Daimler is imported. I fear we have let France and Germany have the lead where motorcar manufacture is concerned. Unless we begin producing English automobiles in England—"

"That's fine, then," the Prince said, standing. "I wouldn't fancy having to give the bloody thing a push." He raised his voice so it could be heard the length of the table. "Brookie! What do you say, Warwick, old chap? Shall we join the ladies? I understand they expect us to dance with them." He turned to Charles with a more kindly look. "You don't have to start those interrogations tonight, Sheridan. I've seen you ogling that auburn-haired American woman. I waltzed with her last night, and she is quite light on her feet. You must ask her to dance."

"Yes, sir," Charles said, not unwillingly. He and the Prince were rising to leave when HRH was accosted by Reggie Wallace, whose face showed signs of nervous agitation.

"Bertie, there's something we must discuss," he said peremptorily. He glanced at Charles and the three or four others in a nearby group. "A private matter, of some delicacy."

The Prince patted his bulging waistcoat and puffed on his cigar. "Let us not speak of unpleasant things tonight, Reggie. I am looking forward to being entertained by the ladies."

Wallace shook his head stubbornly. "This is a matter of urgency, Sire," he said. He dropped his voice. "It concerns your reputation, and that of our hostess."

"Ah, more of that," the Prince said, with irritation. "In that case, it can surely keep until breakfast. Deliver it to me with the sausages, eh?"

Wallace was about to say something more, but a dark look from the Prince silenced him.

Upstairs, a space had been cleared at one end of the elegant gas-lit drawing room. A group of musicians was seated in front of the green velvet draperies and had struck up a gay Strauss waltz. The Prince went to Lady Warwick, bowed low over her hand, and led her onto the floor, which was a signal for the rest of the gentlemen to search out partners.

Charles stood off to one side, watching. Having just been assigned the unwelcome (and to his way of thinking, pointless) task of interviewing a hoard of servants, he did not feel very much like dancing. What he wanted most was to sit and talk quietly with Kate and forget about investigations. He wanted to broach the subject he had been considering before dinner, although he hadn't yet thought of a good way to do it. Charles had never before admitted to being in love, let alone made a proposal, and he felt like an awkward schoolboy. But, he reminded himself, he did not intend to propose marriage, at least not tonight. He intended merely to sound Kate out on the subject, that was all—to see what *her* feelings were. He was about to go in search of her when he was stopped by the man to whom Bradford had been talking at table.

"I don't believe we've met," said the officer, a handsome young man of military bearing. He sported a small blond mustache and his pale hair was brushed smoothly back from a broad forehead. "Andrew Kirk-Smythe," he said. "Scots Guards. Taking a few days off from maneuvers in the New Forest."

"Charles Sheridan." Charles took his hand. The life of a young officer in the Foot Guards could be quite pleasant, he knew. Soldiering here at home was not taken very seriously, and the mess was run by civilian caterers, so that the food and wines were quite civilized. Most officers did themselves well, and it looked as if Kirk-Smythe was no exception. Underneath the young man's smart *savoir faire,* however, Charles thought he detected a certain uneasiness.

"Couldn't help overhearing you and HRH," Kirk-Smythe said. He smoothed his mustache and gave Charles an ingratiating smile. "I say, old man, it's a beastly job you've got there, talking to all those servants."

"Right," Charles said ruefully. "A devil of a job."

Kirk-Smythe straightened his shoulders, as if he were coming to attention. "Well, then," he said crisply, "I shall be glad to offer my services. If it would lighten your burden, I can undertake to interview the outdoor staff."

Charles was mildly amazed. He wouldn't have expected a young Guards lieutenant, particularly one so meticulously turned out, to volunteer for such distasteful duty. What was his incentive? "I appreciate the offer," he replied, "but surely you have more pressing demands on your time."

"Wouldn't want you to get the short end of the stick," Kirk-Smythe muttered. "Been in thankless positions too often myself."

From the young man's sleek, well-groomed appearance, Charles doubted that he had ever found himself in any sort of thankless position. His mistrust must have shown in his face, for Kirk-Smythe added, with clear discomfort, "I've been at Easton several times before, you see. I know my way around. What do you say?"

"Yes," Charles said thoughtfully. "Well, let's talk tomorrow, shall we? I don't expect to start the interviews until sometime in the afternoon, in any event."

Kirk-Smythe drew his heels together, and all but saluted. "Righto, then," he said. "Now, if you'll excuse me, a certain beautiful young lady is waiting to dance with me." He motioned with his head in the direction of several ladies sitting on the other side of the room, among whom, Charles saw with dismay, was Kate Ardleigh.

As it turned out, Kirk-Smythe had another target in his sights. Next to Kate were Lady Verena Rochdale and her daughter Celia. As Charles watched, Kirk-Smythe possessed himself of Celia's hand with a confidence that betrayed a prior arrangement. As they danced off, Lady Rochdale followed them with her eyes, frowning, clearly not pleased with the partner her daughter had accepted with such alacrity. He guessed that the mother had higher marital aspirations, and would remove her daughter from her admirer's grasp. Kirk-Smythe was about to get, in his own words, the short end of the stick.

Charles shook his head. That was what had put him off marriage for so long: the artifice of it, the social maneuvering that went with it, the family ambitions that attached to it. He wanted none of that where his own marriage was concerned—although he suspected that the minute his mother knew of his interest in Kate, the questions would begin. Who was she? Who were her parents and grandparents? Where in England did she come from? When did she come out (which was a decorous way of inquiring about her age)? What were her circumstances—meaning, did she bring her own fortune, or would her family provide her an adequate allowance? At the thought, his insides shriveled. No, if he were to marry, it would best be done without consulting his mother.

He walked across the room, greeted Lady Rochdale more curtly than he might have done, and turned to Kate. She looked more beautiful this evening than he had ever seen her. Her russet hair was piled high on her head and decorated with peacock feathers. She wore a green silk gown that exactly matched the emeralds at her white throat. He found himself thinking that the family diamonds would look much more lovely on Kate than on his sister-in-law, and wrenched his eyes away.

"I'm afraid I'm not a particularly good dancer," he confessed, and saw Lady Rochdale's right eyebrow go up at his unusual candor. "But if you would care to risk a waltz—"

"Thank you," she said promptly, rising from her chair with a smile. "To tell the truth, I am not especially fond of the waltz, Sir Charles." She nodded at Lady Rochdale, whose left eyebrow had risen to match her right, and took the arm he offered her. "Perhaps we could just walk."

They strolled down the ornate room, glancing at the paintings and statuary arrayed along the wall, while Charles, who was not practiced at small talk, tried to find a smooth way into the topic he wanted to open. Try as he might, though, he could not think how to begin. It was not a subject one could come at obliquely, and it seemed much too direct to blurt out, "I have been thinking of marriage, Kate, and would like to hear your views on the topic."

Kate, for her part, thought that Sir Charles was probably preoccupied with the investigation he was carrying out for the Prince. It was a matter in which she had a compelling interest as well, for Beryl Bardwell had decided that a murder in a stable—suitably disguised, of course, so that it could not be traced to Easton Lodge—would lend drama to *The Loves of Lady Lenore*. As to who was murdered—well, that Beryl had not yet determined. She was deliberating between

Lady Lenore's former lover and her husband, and had begun to think that Lady Lenore's present lover might be a reasonable suspect. Or perhaps it would be the other way around: the current lover would be killed, the murderer none other than the jealous husband, with the former lover as one of the prime suspects.

"How are you progressing with your investigation?" Kate asked, hoping he would respond with details that might help Beryl Bardwell with her plot. "What else have you learned about the stableboy's death?"

"There is nothing to tell you," he said. "Only that the Prince has asked me to extend my interviews to all of the servants."

Kate was momentarily taken aback. "*All* of them? The task will take at least a week!"

"It will take days, in any event," he said glumly, "and I have no confidence that anything will be learned." They had come to an upholstered bench at the far end of the drawing room. "Would you care to sit?"

They sat down and Kate folded her gloved hands in her lap, remembering her thoughts of that morning. Like it or not, she had to face the truth. Over the months she had known Charles Sheridan, she had grown to love him, and the thought of it filled her at once with a quiet pleasure and a deep sadness. Sitting beside him now, stealing a glance at his thoughtful face, she was convinced that he cared for her, too. But English men were rarely aware of their deepest emotions, or if they were, they gave little sign of it. He might not be able to say how he felt—nor did she wish him to, for should they marry, Beryl Bardwell would certainly come between them. If he asked her, she would have to decline, for he would not want to marry someone with a secret identity. More, she refused to give up the work that had become such a satisfying and important part of her life. No, it would be much better if she could turn the subject to something else before he could bring up the matter.

Charles, meanwhile, was trying to collect his thoughts. A moment ago, the idea of sounding Kate's feelings on the subject of marriage had seemed quite logical and not at all difficult. Her physical presence, however, was inordinately distracting. She was sitting quite close, pressing against his arm, her scent wafting around them like spring lilacs. For the life of him, he could not focus on what needed to be said, nor think how to begin.

He shifted uneasily. "I wonder if I might ask you your opinion about—"

"If you like—" Kate said at the same moment.

They both laughed self-consciously. Kate colored and looked away.

"Please," Charles said, "go on."

Kate bit her lip. The only subject she could think of was the one they had just left. "I . . . If you like, I could help with your interrogation by speaking with the female servants. It might shorten your work."

Charles found himself sharply annoyed. He wanted to tell the woman about his changed personal situation, explore her feelings about marriage, and *she* wanted to talk about the confounded investigation! He shook his head, bemused. She was a most unusual woman, with quite peculiar tastes. Try as he might, he could not fathom her interest in criminal matters.

"My dear Kate," he said stiffly, "you were of inestimable help on the two other investigations in which I was engaged during the past year, and I am grateful. It is pointless, however, to involve you in the drudgery of this one. While there may well have been a crime, I fear that any evidence has been permanently destroyed." He paused. "It is on another matter entirely that I have been thinking of speaking to you."

"Another matter?" She turned her head to one side. "How can you think of anything else when your investigation is of such importance? Apprehending the boy's killer— if indeed he was the victim of foul play—has the highest priority, does it not?"

He cast about for inspiration. How the devil *did* one speak about marriage with a lady who kept pressing him about murder? But he could think of nothing. Suddenly, and to his enormous astonishment, he heard himself blurting, "Blast it all, Kate, I had meant to ask you to marry me."

She looked at him, her gaze unreadable. She said nothing

for a moment, then asked, in a small voice, "You *had* meant to ask?"

"Yes," he said, wretchedly conscious that he was making a fool of himself and a great mess of the subject he had intended to discuss with rational succinctness. "Yes, I . . . in a word, that is, yes." He cleared his throat. "But something I learned recently has caused me to question whether a union between us would be . . . wise."

She looked down at her gloved hands, tightly clasped. "I think you are quite right to question your impulse, Charles. The subject is not one we can profitably discuss."

He frowned, irrationally seized by a desire to dispute his own statement. "Is the thought of our marriage so preposterous?" he asked. "After all, we have known one another for over a year, and have had a remarkably amiable association." He paused, awkwardly conscious that something more ought to be said in support of a proposal of marriage. "And I do . . . I do care for you, Kate. More than I ought, perhaps. That is, I mean to say—" He stopped, covered in confusion.

She lifted her head, and her eyes met his. "You said that something you learned recently caused you to question your intention. May I know what that is?"

The room had grown so insufferably hot that Charles could scarcely breathe, and he could feel the sweat trickling down his neck under his infernal collar. He could tell her that he would shortly inherit the family title and become the fifth Baron of Somersworth, but that was only the beginning. To enable her to fully understand the heavy burden of duty and responsibility that was about to settle on his shoulders, he would have to tell her his entire family history, which would take hours. And even then, she could not understand the subtleties of the system of primogeniture, or the almost feudal obligations that bound a landowner to land and tenants. How could she, being an American? They had freed themselves of all such restraints.

"The matter . . . is of such gravity and weight that I have scarcely managed to absorb it myself," he said finally, and with far more stiffness than he intended. "Let it suffice to say that my family obligations make it difficult for me to—"

"My dear Kate, there you are!" It was Daisy Warwick, with Lady Lillian in tow. "I do hope I'm not interrupting. I have a proposal to make."

Kate looked up with a strained smile. "Interrupting? Why, no, of course not."

Lady Lillian stepped close to Charles. "While Miss Ardleigh is speaking with our hostess," she said demurely, "perhaps you might ask me to dance."

Charles wrenched his eyes away from Kate. "I regret to say that I am not a good dancer, Lady Lillian. I—"

"Stuff and nonsense!" Lady Lillian exclaimed prettily. "The problem is that you have not yet found the right partner. Do come—we'll have such fun." She took his hand, tugging gently. Before Charles knew it, they were circling the floor.

Deeply shaken, Kate watched Charles put his arms around Lillian Forsythe and dance away with her. A moment ago, he had been about to tell her why he had changed his mind about asking her to marry him. What reason would he have given? That his family would not tolerate his marriage to an Irish-American woman? Or that he had discovered the identity of Beryl Bardwell and had decided he could not marry a woman who practiced such an occupation?

"—and so I would like you to go with us," Daisy was concluding.

"Please forgive me." Kate pulled her attention back to the conversation. "Where are you going?"

"To Chelmsford," Daisy said.

"Oh, yes," Kate said. "To the workhouse." In spite of herself, her eyes had gone back to the dancing. For a man who didn't waltz, Sir Charles was managing quite adequately. She frowned. Was it really possible that he knew about Beryl Bardwell? Yes, of course it was. She had tried to conceal her work from the servants at Bishop's Keep, but she had seen their secret smiles when they came upon her in the act of writing. They undoubtedly knew. It was possible— no, it was quite likely—that Amelia had told Lawrence, who had told his master, who . . .

"Excuse me, you know about the expedition?" Daisy repeated with some annoyance, for what must have been the second time.

With an effort, Kate turned away from the dancers. If Sir Charles had changed his mind about asking her to marry him, that was all to the good, actually. It would have embarrassed them both when she refused him, as she fully intended to do. And if he preferred to dance with a woman so blatantly obvious about her intentions—well, that was his affair. Out of the corner of her eye, she saw Charles step squarely on Lillian Forsythe's instep, and felt wickedly glad.

"My maid mentioned the excursion to me," she said. "I understand that His Royal Highness is going along."

A trace of bleak humor, and then perhaps something darker, flickered across Daisy's face and disappeared. "There's no keeping a secret from the servants' hall," she said with a resigned sigh. "But since you already know about it, I suppose I don't have to explain. The Prince will be riding in Mr. Marsden's Daimler, and Sir Charles and I—he is to photograph our tour—will be following in the brougham. It occurred to me that since you are interested in improving the lot of the poor, you might be interested in seeing the workhouse. And I am sure that your lively company would make the visit more interesting for His Highness."

Sir Charles was going? Then she should not, Kate thought, for it would be too uncomfortable. She spoke regretfully. "Thank you for the invitation. I would like to go, but I fear I must decline. Perhaps another time, when—" Her eyes went toward the dancing couples.

Daisy followed her glance. "Does this have to do with Sir Charles?"

"I'm afraid so," Kate said ruefully. She colored. "You see, he does not— That is, I cannot . . ." She stopped, thinking that her face and manner were giving too much away.

"I fancy I see a great deal, my dear," Daisy said gently. She touched Kate's hand. "These things do work themselves out, though. If you are meant for each other, fate will offer you a way. With Charles's changing circumstances, there will be a great many opportunities, I should think."

Kate frowned. "His . . . changing circumstances?"

"His brother's tragic illness quite alters his situation, of course. When Lord Robert is gone and Charles comes into the title—'' She tilted her head, frowning. ''But you look as though this is news to you, my dear. Am I telling you something you didn't know?''

Kate nodded mutely. She had not known, but it all made perfect sense. Charles's brother was dying, and he would inherit the baronetcy. He cared for her, but he knew she could not bear to live in London during the Season, or go to balls, or host house parties, or—

And even if Kate were willing to try, there was Beryl Bardwell, who would be both a constant thorn and a potential embarrassment. His family—all proper English aristocrats, she was sure—would be mortified if he brought home an Irish-American bride with the unfortunate habit of scribbling stories. No wonder he didn't think it wise for them to marry. She completely agreed. In fact, she thought it a perfectly ludicrous idea!

"I am frightfully sorry, Kate,'' Daisy said. ''I fear I have told you something that Charles intended to tell you himself.''

Kate was about to reply, but she was interrupted by a polite, ''Pardon me, Miss Ardleigh, but I wonder if you might enjoy a waltz.'' The speaker was Sir Friedrich Temple, whose stern eye had fallen on her once or twice during dinner. His face was softer now, and he was smiling. ''If our hostess will permit, that is,'' he said, bowing to Daisy.

"Since when did you need my permission to make off with a beautiful woman, Freddy?'' the Countess asked with careless gaiety. ''By all means, carry Miss Ardleigh away and amuse her. She has been far too serious these last few moments. In any event, I see someone with whom I have been meaning to speak.''

Kate followed her glance. She was looking at Sir Reginald, standing alone on the other side of the room. And then, before Kate realized what had happened, Sir Friedrich had whirled her away among the other dancers.

11

The whole seems to fall into a shape,
As if I saw alike my work and self
And all that I was born to be and do,
A twilight-piece. Love, we are in God's hand.
How strange now, looks the life he makes us lead;
So free we seem, so fettered fast we are!

—ROBERT BROWNING
"Andrea del Sarto"

Charles thought that the column assembled in the courtyard the next morning must be the most extraordinary
ever organized at Easton Lodge. In the vanguard was the
highly polished and finely tuned Daimler, the Royal pennant
fluttering from its standard, the engine idling like a poorly-
maintained thrashing machine. Bradford, wearing duster, motoring cap, and goggles, sat behind the tiller, waiting for the
Prince. Seeing Charles, he gave a cheerful wave.

"A red-letter day in British motoring history," he called,
and Charles suppressed a smile. The Prince was about to
discover that the Countess's stratagem wasn't the only one
to which he would be subject today.

Next in line behind the Daimler was the shiny black four-
seater brougham in which Charles and Daisy would ride,
with room for HRH, should ill fortune befall the motorcar.
Under its seats were several large wicker baskets covered
with red-and-white-checked cloths. Charles supposed them

to be emergency rations, should they be detained beyond lunchtime. The rear guard consisted of a supply wagon which would follow behind, probably at some distance, conveying Bradford's mechanic (his man Lawrence) and a hopefully adequate stock of spare parts, spare tires, and petrol. A good idea, Charles reflected. Motoring was a dodgy business. One never could be quite sure of arriving anywhere without incident.

Charles turned and motioned to Lawrence, who had carried his photographic gear downstairs. "Put that in the wagon," he said. "Carefully, please."

"Yessir," Lawrence replied, and began to stow the various cases.

Charles had brought a camera made in Paris in 1890, a large and fairly cumbersome model, but one that would function under conditions of poor illumination and produce high-quality prints as well. The mahogany front panel folded down when the camera opened, supporting a square leather bellows and a Eurygraphe Extra-Rapid No. 3 lens. He had been intrigued with photography for as long as he could remember, and his collection of cameras now threatened to overtake the room in his Knightsbridge house to which they were consigned. He frowned. Fettered by duty he might be, but photography was one of the interests he intended to pursue.

"'Scuse me, sir," Lawrence said, having stowed the camera paraphernalia. "May I 'ave a word?"

"Certainly, Lawrence," Charles said. Marsden's man had a seedy look about him this morning. Perhaps he had indulged a little too freely the night before. Charles opened a leather valise and began counting glass photographic plates. "What is it?"

Lawrence glanced over his shoulder as though to be sure he wasn't overheard by the stable staff and groundsmen that were gathering to gawk at the motorcar. "'Tis about th' dead stableboy," he said in a low voice. "I've learnt o' someone ye shud talk to."

Charles snapped the heavy valise shut. "I don't know if I'll get to it, Lawrence. As things stand—" As things stood, he had over a hundred servants to question. A damned wild-goose chase.

"Beggin' yer pardon, Sir Charles," Lawrence said urgently. "I know ye've got a lot o' detectin' t' do, but ye ought t' make th' time t' talk t' Deaf John. He *seen* 'im. Or 'er, as th' case may be. 'E cudn't tell which."

"Saw who?"

"Th' killer, that's 'oo." Lawrence leaned closer. "Comin' outta th' stable yestiddy mornin'."

Charles raised his eyebrows. "And who is Deaf John?"

" 'E's th' farrier. Works in th' smithy." Lawrence jerked a thumb over his shoulder. "That way."

"Thank you, Lawrence," Charles said. "I'm very grateful for your intelligence."

"Yer welcome, sir," Lawrence growled. "If ye'll pardon me, there's a thing er two I need t' check on th' Daimler." He glanced at the coachman, a bandy-legged little man named Wickett, and dropped his voice. "An' I need t' talk t' Lord Marsden 'bout a sartin wager."

"What wager?"

"I've laid a bob that th' Daimler'll get t' Chelmsford an' back in three hours, not countin' th' time spent there. Wud ye say that's reason'ble?"

"It's reasonable," Charles agreed. "The Countess is expecting us to return before luncheon, at one." He watched Lawrence walk to the motorcar to talk to Bradford, wondering whether he had time to seek out Deaf John before the expedition got off. But at that moment, he was interrupted.

"Good morning, Charles."

He turned swiftly. Kate was standing a few paces away. She was wearing a gold wool walking costume with a short matching cape around her shoulders, and the rich color of her gold felt hat heightened the russet glow of her hair.

"Good morning, Kate." Charles felt himself flushing. "I regret that we were interrupted last night. I wasn't at all eager to dance with Lady Lillian, but I—" He stopped. The damned woman was trying to hide a smile. "Have I said something amusing?" he demanded crossly.

"It is not to me that you should apologize," Kate said. "I wonder that poor Lady Lillian can walk this morning."

"Lady Lillian doesn't merit an apology," he snapped. Poor Lady Lillian, indeed! He had resorted to rudeness in an effort to be rid of the foolish woman, and even that wasn't enough. It wasn't until Sir Friedrich came up and asked her to dance that Charles was able to make his escape. By that time, Kate was firmly attached to Ellie and Bradford and the opportunity to talk with her had vanished.

Kate's smile was gone and she was looking at him gravely, her head tilted to one side. "Regarding last night," he said. He took a deep breath and plunged in. "What I meant to say to you in our brief conversation, Kate, was that over the past year I learned to care for you very much. I came to believe that I wanted to marry you." He stopped. Why the deuce was he speaking of his desire in the past tense? It sounded as though he no longer cared, and that wasn't the truth. "That is," he said, reddening still more and intent on correcting his error, "I *do* want to marry you. However, I have just recently learned that—"

Kate put out her hand, stopping him. "Charles, please. I own that I, too, had begun to care for you. But it is well that we recognize those feelings as inappropriate to our situation." Her green-flecked hazel eyes were clear, her gaze unswerving. "Speaking frankly—and frank speech is always better than hints and suggestions—a match between us is not suitable. We should be glad that both of us understand and accept that fact."

He blinked, startled into a response he hadn't intended. "Not suitable? For heaven's sake, Kate, what makes you think—"

"Good morning, Sheridan!" came the Prince's booming voice. "A fine morning for a drive, is it not?"

Charles, feeling deeply frustrated by the interruption, turned to greet His Highness and the Countess. Kate, for her part, felt deeply grateful. She had said what she intended to say, and she very much hoped that the matter was closed. Their relationship might be strained for a brief time, but once they accepted the inevitable, they could continue their friendship without complication. She could go on being Beryl Bardwell, and he could go on to the baronetcy of whatever-it-was.

"Good morning to you, Kate," the Prince added in an avuncular tone. He was wearing a Norfolk suit, an ankle-length tan duster buttoned across his bulging middle, and a white yachting cap with the Royal insignia. A silver-headed walking stick was tucked under his arm.

Kate, who was as yet unaccustomed to the idea of being directly addressed by a prince, dropped a nervous curtsy. "Good morning, Your Highness. I trust you will enjoy your drive to Chelmsford."

"Thank you, Kate," the Prince said good-naturedly. He leaned closer and lowered his voice. "Frankly, I can't think why anyone would want to visit a workhouse." He glanced fondly at Daisy, who was dressed in a pale blue duster, her face and hat swathed in blue tulle. "Except our hostess, of course, who feels such sympathy for the poor—and is constantly trying to educate me." He looked around. "By the by, has anyone seen Reggie this morning?" When everyone shook their heads, he frowned. "Well, whatever he wanted to talk to me about can jolly well wait until we get back." He raised his voice. "Well, Marsden, is your motorcar ready?"

"Ready, sir," Bradford said, and saluted smartly. "Come aboard."

The Prince clasped his hands behind his back and paced around the automobile, frowning judiciously. "But where is the man with the red flag?"

Daisy stepped forward. "I hardly think it likely that you will be arrested, Bertie. But if you would be more easy, we can provide a man."

"Oh, pshaw! Let them arrest us." The Prince threw back his head and roared with laughter. "That would be a splendid joke, now, wouldn't it? I can just see the headlines in *The Times.* 'HRH Arrested for Motoring Offense.' It would give Mama something new to complain about." He accepted the goggles Bradford handed him and got into the Daimler, which listed to one side under his weight. "Come on, then," he cried. "Let us be off!"

Kate stepped back a little distance as Bradford pulled out the throttle and the rattle of the Daimler's engine increased to a smooth chatter. At the last moment, Andrew Kirk-

Smythe raced out of the stable and hopped into the motor-car's jump seat, a vis-à-vis arrangement that faced passenger and driver. Sir Charles, surprised that Kirk-Smythe was going along, handed Daisy into the brougham and got in himself, and the coachman shook the reins, clucking to the horses. Behind them, Lawrence and another coachman climbed into the supply wagon. The parade clattered off at a smart pace, the Daimler at its head.

At Kate's elbow, a man spoke dryly. "An impressive entourage, is it not? Ironic that they are so elegantly equipped for a visit to a workhouse."

Kate turned, recognizing her dancing partner of the evening before. "Impressive, yes," she agreed. "I wonder, though, whether His Highness is quite prepared for the journey. Twenty-six miles seems a long way to ride in that noisy contraption."

"My thought exactly," Sir Friedrich said, and gave a dry chuckle. "I should have expected Daisy to pay more attention to HRH's creature comforts." He offered her his arm. "Since you are about so early, Miss Ardleigh, what would you say to a walk? Or may I call you Kathryn?"

"Certainly," Kate said, watching the procession as it disappeared around the curve. "Please do, Friedrich." She hadn't quite got into the habit of calling princes and lords by their familiar names.

As they drove off, Charles waved good-bye to Kate, but she was talking to Friedrich Temple and did not notice. He leaned back and folded his arms, feeling quite out of sorts.

"I didn't know Kirk-Smythe was meant to come along," he said darkly, although that had nothing to do with his pique.

Across from him, Daisy was settling her skirts into the seat. "You didn't?" she asked with some surprise. "But then, I suppose no one has told you that he is Bertie's personal bodyguard."

"Ah," Charles said. There had been several attempts on the Queen's life, and in the current time of unrest, it was only prudent to assign a man to protect the Royal person. It occurred to him that this intelligence explained Kirk-

Smythe's offer of the preceding evening. As a Royal body-guard, it was his business to know the servants.

They rode in silence for a time. It was difficult to see through the blue tulle that swathed the Countess's face, but Charles thought she looked pale and drawn, as if she had spent a sleepless night. He was intrigued again, as he often was, by the complexity of her character. Daisy Warwick appeared to have everything a woman could want—beauty, fortune, a congenial husband, the attentions of a prince. But beneath these superficialities, what were her real desires? What did she imagine she was born to be and do? What dreams compelled her onward?

"I have been wanting to talk to you, Charles," she said, in a voice that he had to strain to hear. They had turned out of Easton lane and into the road to Chelmsford. "The accident that befell Bertie's groom yesterday—I understand that you are looking into it. What have you learned thus far?"

"Precious little, I fear. The boy died from a blow to the head. I am inclined to believe that it was inflicted by some means other than a horse's kick, but I cannot be sure. What clues there might have been were destroyed by the staff when they took him out of the stall."

Daisy clasped her hands in her lap and looked out across the landscape. "What . . . what sort of clues would you have looked for?"

"The exact position of the body would have been instructive," he replied. "Or evidence that someone else had been in the stall, or that the boy had been in the loft above. But I could find nothing, and failing that—"

"Then it is best to accept the obvious explanation. The lad simply had the misfortune to be kicked by a horse." Daisy leaned against the seat with an expression, Charles thought, almost of relief. "I'm sure it would be of some comfort to his mother to know that her poor boy died while he was doing his duty. I think we may consider the matter closed."

Charles raised his eyebrows. "I fear," he said, "that His Highness thinks otherwise."

Daisy frowned. "Bertie wants you to continue your investigation?"

"He has taken quite an interest in this matter. He asked me last night to interrogate the servants."

She looked alarmed. "My dear Charles, that is out of the question! You know how servants gossip. Every question will spawn some wild tale or other. Rumors of murder are certain to reach the guests, and then the newspapers. The whole thing will be an appalling embarrassment for all concerned, Bertie, most especially." Her lips firmed. "He has not thought the matter through to its logical conclusion."

Charles sat back, pondering. He understood Daisy's desire to bring the matter to a close, and he himself saw little usefulness in questioning all the servants. But a thorough investigation would do more to allay rumor than a quick cover-up, and he did mean to talk to Deaf John.

"I think you can trust me to proceed in a way that will keep rumor to a minimum," he said. "And I must follow HRH's instructions."

She considered for a moment, then said with a sigh, "Oh, very well. But I really do mean to speak to Bertie about this." She was silent for a longer time, and her face softened.

"On quite another subject, I fear I must make a confession, Charles. Last night, after you and Lillian left to dance, I told Kate about your brother Robert's illness, and about your expectations."

Charles looked at her, startled. "You told her?"

"I am *dreadfully* sorry," Daisy said contritely. "I realized immediately, of course, that she did not know. I hope I have not made things difficult for you." She was watching him closely, her dark blue eyes intent. "She is a beautiful woman, although I think not schooled in the ways of our society. Do you care for her, Charles?"

Charles managed a half smile. "That's hardly the point, is it? She told me this morning that a match between us is unsuitable, and I daresay she's right. When Robert is gone, I must do what I was born to do—take my place at Somersworth."

Daisy raised her eyebrows. "That is not all bad, I hope."

He shook his head, feeling suddenly quite dismal. "It is hardly a life for Kate. She is an independent-minded woman. The Americans have spent two hundred years cutting themselves free of tradition, you know. They fancy themselves more spontaneous, more impulsive than we—and they are, to a great extent. They have no patience for the fetters of duty.'' If he and Kate were by some miracle to be wed, it would not be long before she became irritated by the restraints under which they would perforce live.

Daisy leaned forward. ''Forgive me for speaking frankly, Charles, but I know from my own experience how it is to be confined in a life of obligation when your own desires call you to something else. As for what lies ahead, you must honor your *own* wishes, not those others may have for you. And you must speak more frankly to Kate. If you love her, tell her so. Permit *her* to choose her life as she would have it. It is arrogance to assume that you know what her choice would be before it is put to her.'' Her smile was gentle. ''Especially since, as you say, she is a woman of independent mind.''

Charles sighed, thinking that Kate had already announced her choice. As far as she was concerned, the match was unsuitable. But he only said, ''Thank you for the recommendation, Daisy. I shall consider it.''

Daisy sat back, smiling a little, and once more Charles thought how drawn and pale she seemed. ''It is easy to speak with assurance of another's life, Charles. If only I could speak so confidently of my own.''

12

Stone Hall, furnished and decorated as a museum of past ages, was a paradise for illicit assignations, with quaint Elizabethan rooms where the lovers could sit and talk seriously of politics and literature, or no doubt, in many cases, cover more dangerous ground.

—MARGARET BLUNDEN
The Countess of Warwick: A Biography

The night before, Friedrich Temple had proved to be an accomplished dancer whose skill had brought out the best in Kate, and she had enjoyed their waltz. This morning, she was pleased at his invitation to walk, for the air was cool and clear and the season more nearly resembled October than November. The hawthorn and bittersweet were decorated with tiny bright fruits, a few glowing leaves still clung to the lower branches of the service trees, and the thick grass was littered with acorns, hazelnuts, and beechnuts. A few finches fed on dogwood berries and yew, and a thrush sang throatily from its perch on a half-bare oak.

It was indeed a glorious morning, and Kate almost wished that she had accepted Lady Warwick's invitation to drive to Chelmsford. Her short exchange with Charles had been terribly uncomfortable, however—she had not expected to hear him say, "I *do* want to marry you" in quite so forthright a way, and the feelings his words had awakened in her had nearly unsettled her resolve. But a match between the fifth Baron of Somersworth and Irish-American Kate Ardleigh (alias Beryl Bardwell) could only make them both desperately unhappy. No, it was well that she had not gone on the expedition, and for the rest of the weekend she would have as little to do with Charles as possible. With that firm determination, she turned her attention to the man beside her.

Friedrich, who was in his early forties, was tall and sandy-haired, with a Germanic stiffness of manner and an imperious glance that at first had rather taken her aback. But last night she had learned that his mother was a German countess and his father a military man, which accounted for a great deal. This morning, she decided that he was no stiffer than other British gentlemen and that it was his erect bearing and scholarly-looking gold pince-nez that made him seem imperious. And he was interested in her American point of view. After strolling for a time in silence, he quizzed her on what she thought of the house party.

"It has been quite interesting so far," she replied truthfully. Beryl Bardwell, in fact, had sat up past two a.m., making notes on everything she could remember of the snippets of dinner-table conversation she had overheard and the drawing-room exchanges she had witnessed afterward. "I am learning a great deal about the rules of English society. We Americans pay much less attention to social rules, I have found."

Friedrich turned a frowning look on her and said, "My dear Kathryn, what you see here this weekend are not the rules of *English* society."

She tugged the skirt of her gold-colored walking suit away from the thorny branch of a rosebush and glanced at him. Behind his glasses, his eyes were a sharp, pale blue. "Not English?" she asked lightly. "Then what rules are they? Russian? German? French?"

Friedrich pursed his lips. "What I mean to say," he replied with some care, "is that the company gathered here at Easton is a very small segment of English society, which can afford to make its *own* rules." He gestured at the smooth green lawn to their right, where the yellow silk tent was being set up for the refreshments that would be served at the evening's fireworks entertainment. "The glamour and luxury that you see around you, the extravagant food and clothing and jewels, the idle pleasure and easy flirtatiousness—all this is peculiar to the Marlborough set. It is not typical of English society at large—and, I fear, not the best of society for our future king.'' The last had a moralistic ring and he bit it off, as if he had not meant to speak with so judgmental a tone.

For a few moments, they stood watching the workmen. Some were anchoring the tent, others were laying out the fireworks at the far side of the lawn, still others were setting up a small outdoor dais for the musicians.

"I suppose it is the wealth that sets them apart,'' Kate replied thoughtfully. "People who have a great deal of money are inclined to behave as they wish, without regard for the feelings of others. But there is a paradox here, for the women I have met this weekend seem inordinately concerned about scandal. The rule seems to be that what they do or feel in private is their own affair, but they must do nothing that courts public censure.''

Friedrich seemed pleased by her observation. "Exactly so, Kathryn. Wealth insulates, to a great degree, and certainly leads to carelessness. But any kind of public scandal is a great deal feared.'' They had come to the path that led to the Folly, and he paused. "Shall we walk this way?''

Kate nodded, so absorbed in the conversation that she would have walked in any direction. "From that point of view,'' she went on thoughtfully, "I am sure there are those who feel that it would be better if the Prince were to choose less frivolous companions. I don't mean to be critical of His Highness's friends, of course,'' she added, thinking that it was her turn to sound judgmental.

Friedrich's voice was hard-edged. "It might be well,'' he said, "if we were all so critical. If Lady Warwick, for instance, would exercise a more careful judgment, especially in the matter of those with whom she—'' He shrugged. "Ah, well. One does not castigate a lady in matters of judgment. I am merely delighted to find yours so well formed.''

Kate raised her eyebrows at the compliment, which seemed to her undeserved, and perhaps a bit odd. Friedrich Temple struck her as a cautious man, but their conversation seemed to have touched upon deep convictions, prompting him to speak freely. She rather liked that, she decided. English men, including Charles, usually responded with calculation and restraint, making them seem stiff and wary. She sighed to herself, thinking that this was more evidence of the fundamental incompatibility between Charles and herself. She was impulsive of speech and manner, and her quickness sometimes got her into difficulties. If she and Charles were constantly together, it would not be long before he became annoyed with her impetuosity.

They walked for quite some moments without speaking. Then, as they mounted the steps to the veranda of the Folly, she smiled up at him.

"And you, Friedrich?" she asked, wondering idly if she could provoke him to unbend even more. "If the Marlborough set is not to your liking, I wonder that you should devote an entire weekend to its company."

He gave a little shrug. "It's not a question of my liking or not liking, Kathryn. I have been acquainted with the Warwicks for many years, and I enjoy my visits to their estates." His pale eyes lingered on her face. "I feel I have found in you a kindred spirit. Perhaps that has made me speak more openly than I might have done." He looked around. "Ah, we have come to Daisy's Folly. Did you know that this was once a monastic house?"

"Indeed," Kate said. They were standing on the veranda where they had lunched the day before. It was empty now, except for the statuary and pots of shrubbery with which it was decorated. Directly ahead of them were the glass doors that opened into the house.

"Yes, quite a famous monastery, in fact, Built in the time of the Angevin kings, but reduced to ruin by Henry the Eighth. Daisy had it rebuilt, with certain . . . pleasures in mind." He smiled slightly, tipping his head to one side, his eyes still on her face. "It is quite a celebrated trysting spot."

"I . . . didn't realize," Kate said, seeing too late the trap she had stepped into. The man's aloofness had deceived her.

His chuckle was wry and ironic, even slightly sarcastic. "Did you not?" He moved a step closer. "If you have not seen the rooms already, you must view them. Daisy has furnished them with some rare old pieces of furniture and a great deal of fine art, all quite valuable. In fact, she has spent a fortune on her Folly." He took her hand, the corners of his mouth curling up in a smile. "You must come and see, Kathryn."

With a small smile, Kate retrieved her hand and made a show of consulting the watch pinned to her jacket lapel. It was almost nine. "I think it is time we returned to the Lodge. I have some letters to write before the post goes."

Friedrich took a step back and bowed at the waist. If he was disappointed, Kate thought with relief, he was too much of a gentleman to show it. "In that case," he said, "it is quicker to return by this path." He pointed to a walk that angled across the Friendship Garden.

"Thank you," Kate said, and then could not think of anything else to say, until they rounded a corner and she suddenly put her hand to her mouth and cried, "Oh!"

Friedrich put a protective arm around her shoulders, saying, in a stunned whisper, "Dear God!"

They had come upon Reginald Wallace. He was lying on his back, a look of shocked surprise on his face, his wide-open eyes staring upward. There was a bullet hole in the center of his forehead.

13

There is always more misery among the lower classes than there is humanity in the higher.

—VICTOR HUGO
Les Miserables

Royal pennant fluttering, the Prince's entourage made steady progress along the narrow track toward the market town of Chelmsford. The day was warm for November, the sky a brilliant blue, and Charles sat back, willing himself to enjoy the ride. The beeches had lost almost all their golden leaves and their limbs were stark against the sky, but the oaks still kept their bronze-brown foliage and the hedges and banks were bright with the warm gold of nut leaves and bracken, the red of creeper and bramble. Noisy flocks of starlings, sparrows, and finches scoured the stubble fields, and along the hedges, redwings and fieldfares foraged for seeds of cow parsnip and dock.

While the Daimler generally outpaced the other two vehicles, it was seldom out of view for long. The motorcar would disappear for a time, then they would overtake it sitting along the verge while its pilot attended to some necessary lubrication or demonstrated some point about the operation of the automobile or indicated some scenic view to his two passengers. The Prince, who had seemed at best resigned to the excursion, now appeared to take it as a holiday, waving to workers in the field and saluting those they passed, who appeared surprised and not a little frightened by the motorcar and the noise and clouds of dust that attended it. Charles thought that their parade must make an odd impression on its witnesses, and he wondered if they realized it was led by their future king. He also wondered if Bradford was making any headway in persuading the monarch-to-be to take a more liberal view of motoring.

As the entourage approached the outskirts of Chelmsford it began to take on a carnival air. The vehicles were joined by a ragtag gang of boys rolling iron hoops and racing alongside with gleeful shouts, then by a baker's boy in knickers riding an old-fashioned high-wheeled bicycle with packets of fresh-baked bread lashed to his back. Charles heard more shouting and turned to see a brewer's dray falling into line behind the wagon, trailed by three or four barking dogs and an aproned girl with a flock of raucous white geese. It looked like a gypsy troupe had come to town.

Daisy turned to peer over her shoulder. "What we need," she remarked wryly, "is a brass band marching in front."

"No," Charles replied, "what we need marching in front is a man with a red flag."

He was right. As they approached a dusty intersection, a uniformed constable suddenly pedaled up on a safety bicycle, skidded to a stop, and raised his white-gloved hand.

"Halt!" he cried. "In the name of the C-C-Crown!"

"Oh, dear," Daisy said.

The constable pulled a black book from his pocket, opened it, and began to read, as loudly and as rapidly as he could, given that he was afflicted by a violent stutter.

"It is my d-d-duty to advise you that you have violated the first t-t-two sections of the Locomotive Act of 1865, t-t-to wit, Section One: P-p-persons exceeding the sp-sp-speed limit of t-t-two miles p-p-per hour are in violation of this act." He paused in his recitation, wiped his mouth with the back of his white-gloved hand, and went on. "Section T-t-two, P-p-persons failing to p-p-post a man b-b-bearing a red flag t-t-two hundred yards in front of a moving vehicle are in violation of this act." He lowered the book. "Inasmuch as you are in violation of t-t-two sections of the aforesaid act, it is my d-d-duty to arrest you in the name of Her Majesty the Q-Q-Q—'' He stopped and tried again. "In the name of Her Majesty the Q-Q-Q—''

Bradford sounded his electric bell. Startled, the constable looked up. His gaze alighted upon the Royal pennant. His mouth fell open and he gaped at the unmistakable outline of the stout passenger in the passenger seat.

"Your . . . Highness?" he asked faintly.

The Prince pulled off his goggles. "Good show, old chap!" he chortled. He leaned over and punched Kirk-Smythe's arm. "I've never been arrested before!"

Somebody shouted, "Three cheers fer 'Is Rile 'Ighness!" and the assembled crowd, which now included a ruddy-cheeked fishmonger with a wooden tray suspended from his neck and a group of pinafore-clad schoolchildren with their slates, began to huzza. Hats flew in the air, boys whistled, girls clapped, dogs barked, geese honked. The fishmonger and the brewer's drayman broke into a chorus of "Fer 'e's a jolly good fellow." Charles couldn't help feeling enormously relieved. One never knew these days whether the people would respond to Royalty with respect or resentment. If an Anarchist had been in the crowd, the welcome could have turned nasty.

Daisy was chewing on her lip. "I do hope Bertie does not resent the familiarity," she said nervously.

"He seems to be enjoying himself," Charles observed.

He did indeed. The Prince had disembarked from the Daimler and was standing beside it, ready to receive the constable. That nervous gentleman pulled off his hat and approached the Royal presence with obvious trepidation.

"Good morning, Constable," the Prince said genially.

"G-G-Good mornin', Your Highness, sir," the constable managed. Thrusting his hat under his arm, he came to rigid attention, his face as red as a brick, and saluted.

"At ease," the Prince said. "Now, what was it you wanted, Constable?"

The constable could barely manage the words. "It seems, Yer Highness . . ." He was suddenly seized by a fit of coughing. "B-B-By yer leave, Yer Roy'l Highness—" He cleared his throat mightily and tried again. "I fear I must p-p-point out, sir . . ." He faltered once more.

"You must point out that His Highness's motorcar is breaking the law." The Prince tactfully finished the constable's sentence, since the constable seemed unable to do so.

The constable had gone quite pale. "Yes, sir," he whispered wretchedly.

"And we can't have that, now, can we?" the Prince said, with great good humor. "It wouldn't do, wouldn't do at all, would it?"

"No, sir," the constable said, biting his lip.

"Well, then," the Prince said affably, "what we need is a red flag." He turned and spotted the fishmonger, who was wearing a dirty red bandanna tied around his neck. "My good man, what will you take for your neckerchief?"

"A shillin', sir," the fishmonger replied, whipping it off and handing it up through the crowd to the Prince.

"Done," said the Prince, and tossed the fishmonger a coin, as the crowd cheered and others clamored to trade their neckwear for a Royal coin. Holding the filthy neckerchief delicately by one corner, he turned to the constable. "We shall also require a man to lead us. Would you be so kind, Constable?"

Thus presented with an ingenious resolution of the difficulty, the constable gave an audible sigh of relief. "Oh, yes, *sir*," he cried. He looped the handkerchief around the handlebar of his bicycle. "And where are we g-g-goin', sir, 'f I may ask?"

"To the workhouse!" the Prince exclaimed, and climbed back into the Daimler.

"To the . . . w-w-workhouse?" the amazed constable stammered, as the assembly applauded and whistled.

"Let us be off!" the Prince cried and flung up his arm. In a moment, the parade was moving again, led by the dazed constable on his bicycle, flying the fishmonger's dirty neckerchief as if it were His Highness's very own pennant.

Afterward, Charles had occasion to ponder on the ironic contrast between the lighthearted prologue of their comedic journey and the tragic despair of the bleak place at which they arrived. The workhouse was surrounded by a neighborhood that belonged in one of the circles of Dante's Inferno, and

Charles would not have been surprised to see over one of the doors a sign that read, "Abandon hope, all ye who enter here." A filthier or more wretched collection of buildings and alleys he had never seen.

The sun had disappeared behind a bank of dark gray clouds, and the air was heavy with fetid odors. The cobbled street—so narrow that he could almost reach out and touch the dingy buildings on either side—was lined with ragged children who gaped at the Royal parade as if it conveyed beings from a distant country. And perhaps it did, Charles reflected, contrasting the splendor of the estate they had left to the dirty doorways and foul gutters. He wondered what the Prince made of the scene. Was he moved by the misery of his poorest subjects, or was he so thoroughly cocooned in Royal cotton wool that he could neither see nor hear nor smell it?

Ahead of them, the Daimler slowed, and Kirk-Smythe jumped out and began to walk alongside, watching the bystanders warily. Charles wondered if he were carrying a pistol.

"Perhaps this expedition wasn't such a good idea," Daisy said, glancing nervously at a pair of ill-looking fellows lounging against a rubble heap. "Bertie is often offended by unpleasant sights and smells. Perhaps you had better tell Bradford to remain with the motorcar and prepare to leave at a moment's notice."

Charles nodded. Given the neighborhood, he felt certain that Bradford needed no encouragement to remain with the motorcar. "Is that the workhouse?" he asked, glancing ahead, and Daisy nodded, tight-lipped.

Built of red brick stained with fifty years of black soot, the workhouse stood atop a small rise at the end of the street, which led up to it and stopped at its door. A welcoming party was assembled at the top of the three front steps, upon which a tattered and stained red carpet had been laid—borrowed, as its conspicuous gold insignia indicated, from the office of Chelmsford's Lord Mayor. Indeed, the mayor himself, a cheerful, smooth-cheeked individual wearing a red velvet cap and a matching ermine-trimmed cape, had come to receive the Prince, along with two more somber men in black frock coats and a small round lady in black silk with an old-fashioned lace cap perched on her fuzzy gray curls.

The entourage came to a stop. Kirk-Smythe helped the Prince alight, while Charles handed Daisy out of the brougham. The mayor doffed his large red hat and bowed low, and there followed a good deal of bowing and curtsying as Lady Warwick, who was already acquainted with the welcoming committee, introduced to the Prince the mayor, Warden Holden, Matron Kingsley, and Guardian Brocklehurst, the latter a member of the Workhouse Board of Guardians. Each of these persons in turn expressed his or her humble gratitude for His Royal Highness's concern and her ladyship's compassion, and hoped that the visit would not prove too trying.

While this was going on, Charles retrieved his camera, mounted it on its stout wooden tripod, and got down to the business of documenting the Prince's visit. He was hunched under the black shroud, planning his first photograph, when Guardian Brocklehurst, a burly man with sandy whiskers and hairless brows, came toward him.

"You, there, stop!" he growled. "No one has been authorized to take photographs." He had his hand on the camera, about to wrench it away, when Kirk-Smythe intervened.

"This is the Royal photographer," he said sternly.

The Prince turned around. "I say," he called out. "Is there a problem?"

Warden Holden stepped forward. "If it please Your Highness." He extended a soft white hand that would have done justice to an undertaker. "The Board of Guardians has ruled that photographers are not allowed within our doors. We have had several unfortunate experiences with—"

"That is to say, sir," Matron Kingsley put in, "there are those who would portray our good work here in an unfavorable light." Her gray curls bobbed earnestly. "Our funds are woefully inadequate, sir. We cannot do all we might wish to assist the poor souls under our—"

"Well, then," the Prince said briskly, "I should think that photographs of these woeful inadequacies could be used to wring the hearts and purses of the rich." He smiled. "I promise you, Matron, that my personal photographer will capture as many unfortunate scenes as possible.''

Guardian Brocklehurst continued to glare at the camera, and Warden Holden bit his lip nervously. But at Charles's request, the party stood for a photograph on the front steps, the Prince in the middle with Daisy on one side and the mayor on the other, the remaining three behind. Then, leaving Bradford, Lawrence, and the two coachmen to guard the vehicles, they went around the building to the back, where there was a walled-in recreation ground. In the middle were three long wooden benches on which were seated forty or so well-scrubbed and tractable inmates wearing what looked to be freshly ironed clothing, the men on one bench, the women on another, the children on a third.

''And what have we here?'' asked the Prince, striding in front of the benches, swinging his silver-headed walking stick as if he were reviewing the Guards.

''Takin' the air, sir,'' Warden Holden said.

''They take the air several times a day, sir,'' Matron Kingsley added. She turned to Sir Charles. ''This 'ud make a good photograph.'' Charles set down his tripod, thinking that the scene was so obviously staged that it was hardly worth wasting a photographic plate on it. But there was a sad pathos on the scrubbed faces that pulled at his heart.

Daisy was frowning. ''When I visited here, unannounced,'' she said, ''the inmates were not so clean as this, and there were three or four times as many.''

''Today is bath day,'' explained Matron Kingsley. ''I believe that you were here on the day *before* bath day, Your Ladyship.''

Daisy's dark blue eyes narrowed. ''And how many souls do you care for in this place?''

The mayor spoke up proudly. ''A hundred and thirty-seven last night, Your Ladyship. More every day as the weather turns chill. Winters is always the worst, of course. That's when the casuals all try to crowd in, whether they need charity or not.''

''That's right,'' said Guardian Brocklehurst. He looked down his long nose. ''Why, last night, when the men applying for shelter were searched, one had a whole shilling. He claimed he was saving it for his family, but with that kind of money, he could have paid for a bed at an inn.''

"You searched him?" Daisy asked. "Do you search all
the men and women who seek shelter from you?"

Warden Holden folded his soft white hands. "Beg pardon,
Yer Ladyship, but our aim is to confiscate pipes, tobacco,
and matches, which are not allowed. Each inmate may keep
fourpence.''

The Prince was looking impatient. "Where are we off to
next?" he demanded.

Matron Kingsley had developed a nervous tic at the corner
of her mouth. "We thought, sir, that a view of our Recreation
Ground would suffice.''

"But there are no more than forty persons on these
benches," Daisy objected, "which leaves nearly a hundred
unaccounted for. And I particularly wanted His Highness to
visit your brickworks.''

The mayor stepped forward. "I must suggest to Your Ladyship," he interjected, "that the sight of too much wretch-
edness would tire the Royal eyes. I humbly entreat—"

"Damn it!" the Prince said pettishly. "I have ridden thirteen miles in a rattletrap motorcar with the express intention
of seeing the unspeakable inmates of your wretched workhouse. Now, I mean to see them—*all* of them, whether the
sight tires the Royal eyes or not!" He aimed his walking
stick at the mayor. "Do you take my point, sir?"

"Y-Y-Yes, Your Highness," gabbled the mayor.

"Well, then," His Highness said grimly, "let's get on
with the miserable business." He tucked his stick under his
arm. "Come along, Your Ladyship. You too, Kirk-Smythe.
Bring the camera, Sheridan.''

And so it was that Charles, pausing every so often to
photograph a scene, followed the Prince and Daisy as they
surveyed the dismal interior of the Chelmsford Workhouse,
Kirk-Smythe at their heels. They walked hurriedly through
the men's, women's, and children's wards and the nursery,
where miserable, half-clothed inhabitants huddled in unclean
corners and on filthy beds. Picking up their pace, they
quickly toured the kitchen, where a gang of ragged, dirty
women was stewing up small quantities of mutton with large
quantities of cabbage and potatoes in huge copper kettles on

massive stoves, while others made coarse flour into bread.
To Daisy's inquiry, the matron reported that the luncheon
menu was the same each day: three ounces of meat, six of
cabbage and six of potatoes, and four of bread.

"With four of bread and a pint of broth for supper," she
added hastily, "and four of bread and a pint of porridge for
breakfast. So you see they are adequately fed."

The Prince shuddered. Charles wondered whether he was
comparing the meager meal to the enormous breakfast he had
put away this morning—ptarmigan pie, deviled kidneys,
eggs, bacon, bread, several kinds of fruit. But he only said,
"I cannot abide the odor of cooked cabbage," and left the
room.

From the kitchen, they went across the Recreation Ground
again—the benches still filled with their sad-faced occupants—to a large barnlike structure at the rear. Inside, several
dozen men, women, and children were laboring in the dusty
dimness. The children were chopping straw and carrying it
to a pug mill turned by a trio of men, while women broke
up chunks of clay and mixed it in the mill with buckets of
water. Other women were filling molds with the stiff paste
that came out of the mill. Men knocked the bricks out of the
molds and stacked them to cure, while other men carried the
cured bricks to the outdoor kiln that roared like the flames
of Hades in the yard behind. The ragged clothes and the
weary faces of the laborers were covered by a powdery dust-
ing of clay particles, so that they looked like walking ghosts,
and except for the roaring of the kiln and the squeaking of
the pug mill, not a human voice was raised. It was a scene
of such somber melancholy as Charles had never seen before.
In the unnatural quiet, he set up his camera, hoping that his
photographs would capture the speechless despair on the
workers' faces.

"Our brickworks, Your Highness," the warden said nervously, glancing at the camera.

"Capital idea," exclaimed the Prince, looking around and
apparently seeing, for the first time, something to admire.
"You are to be congratulated upon the industry of your
workers. I imagine your bricks fetch a pretty price."

"Quite so, sir," Guardian Brocklehurst replied, as the

warden seemed to relax. "We supply the local market and ship by railway as far as Colchester. It is a modestly profitable operation."

Charles, enshrouded in his black hood, thought the man was understating the situation. Brick-making on this scale, with no rent, low-cost supplies, and free labor—it was a recipe for enormous profits.

"Brick-making is an ideal occupation for our inmates, sir," Warden Holden explained, gathering courage from His Highness's approval. "It requires limited skill, except for making the forms and laying the courses for firing. Two trained craftsmen supervise that work."

"And as you see," the matron put in helpfully, "tasks may be found for all. Even small children can be set to work preparing the straw and grinding the clay. With such a ready labor supply, the brickworks operates the whole day around—two shifts."

That meant that the women and the children were working twelve-hour shifts, Charles thought sadly. No wonder they looked so worn and weary. His sadness turned to anger as he thought of the irony of the situation. Under the Factory Act that had been passed almost two decades before, children under ten could not be employed in a mill or a mine, and children under eighteen had to be given a Saturday half-holiday. But the managers of a workhouse, which was not regulated under the law, could employ children with impunity—and pocket the profit from their labor.

"With half of your inmates always at work," Daisy said, "you require only enough beds for the other half. Is that not so?"

"Exactly," Matron Kingsley replied triumphantly. "It is a great economy."

"You see, Lady Warwick?" the Prince asked, smiling. "Things are managed so that the workhouse is supported by the labor of the very people who depend upon its services. A tidy solution. By Jove, I like it!"

Charles shook his head. It was a sentiment to which even the staunchest Conservative could have agreed. If Daisy had brought HRH here in the hope of turning him toward Socialism, it looked as if she had lost.

But Daisy was undismayed. Without hesitation, she launched her counterattack. "And how much do you pay your workers, Warden?" she inquired icily.

Warden Holden's eyebrows shot up. "Inmates of a workhouse are not paid wages, as Your Ladyship knows very well." His voice was huffy. "They labor for their beds and board, according to the provisions of the Poor Law Act of—"

Daisy did not allow him to finish. "You require these men, women, and children to work at this backbreaking labor without wages?" She turned to the Prince, imploring. "Don't you see, Your Highness? These wretched people are no better than slaves."

The mayor pulled himself up. "Oh, no, Your Ladyship!" he cried in horror.

Lady Warwick whirled on him. "Your inmates are *slaves*! You pay no salaries, so your bricks can be sold for far more than they cost to produce. And to judge from the appalling conditions we saw today, only a fraction of these people's earnings go to provide for their food and shelter. What happens to the rest?"

Guardian Brocklehurst cleared his throat nervously. "I assure you, Your Ladyship, the Board of Guardians follows the most stringent accounting practices in apportioning its funds."

The Prince frowned. "I'm not sure I follow your argument, my dear Lady Warwick. The inmates are free to leave if they wish, are they not? No one confines them here. Ergo, they are not slaves."

"But where are they to go?" Daisy asked passionately. "They have come here because they could not find work, so where are they to turn?" She threw a dark glance at Guardian Brocklehurst. "Of course, if the workhouse were not in the business of brick-making, some local brick maker might employ them. Or if they were paid a fair wage for their labor here, they might be able to afford housing and food for themselves. But as it is, they are condemned to—"

"Ahem." The Prince coughed delicately. "This is all quite interesting, Lady Warwick. But I fear that my throat is growing raspy from the dust in the air, and the time for luncheon is rapidly approaching. We must let these good people go on with their work.''

Daisy's face registered disappointment and a sharp dismay. "But, Bertie," she said, "I hoped that—''

She didn't get to finish her sentence. She was interrupted by a dour-faced woman who opened the door and stepped inside. The woman was followed, to Charles's great surprise, by the lanky young man who had been sent to fetch the doctor yesterday—Tom, his name was. He whipped off his cap and bowed to the Prince, then turned to Lady Warwick.

"Lord Warwick wants that Yer Ladyship an' 'Is 'Ighness come back t' Easton as quick as ye kin, ma'am. There 'as bin a misa'venture.''

"Another accident?" The Prince frowned. "We haven't untangled the last one yet. Who's been hurt?''

"It's Lord Wallace, sir," Tom said. He shifted his feet uncomfortably. "'E's dead, sir.''

"Dead?" Lady Warwick asked. She had grown suddenly very white. "Was it a shooting accident? Did he take a fall? How—?''

Tom twisted his cap in his hands. "No, ma'am," he said. "'E was murdered, ma'am. Shot, 'e was. Right i' th' middle o' 'is for'ead.''

With a little moan, the Countess sank to the ground.

14

Our rule was, No Scandal! . . . Whenever there was a threat of proceedings, pressure would be brought to bear, sometimes from the highest quarters, and almost always successfully. We realized that publicity would bring us into disrepute, and as we had no intention of changing our mode of living, we saw to it that five out of every six scandals never reached the outside world.

—FRANCES (DAISY) BROOKE, LADY WARWICK
Discretions

There was a metallic clatter in the lane beyond Stone Hall. "The Daimler, at last!" Lord Warwick exclaimed, rising from the carved wooden bench on which he and Friedrich Temple had been sitting for a good part of the morning. Kate rose, too, glad that the long wait was over.

A few moments later, the Prince strode impatiently onto the scene. "What's all this about a murder?" he demanded of Lord Warwick, who had stepped forward to meet him. "Do you have any idea how fast we drove to get back here?" He turned to Bradford Marsden, who, with Sir Charles and Andrew Kirk-Smythe, was at his heels. "How fast *did* we drive, Marsden?"

"By my watch, sir," Bradford said, "we covered the thirteen miles in fifty-two minutes."

"Astonishing," the Prince said. He shook his head. "P'rhaps you're right, Marsden. P'rhaps this machine *is* the wave of the future." He turned around, remembering why they had come. "I tell you, Brooke, if this murder business is someone's idea of a practical joke, I will personally have his—"

Wordlessly, Lord Warwick reached down and removed the horse blanket covering the dead man. The Prince stared down at Wallace's unmoving body, which lay on the path in front of a low stone bench. Then he bent over and examined the hole in the center of the dead man's forehead.

"Jupiter!" he breathed. "So that's why he didn't appear for breakfast." He straightened up. "Come here, Sheridan, and have a look!"

"I did not think it right to move him until you arrived, Bertie," Lord Warwick said. He looked down sadly. "Poor old Reggie. We had words occasionally, but he was a gentleman through. Absolutely fair, you know, and quite discreet. Could be trusted with any secret—"

Kate's nose tickled and she suddenly sneezed, startling Lord Warwick into an awareness of her presence. He closed his mouth firmly, just as she was wishing that she could hear what secrets had been entrusted to Lord Wallace. It did seem curious that a man would praise his wife's former lover for his fairness and discretion. What a complicated web of relationships was woven by these affairs. Before her stood a husband and a current lover, conferring over the body of a former lover!

"Miss Ardleigh?" Charles asked in surprise, apparently just noticing her.

"It was Miss Ardleigh's and my misfortune to discover the body," Sir Friedrich said smoothly. He moved close to Kate. "We had come to have a look at the Folly—"

Kate stepped away, conscious that Temple's tone might be wrongly interpreted—and from Charles's frown, she could see that it had been.

"It is more accurate to say that I was returning to the Lodge from a brief walk through the garden, accompanied by Sir Friedrich," she amended tartly.

"In any case, gentlemen," Sir Friedrich said with a slight smile, "I must report that Miss Ardleigh has been reading detective stories. She forbade me to touch the body and in-

sisted that I send one of the gardeners in search of Brooke."
He glanced at Charles. "She was most emphatic that you be
summoned, Sheridan. She said, and I quote, 'We must not
disturb the crime scene until Sir Charles has arrived.' " His
tone became patronizing. "We should congratulate the lady
for her knowledge of police procedures, wouldn't you say?"

"Quite right," the Prince said briskly. "Good girl, Kate."
He turned to Charles. "Well, Charles, it looks as if you have
another corpse on your hands."

"Forgive me, sir," Charles said. "This is clearly not a
case of accidental death. The investigation is a task for the
police."

"It might be suicide, of course," Kirk-Smythe said
thoughtfully.

"Suicide?" Kate asked. "But there is no weapon. At
least," she added less eagerly, sensible that the men had all
turned to stare at her, "there is none in sight." While she
had been sitting on the bench, Kate (or rather the irrepressible Beryl Bardwell, she of the avid interest) had been
searching with her eyes and had detected no gun. She had
seen one or two other things, however.

"It is possible, Miss Ardleigh," Charles said, "that someone else might have happened on the body before you discovered it, and taken the weapon." He turned to the Prince.
"But suicide or murder, the fact remains that the investigation is police business. Brooke must summon the local constable at once."

Lord Warwick shook his head. "I don't like the idea of
the police." He looked at the Prince and Sir Friedrich. "Gentlemen, perhaps we should discuss—"

While the three men drew together to talk, and Bradford
and Kirk-Smythe were bending over the body, Kate went to
Sir Charles. "Charles," she said in a low voice, "there's
something I must tell you."

He pressed his lips together. "If it is about you and Temple," he said, "I don't want to hear it. What you do is your
own private—"

"Fiddlesticks," Kate retorted smartly. "You know me
better than to think I would allow myself to be compromised

by a man like Temple. What I have to tell you concerns the handkerchief and the—''

''What handkerchief?''

''The one about eighteen inches to the right of your left foot, caught on that rosebush.'' She saw his eyes go to the small scrap of white. ''I didn't want to call Lord Warwick's or Sir Friedrich's attention to it, since they would most certainly feel compelled to take it up and I knew that you wouldn't want the crime scene disturbed.'' She glanced over her shoulder. ''No one is looking. You have the opportunity of retrieving it.''

''No,'' Charles said. ''I would rather first photograph it in place.''

Bradford straightened. ''Clever of you to stow the camera in the motorcar,'' he remarked. ''Shall I fetch it?''

''Please,'' Sir Charles said. He turned back to Kate. ''No one has moved the body, then?''

''Not while I have been on the scene,'' she said. She consulted the watch pinned to her lapel. ''Sir Friedrich and I stumbled onto the corpse at a moment or two past nine. It is now just past noon.''

Charles gave her a brief smile. ''I must compliment you. If the police manage to solve this, their success will largely be due to your insistence that the scene remain undisturbed.''

''But I am afraid I did disturb the scene,'' she said ruefully. ''When I first saw the body, I observed a piece of paper protruding rather obviously from the breast pocket. I asked Sir Friedrich to step away and send a nearby gardener for Lord Warwick. While he was thus occupied, I took the paper out of the pocket, only because I feared that someone might see it and become curious about it before you arrived.'' She reached into her reticule, took out a folded piece of paper, and pressed it into his hand. ''Here it is. I have not had the opportunity to read it.''

There was no opportunity for Charles to read it, either. The three men had completed their consultation.

The Prince turned, grim-faced. ''Charles,'' he said, ''I don't need to tell you what will happen when the police arrive, with the press hot on their heels. The Tranby Croft fiasco—which involved merely a bit of gaming, not murder—will be as nothing compared to the stink that will be raised about the two deaths that have occurred this weekend. To exclude the press, we must exclude the police.'' He paused for emphasis. "Do you take my point?"

Charles shifted his weight uneasily. "I understand the difficulty of dealing with an inquisitive press, sir. But anyone who conceals a murder may be judged an accessory to it. Have you considered that?"

"Indeed I have," the Prince replied severely. "Which is why you have just been commissioned an officer of the law."

If His Highness had not been so serious, Kate would have smiled. Sir Charles Sheridan, about to become the fifth baron of something-or-other, an officer of the law?

Charles's jaw tightened. "Forgive me, sir," he said, "but I am not—"

"Oh, yes, you are," the Prince replied. He raised his walking stick. "I hereby appoint you, Sir Charles Sheridan, as temporary captain in the Household Police of His Highness the Prince of Wales, and invest you with the authority to investigate this conspiracy."

Charles tried one last time. "But I must point out, sir, that the local authorities have jurisdiction—"

"Sheridan," the Prince thundered, "this investigation is your *duty*!"

Kate flinched. Charles straightened and looked the Prince in the eye. "Yes, sir," he said. "Forgive me, sir, but you mentioned a conspiracy. Might I ask—"

"It also involves the death of the boy. I don't for a minute believe the horse had anything to do with it."

"A conspiracy, Bertie?" Lord Warwick looked uneasy. "You mean, you think there's a link between your stable-boy's getting a knock on the head and somebody doing in poor Reggie?"

"It's possible," the Prince said. "What if Harry saw or heard something he shouldn't have—something that made him dangerous?"

"Entirely correct, sir," Kirk-Smythe put in. "The lad might have eavesdropped on some sort of plot, and then—"

"—and then was killed to keep him from revealing his

suspicions to me. Ah, yes, of course!'' The Prince, pleased, turned to Charles. ''There, you see, Charles? Half of your work—the logical half—has been done for you. All you have to do is find the evidence. What do you say?''

Charles said the only thing he could say, under the circumstances, Kate thought. He said, ''Yes, sir.''

''Excellent,'' the Prince exclaimed. ''And one more thing. Since this matter so obviously involves the security of the realm, I must instruct you to maintain the strictest secrecy in your investigation. No word of this is to get through to the outside world.''

''I fail to see,'' Charles said carefully, ''how the security of the realm got into the matter.''

The Prince assumed a patient expression. ''I am now compelled to believe, Charles, that this crime and the other are part of a plot. Your investigation must be kept secret in order to ensure that no word of it disturbs the populace or alerts Anarchists who might use it to seize some villainous advantage.''

Charles was stroking his brown beard. ''Suppose for a moment, sir, that this is not an Anarchist plot but a simple case of murder. Suppose—hypothetically, of course—that my investigation reveals that the murderer is one of the servants, or perhaps one of our party. What then? Will that person be turned over to the proper authorities?''

''In this matter,'' the Prince said decidedly, ''*I* am the proper authority. Now, get to it, Charles. Question whom you will, investigate as you must. No holds barred, as it were. We must have the truth of this matter. I shall want your first report in an hour.'' He pulled out his heavy gold pocket watch and frowned at it. ''No, make that two hours. We are abominably late for luncheon as it is.''

From his half-audible sigh, Kate understood that Charles had unwillingly resigned himself to the task. ''Perhaps, sir, I should consult with you when I have something to report. It may be two hours, or—''

''Oh, very good,'' the Prince said impatiently. ''Now, shall we—''

''Speaking of luncheon,'' Charles went on, ''it might be a good idea if you announced the murder and requested the cooperation of the guests and their servants. The Easton servants, as well.''

''The guests?'' Sir Friedrich asked with a small laugh. ''Surely you don't for a moment imagine that one of us would—''

Charles looked at him. ''I have no way of knowing, Temple, where this investigation will lead. With that in mind, sir,'' he said to the Prince, ''no one who is here now must be allowed to leave.''

''Good thought,'' the Prince agreed. ''Put a cork in the bottle, as it were. Well, then. I will make the announcements. The murder is likely known, anyway.'' He turned to go.

''And there is the corpse,'' Charles said.

The Prince paused. ''Oh, yes. Poor Reggie. We can't just let him lie here, I suppose.'' He pulled his brows together. ''But we can't have him in the house, either, disturbing the ladies' sensibilities. Where then—''

''How about the game larder, Bertie?'' Lord Warwick suggested.

''The game larder? Capital!'' The Prince thumped his walking stick on the ground. ''Get some men and take him there at once.''

''I shall need to photograph the scene first,'' Charles said. He stepped forward, knelt beside the body, and lifted the head, turning it slightly. After a brief examination, he stood again. ''I shall also require the services of a competent surgeon.''

Sir Friedrich frowned. ''A surgeon? But the man is quite dead.''

''Since there is no evident exit wound, the bullet must still be in the body. I would like to recover it.''

The Prince grimaced. ''It seems a rather macabre souvenir.''

''Not a souvenir, sir, evidence. With luck, a bullet can be traced to the gun that fired it.''

''The exact gun?'' Sir Friedrich asked curiously.

Lord Warwick looked skeptical. ''I have had a great deal of experience with guns, Charles. A bullet might reveal the caliber and type of the gun that fired it, but beyond that—''

''When I was visiting the Krupp munitions works,''

Charles said, "I noticed the driving bands with which the shells are fitted. When the shell is fired, these copper bands are forced into the spiral grooves that are cut into the inner surface of the gun barrel—its rifling, that is. These grooves, as you may be aware, force the projectile to rotate."

"Every sportsman knows as much," Sir Friedrich said impatiently. "The rotation prevents the projectile from tumbling while in flight, and increases its range and accuracy. But I fail to see what that has to do with—"

"As I studied the copper bands," Charles said, "I noticed that the shells fired from the same weapon bore identical markings, but that these were different from the markings on shells fired by another weapon. As I looked into the matter further, I discovered that different arms manufacturers use different riflings. From model to model, there is a great variation among the number of grooves, their angle and twist, and the width of the grooves and the lands—the smooth surfaces between the grooves. Theoretically, at least, it is possible to identify the weapon from which a particular bullet was fired."

"Amazing!" Lord Warwick exclaimed. He frowned. "I'm not sure I see the practical application, though."

"Don't you?" the Prince asked. "I daresay the police do."

"As a matter of fact," Charles said, "a murder conviction was obtained in Lyons in '89 upon the testimony of Professor Lacassagne, who compared the marks on a fatal bullet and found them identical to the rifling of a gun owned by one of the suspects. While his conclusion is open to question, the conviction demonstrates that such evidence is useful in prosecution."

"By Jove!" the Prince exclaimed. "What wonders science is visiting upon us!" He frowned down at Wallace's body. "The projectile is of no use, however, unless there is a weapon against which it may be compared."

"Precisely. But the weapon may come to light. Meanwhile I should like to retrieve the bullet. There is a surgeon in Chelmsford who has my trust—a Dr. John Miles."

"I shall be glad to send the carriage," Lord Warwick offered.

There was a rattle of footsteps on the gravel, and Bradford appeared with the camera gear. "Sorry to be delayed," he said to Charles. "Your gear had been unpacked and taken to your room."

"Send Marsden," the Prince said. "He's eager enough to put that motorcar of his into use."

"Oh, absolutely, sir," Bradford said, setting down the camera. "Where am I going?"

"To Chelmsford, for a surgeon," Charles said. "His name is Dr. John Miles. You will find him in the High Street, at Number Twenty-two." He turned to the Prince. "In the meantime, I suggest that Your Highness have Wallace's room sealed and post a guard at the door."

"Excellent idea," Sir Friedrich put in. "Reggie's belongings may contain vital evidence."

"Yes," Sir Charles agreed. "We need someone reliable. Everyone must be kept out."

The Prince turned to Kirk-Smythe. "Room-guarding is up your line, Kirk-Smythe. I'll have a lunch plate sent up to you."

Kirk-Smythe came to attention. "Your Highness will be safe?"

"Of course I'll be safe," the Prince said testily. "After all, I am among friends. This body-guarding business can be carried a bit too far, if you ask me."

Kate looked at Kirk-Smythe, suddenly realizing what she might have guessed before: that the man was assigned to protect the Prince. It must not be an easy job.

"But, sir," Kirk-Smythe objected, "the Queen is quite concerned about Anarchists. And when she learns of Lord Wallace's murder, she will be deeply worried that—"

"Oh, blast the Queen," the Prince said. "Anyway, I don't intend Mama to learn of the murder until Sheridan has solved it for us." He waved the young man off. "Go on and guard that room." He turned to Sir Charles. "Are we quite finished? While we dawdle here, our food is getting cold."

"There is one thing more," Charles said. He glanced obliquely at Kate. "I would like Miss Ardleigh to serve as my assistant. She has an access to the female guests and servants that I could not possibly obtain."

Kate pulled in her breath. His assistant? Beryl Bardwell felt like shouting and throwing her hat in the air. Access to the details of a criminal investigation—no, more than access, participation in the investigation itself! What a wonderful way to gather new materials for—

But then her heart sank. If she had any doubt that Sir Charles knew about Beryl Bardwell, this kicked it into a cocked hat. Of course he knew—and thought that since she practiced the solution of crime on paper, she might have a talent for the thing itself.

"Miss Ardleigh? Kate?" The Prince was staring at her, perplexed. "But she is a woman!"

Sir Friedrich looked through his pince-nez. "One reads of such things in popular fiction," he drawled in a condescending tone, "but confidential investigation is hardly a suitable occupation for a lady."

"I can vouch for Miss Ardleigh's powers of observation," Charles said. "She will be a most competent assistant." Kate, taken totally aback by this turn of events, could think of nothing to say on her own behalf.

"Observation and competence are all very well," the Prince said, twirling his walking stick, "but there remains the question of trust." He peered at Kate. "Can she hold her tongue?"

"Miss Ardleigh can be trusted absolutely," Sir Charles said, before Kate could speak. "I have no qualms regarding her ability to maintain a confidence."

Sir Friedrich was frowning. "All this is well and good," he said, "but don't forget that she is an American." Suitable for enticing into Stone Hall for a spot of seduction, Kate thought with wry amusement, but fundamentally unreliable.

"Her viewpoint is all the fresher for it," Sir Charles said. "She can see through our pretenses." He glanced at her and added, as if he were suddenly struck by the thought, "She will not be dismayed by rank and privilege."

"And," Lord Warwick said practically, "since she's not one of us, she's not likely to have had a motive to kill Reggie."

"Quite so," the Prince said. "Well, then, Charles, Kate shall play Dr. Watson to your Holmes." His good humor seemed entirely restored now that luncheon was at hand. He lifted his hand to Sir Charles. "Carry on, Sherlock." He bowed to Kate. "And you, too, my dear Miss Watson."

He strode off, chuckling at his little joke. As he rounded the corner in the path, they heard him say, "Her Watson to his Holmes. Quite apt, that. Quite apt!"

15

It is impossible to love and be wise.
—FRANCIS BACON
Essays, 1625

Charles watched the Prince stride jauntily away, wondering whether to laugh or be angry. He seemed to have very little comprehension of the dreadful reality of this situation. Two people dead, and His Highness was concerned with getting to luncheon on time!

Kate was also staring after the departing backs. "So I have been given permission to assist you," she said, obviously annoyed, "even if I am a woman—and an American." She paused, narrowing her eyes. "You don't suppose the Prince really believes that silly business about the security of the realm, do you?"

"I think he will seize any excuse to keep this crime out of the public eye," Charles replied, "particularly if the killer turns out to be one of his friends. He has a terrible fear of scandal."

"As do they all," Kate replied, "the women even more than the men."

She frowned, and Charles noticed again, not for the first time that morning, how striking was the intelligence in her hazel eyes, and how lovely her russet hair, piled high on her head under that foolishly tipped gold hat. But his thoughts were wrenched back to the subject by her next question.

"Do you suppose, Charles, that fear of scandal might have been a motive for this murder?"

"It is certainly possible," he replied, and wondered again why this woman was so infernally interested in crime. Of course, it was that very interest which had prompted him to suggest her as his assistant. Remembering something Temple had said, he muttered, half to himself, "It is almost as if you *have* been reading detective stories."

"Pardon me?"

He smiled, thinking that this one small revelation made light of a great deal that had puzzled him about the hitherto enigmatic Kate Ardleigh.

"Was Temple right?" he asked. "Are you one of Doyle's devotees? *Do* you imagine yourself Dr. Watson to Sherlock Holmes?"

The minute the words were out of his mouth, he realized how patronizing they must sound and hoped he had not offended her. Where was the fault if a lady read crime stories for her amusement?

But it was not offense that he read in those green-flecked eyes. She searched his face intently; then, as if she had come to some conclusion, squared her shoulders, raised her chin, and said, "I think, Charles, that it is time we spoke straightforwardly to one another. You know that I do not just read detective stories. I write them."

Charles frowned, not quite sure he had heard her correctly. "Forgive me," he said, "I fear I don't—"

She sighed. "Let's not play games, Charles. I know you have guessed."

"Guessed what, for heaven's sake?"

"That I am ... Beryl Bardwell."

"Beryl Bardwell?" He searched his memory. "The author of 'The Duchess's Dilemma'? The writer who is being spoken of as a female Conan Doyle?" He stared at her. "You are telling me that you—? I don't believe it!"

She gave a little gasp. "You mean, you had not guessed?"

"Guessed?" he exclaimed, throwing up his hands. "Great God in heaven, how could I have guessed a thing like that?"

There was an audible outbreath and she turned away so that her face was hidden. "You have read 'The Duchess's Dilemma'?"

"A day or two ago, upon the recommendation of Bradford Marsden. He thought the setting and characters fit a situation that occurred in his family last spring. He wanted my opinion."

Her cheeks reddened. "I should not have stayed so close to the facts."

Charles shook his head, still bemused, still only half-comprehending. "The description of the duchess—I recognized the similarity to Bradford's mother, of course, and wondered if the author might be acquainted with the family. But I never surmised that *you*—"

"I'm sorry," she said in a small voice. "I thought you knew."

"Thought I knew!" he exclaimed, seized by an unexpectedly wild feeling. "I *should* have known, damn it! The truth was right there in front of me. Since the very day I met you, you have been absorbed in such matters!"

As he spoke, he heard the passion in his words, revealing his feeling for this confounded American woman who refused to know her place.

"That is," he said, "I mean to say . . ."

He stopped, lost in her eyes, unable to remember what he had meant to say. He lifted his arms and drew her into his embrace, feeling the fragrant sweetness of her body against his. Then his lips were on her mouth and he was devouring her in a kiss that seemed to him to divulge every confused feeling in his heart. But a moment later, he was wrenching himself free.

"Forgive me," he muttered, gasping for breath. "I am . . . dishonoring you, and myself."

Kate put her fingers on his cheek, turning his face so that he had to look into her eyes. "What is the dishonor in loving, Charles?" she asked gently.

"Not in loving," he said. He took her hand and held it. "I do love you, Kate. I had made up my mind to ask you to marry me. But after I learned about Robert's illness, I. . . . I must agree with your conclusion. It is not wise." He stopped. "Daisy tells me that you know about Robert."

"Yes," she said and looked him full in the face. "I am sorry for you, Charles. Losing a brother is a sad thing."

"It is only one of the sadnesses," he said. "Robert enjoys the baronial life and has lived it with great pleasure. I have already determined that if I must take his place, I will continue to pursue my own interests, insofar as I can. But there are certain obligations I cannot avoid. I must manage the estates, assume the family seat in the House of Lords, occasionally appear socially. In this situation, a marriage between us—"

She lowered her eyes. "I know. In this situation, a marriage to an Irish-American wife with a secret life as a writer cannot be wise."

"But that's not what I mean at all! In such a situation, you would be terribly unhappy. It is not a life you would enjoy."

She was startled into looking at him. "If I were your wife, you would not see my writing as a thorn, or as a potential embarrassment?"

"If I were your husband," he countered, "would you not see my family, and the estate, and the damned social appearances as thorns? For they are, certainly."

She considered for a moment. "I see that we would both bring certain liabilities to a marriage. Although, should I retire to the garret and scribble for days on end, you might begin to feel that you had the worst of the bargain. Or should my name—*your* name—be somehow associated with Beryl Bardwell's stories."

"You may scribble at will!" he exclaimed. "And if your identity should come to light, we shall have plenty to talk about at dinner parties."

"If we are invited."

"Oh, but we shall be. Almost any hostess in the land would welcome Beryl Bardwell. But do not assume that anyone will tell you anything they don't want to see in print."

Her lips were trembling. "Then you are asking me to marry you, in spite of . . . everything?"

He put his arms around her. "Will you, in spite of everything?"

She hesitated for only a moment. "Yes," she said, her voice low but resolute. "Whether it is wise or not."

He kissed her again, delighting in the way her arms

slipped eagerly around his neck. It seemed to him that he could go on kissing her into the afternoon and the night and the next morning, and he reflected with stunned delight that soon—very soon, perhaps—he would be free to do just that.

But a moment later, she pulled away and straightened her hat, which had tipped over one ear. She looked down. "I fear," she said, "that we are not showing the proper respect."

He followed her gaze to the blanketed corpse lying on the path. "Good Lord," he groaned, "I forgot all about Reggie."

16

In the late Victorian and early Edwardian periods, the servant class underwent a dramatic change. Many individuals began to perceive opportunities for betterment in other situations and resent their paltry wages and low status in the great houses. This resentment was expressed, in some instances, by a sullen sluggishness; in others, by outright belligerence and a more or less open rebellion. Such individuals could be easily influenced by the Anarchist sentiment which abounded in the last decade of the century.

—THOMAS SEYMOUR
Social Precursors of the Great War

Half-stunned by what had just occurred between them, Charles sent Kate off with instructions to see what she could learn from the women guests and upper servants and upstairs maids—a daunting task, for there were quite a number to interrogate. It was a delicate task, too, requiring not only finesse in asking questions but an ear for lying answers. He did not doubt that Kate was up to it.

When she had gone, he set up his camera and took the necessary photographs. Then he summoned the men who had been promised and oversaw the removal of Wallace's body to the game larder, a low building with a stone floor, a wooden sink and large table for cleaning and butchering game, and heavy plank shelves suitable for laying out a corpse. He left Wallace in the company of a number of naked

grouse and pheasants dangling from hooks in the rafters, with
a man to guard the door. Then, after making inquiries as to
the whereabouts of Deaf John, he went off to the nearby
forge, where the man was said to work. With luck, it would
take only a minute to question him and discover whether he
could shed any light on the groom's death.

But questioning Deaf John took longer than he expected.
Encountering the smith on the path to the forge, he was directed to the old man's cottage. According to the smith, the
farrier (who worked under his supervision) had come to the
smithy with chills and a fever that morning and had been
sent back to his bed.

"Perhaps," Charles said, "I should ask you to go with
me to see him. If the man is truly deaf, I may not be able
to make my questions understood."

"Ye'll 'ave no trouble," the smith said, wiping his nose
on his coarse sleeve. "People think John's simple an' doan't
give 'im credit. But 'e's canny, right 'nough, an' clever at
readin' lips. Anyway, I seen 'is girl Meg goin' that way, too,
a little bit agon, carryin' a pail o' soup fer 'er faither's lunch.
She'll 'elp ye talk t' 'im."

The cottage stood at the end of a dirt lane lined by several
such cottages, all rented to estate workers. The dooryard was
mostly packed dirt, with the frosted remains of a few summer
flowers under the window. The thatched building had only
one room downstairs, with two small casement windows set
into the thick walls and a Dutch door, the top half of which
stood open. Looking in, Charles saw that the dim room was
furnished with a table, several chairs, and a narrow bed, with
a potato sack thrown down by way of hearth rug and a par-
affin lamp set on the table for light.

But the room was clean-swept and neat, there was a small
fire in the grate and a potted geranium on the windowsill,
and the thin mattress was covered with a bright green cov-
erlet, which had been thrown back. A stooped old graybeard
whom Charles took to be Deaf John, his shoulders hunched
under a blue knitted shawl, sat in a wooden chair before the
fire, his large, calloused hands holding a bowl from which
he was drinking a thick soup. A slight, pretty girl of sixteen
or seventeen sat on a stool at his knee, a worried expression

on her thin young face. She was wearing a maid's working dress of blue stuff, covered by a white apron, and her curly brown hair was tucked under a white cap. The evident tenderness of her concern for her father warmed Charles's heart, and he was hesitant to intrude. But he had come here to question the old man, and question he must.

He cleared his throat quietly, so as not to startle the girl. Even so, she whirled around, her mouth falling open at the sight of a stranger in the doorway. "I'm sorry to have frightened you, Meg." He took off his hat. "My name is Charles Sheridan. I've come to—"

The girl's brown eyes became very large, the eyes of a frightened doe, and the freckles showed against the sudden pallor of her cheeks. "Yer th' one wot's doin' th' investigatin'?" she asked in a small, frightened voice that was barely more than a whisper. "Wot d'ye want wi' me? I doan't know anything."

He smiled to allay her fears. "My business is with your father," he said, opening the bottom half of the door and stepping in. The old man, gray hair straggling on either side of his weathered face, was watching him intently. "I understand that you can help me communicate with him."

The girl looked at her father, trading fright for worry. "But 'e doan't know anything neither, sir. 'E took bad sick this mornin' an' can't work. 'E's bin right 'ere, either lyin' in bed er sittin' in front o' th' fire, since arter breakfast. Why, 'e ain't even 'eard 'bout Lord Wallace gettin' shot."

Charles was not surprised at the speed with which news traveled on the estate. He suspected that rumor of Wallace's murder had reached the Lodge before the messenger left for Chelmsford. And in spite of the Prince's concern for secrecy, the news had by now reached the far outskirts of the Park and was on its way to Dunmow.

"It is not about Lord Wallace's death that I wish to inquire," he said, and was startled by the sudden and involuntary relief that flooded the girl's face. Struck by the idea that she knew something, he was about to question her. But he caught himself. Kate—a woman, and less intimidating— would be better able to persuade the girl to reveal anything she might know. "I have been told that your father saw

someone coming out of the stable yesterday morning, about
the time the Prince's groom was killed. Will you ask him if
that is so?''

Deaf John put his hand on his daughter's arm, made a
gruff sound, and nodded vigorously.

'' 'E's sayin' 'e wants t' tell ye wot he knows,'' she said
nervously. '' 'E read yer lips, ye see, sir, although sometimes
it's better if I ask 'im, too, t' make sure 'e's got it right.''

''Does he know the name of the person he saw coming
out of the barn?''

The girl put her lips close to her father's ear and shouted.
'' 'E wants t'know 'oo 'twas, Dad. D'ye know 'is name?''

The old man shook his head, then grasped the shawl,
lifted it and settled it again on his shoulders, saying something that sounded to Charles like a harsh, confused garble.

'' 'Twere a person in a cloak, 'e says,'' the girl interpreted. She seemed to Charles to be less apprehensive about
this subject.

''A man or a woman?''

Another shout, another garble. The old man pointed at
Charles's boots.

'' 'Twere a man, by 'is boots,'' she said. The old man
said something, amplified by signs and gestures. ''Black
boots,'' the girl went on, watching her father. ''Dad doan't
know 'is name, but 'e owns a big gray mare.'' There was
another consultation, and she added, ''A big gray mare wi'
a new shoe on 'er left 'ind foot.''

''Thank you,'' Charles said, inwardly exultant. With such
a clear description, it should be easy enough to discover the
cloaked man's name. He was thanking her for her help when
a shadow blotted the light from the door.

'' 'Oo's 'ere?'' a man's voice inquired, with rough concern. '' 'Tain't th' doctor, is't? 'E ain't took that bad, I
'ope.''

''Marsh!'' Meg exclaimed, and jumped to her feet, her
eyes going from Charles to the other with a return of the
fear Charles had seen earlier. ''No, no, 'tain't th' doctor,''
she said hurriedly. ''Dad's eat up all 'is soup an's ready fer
'is nap. 'E'll be back t'work termorrer, sure. So ye doan't
need t' stay.''

Marsh, a surly, pock-faced young man wearing the green and gold livery of a footman, looked a little surprised at her sudden dismissal. He dropped an armload of wood beside the fire and brushed the bark off his sleeve. "Th' smith wants 'im back termorrer? I doan't think so." He raised his voice and bent over the old man. "Ye wants t' stay i' bed another day er twa, ol' John," he shouted. "They kin do without ye at th' forge." He lowered his voice and added, to the girl, "Lit'le as they pay, they'll scarcely miss 'im." He turned to face Charles, his eyes angrily slitted. "An' 'oo be ye?"

"It's all right, Marsh," the girl said. With an obvious effort at intervention, she stepped between them. " 'E's only somebody 'er ladyship sent to—"

"Yer th' one 'oo's doin' th' job fer th' police, ain't ye?" Marsh asked belligerently. He pulled his black brows together and thrust out his jaw. "Well, ye might as well git yersel' gone, then. This 'ome's private. There's nothin' t' be learnt 'ere."

Meg touched the young man's sleeve. "It's all right, Marsh," she repeated. "Th' gentl'man's done 'is askin' an' he's leavin'." When Marsh did not respond, she leaned closer and added, so low that Charles had to strain to hear, " 'E was only askin' 'bout th' stableboy."

"I doan't like it, Meg," Marsh muttered. The glance he cast at Charles was half fight, half fear. "I doan't like 'is bein' 'ere, snoopin' in pore folks' bus'ness."

The young man was something less than one-and-twenty, Charles thought. It was unusual for a footman—Meg's brother, was he, or her sweetheart?—to be so bellicose. At Somersworth, in the lifetime of his father, such an attitude would have been grounds for instant dismissal with a bad character. But times were changing, and with them the demeanor of the servants. Their submissive obedience was giving way to a natural and irrepressible wish to better themselves and, when that wish was thwarted, a sullen resentment. That, he suspected, was what lay behind the young man's antagonism. If Marsh were in his employ, some more challenging and interesting work would have to be found for him, with opportunities for advancement.

He bowed to the old man, nodded at Meg and Marsh, and

went to the door. "Thank you for your help," he said.

"Yer welcome," Meg said, with an attempt at civility. Marsh growled something unintelligible, and they both turned back toward the fire and the old man.

Charles retraced his steps to the smithy, a three-sided stone building with a tiled roof, as dark as a cave. The roof and walls were black with the soot of the many coal fires that had been built in the enormous stone forge at the back, and the place rang with the infernal clanging of the smith's heavy hammer. The air was acrid with coal smoke and the smell of the hot oil that was used for tempering. Walking into the place was like walking into the devil's den.

On one side of the forge, Charles saw a sturdy boy of hardly more than twelve, pumping a large ox-hide bellows fixed flat to the dirt floor. The bellows directed a stream of air into the furnace, fanning the hungry flames. On the other side of the forge, the smith was bent over an anvil, punching holes in a hot ox shoe he was fashioning from an iron bar. Behind him stood the huge beast, docile in the elaborate leather and canvas sling that supported his weight while the smithy shod him, one hoof at a time. The smith, a burly man in a leather apron, his face blackened with coal smudge, looked up as Charles approached.

"Git wot ye was after?" he asked, with a certain familiarity. Charles had long ago noticed the easy address of craftsmen, whose skill and experience seemed to give them the right to speak as an equal to almost anyone. With the skill of long practice, the smith picked up the hot shoe with his forge tongs, turned swiftly to hoist the ox's right foreleg, and applied the shoe against the horny wall of the hoof. There was a great sizzle and smoke, but the animal stood compliant as before, appearing not to notice.

"I made a start," Charles said. He waited until the smith had finished putting in the nails, nipped them off, clinched them over, and dropped the beast's leg. "I wonder," he said. "Do you know the name of a man whose large gray mare has a new left hind shoe? I should like to interview him."

The smith seemed to find this funny. Chuckling broadly, he took another piece of metal and, placing it on the forge, waited for it to glow red. Motioning to the boy to increase the rhythm of the hissing, wheezing bellows, he said, "Ye wud, eh? Well, sir, I doubt ye'll be interviewin' 'im anytime soon."

Charles raised his voice. "And why is that?" he asked, over the roar of the forge.

"Because 'e's dead, that's why. 'E's th' gentl'man 'oo was found shot this mornin'." The smith picked up his hammer and began to pound the glowing metal. "Lay t' it, boy!" he shouted over the ringing of iron on iron. "Lay t' it, m'fine lad!"

Outside the forge and down the path, it was so quiet that Charles could hear the dry leaves rustling. So Reginald Wallace had been in the stable around the time of the boy's death. Did this fact suggest that Wallace himself was the killer, and his murder an act of revenge by one of the servants? Or was he a witness, murdered to keep him from revealing what he knew?

He was some distance away from the forge before he suddenly remembered something he should have dealt with prior to any interviews. He took out the folded paper Kate had given him, which she had pulled from Wallace's pocket as he lay on the ground. He opened it and scanned the page quickly. When he finished reading it, he had a firm grasp of the direction in which this investigation must proceed.

But it was a revelation that brought him no joy.

17

Love, pain, and money cannot be kept secret. They soon betray themselves.

—*Spanish proverb*

To know that one has a secret is to know half the secret itself.

—HENRY WARD BEECHER

It was already lunchtime, and Winnie Wospottle had not yet recovered her customary good humor, so sharp had been her disappointment of the evening before. Remembering Lawrence with pleasure from the dear old days in Brighton, she had fully expected him to accept her invitation to join her in the laundry room. With that expectation, she had arranged the cozy corner behind the hot water boiler with all the care which a lady, anticipating a clandestine visit from her lover, might lavish on her boudoir.

Winnie was a resourceful woman. When she first arrived at Easton, she had made it her business to learn what was available in the kitchens, pantries, closets, cupboards, stillrooms, butteries, game larder, and wine cellar. In Winnie's considered opinion, this plenty was free for the taking, as long as she kept a vigilant eye out for Buffle, the house steward, who was reputed to glue pieces of felt on the soles of his shoes so that he might step noiselessly in the halls. Even when she had nothing special to celebrate, she regularly availed herself of the abundance, just to keep in practice.

On this occasion, Winnie had already filched a dozen

sprigs of hothouse stephanotis and some stems of fern from the fragrant vases in the pantry, standing ready to be distributed to the bedrooms upstairs. While Buffle was counting the plate, she purloined two crystal goblets from the sparkling rows arrayed on the shelves, reasoning (rightly) that with so many goblets displayed, two would not be missed. And while the undercook was scolding the scullery maid for inattention to the floor, she made off with half a baked chicken, a plate of cucumber sandwiches, and a dish of crystallized fruits. A bottle of fine French wine from the cellar completed her acquisitions.

The plunder safely transported to the ironing room, Winnie hung a sheet behind the boiler to screen off the corner, draped a board with a lace tablecloth and centered it with the flowers and a pair of candles, and fluffed up the down pillows that made a soft, warm bed behind the hot water boiler. Surveying her seraglio, she was entirely pleased. Full of warm anticipation, she went off to her attic bedroom to ready herself for an evening of revel in the servants' hall.

The festive evening, however, had come to a fruitless and bitter conclusion. The fickle Lawrence danced but once with her and was then lured away by a brazen young girl named Amelia, lady's maid to the red-haired American woman, who seemed to think she had some sort of claim on his affections. And even though Winnie went alone to the ironing room and comforted herself with wine, baked chicken, cucumber sandwiches, and candied fruits, all she earned thereby was a headache and a bellyache, causing her to miss breakfast and further adding to her surliness. By lunchtime, working like fury, she had overseen the washing and hanging of a dozen baskets of towels and linens and had personally fed two dozen sheets through the mangle, which she did not trust the maids to operate. She was hot and cross, and the discovery that she was to be in the second shift at table (there being too many servants to seat all at once) destroyed what remained of her disposition. By the time she sat down to lunch and heard about Lord Wallace's death and the Prince's command to cooperate with the investigators he had appointed, she was in a fine stew.

"Wot's wrong wi' th' constable, I wants t' know," she

demanded truculently. "Why is't we got t'ave some 'igh-toned nob askin' us questions?"

"Ye won't be answerin' t' a nob, Winn," said Wickett, the bandy-legged coachman. He grinned mischievously. "A lady nob is 'oo ye gits t' talk to."

"Not that, neither," said Marjorie, an iron-faced under-cook whose reputation for temper was second to none, not even to that of Winnie herself. She added, in an acid tone, "'Tis th' red-haired American 'ooman. She's already 'ard at it, in th' mornin' room. Arter lunch, th' upstairs maids are t' line up, six at a time, as they're called. She'll call fer us later."

"Th' American?" Winnie asked, affronted and dumbly amazed. "Why, she's not even a lady! She 'as no rank wot-somever."

"Ooh, aye," said Marjorie, becoming increasingly in-flamed. She jerked a stained and calloused thumb in the di-rection of Amelia, who was seated a little way downtable, next to Lawrence. " '*Er* miss."

Winnie's amazement turned to disgust. She glared at Amelia. "Be careful wot ye say, then," she said to Marjorie, and added, with the force of inspiration, "I don't doubt she's a spy."

Wickett leaned over to look downtable. "A *spy*?" he asked incredulously. "Why, she's jes' a lit'le thing, no big-ger'n a mite. Pretty, too, 'f ye ask my 'pinion."

Marjorie's fancy had been tweaked by Winnie's assertion, and she curled her lip at Wickett. "Pretty she may be, but she's cert'n'y a spy," she said with conviction. "A spy fer 'er mistress, is wot she is. I read 'bout spies in a story once. They listen t' secrets, then run upstairs an' snitch t' their mistress." She raised herself off the wooden bench in order to get a look at Lawrence. "D'ye s'pose 'e's another one?" she asked in a shrill stage whisper.

"Now, I wudn't doubt *that*," Wickett growled vindic-tively. He had lost a bob to Lawrence that morning when the Daimler had completed the round-trip run to Chelmsford in something under two hours and thirty minutes and he was still smarting. "Lookit 'is eyes. Shifty-like, wudn't ye say?"

"Foxy eyes," Winnie agreed. She raised her voice so it

could be heard the length of the table. "Watch yer tongues. There's spies among us. Don't tell no secrets."

A sudden hush fell over the table, as all eyes turned questioningly to Winnie. Peyton, the bootblack, who was reputed to have a level head, looked up with a frown.

"Shudn't think we'd 'ave a spy 'ere," he said mildly. " 'Oo d'ye mean?"

Winnie might have spoken, but Marjorie, whose excitement had been growing by the moment, jumped to her feet. " 'Tis them!" she cried, pointing her knife at Lawrence and Amelia. "Them two. Spies!"

Amelia looked one way, then another, confused. "Spies?" she cried, her hand going to her mouth. "Oh, no!"

"Spies?" Lawrence demanded. He stood up, leaning on his hands, palms down, his head wagging like an angry bull. " 'Oo says we're spies?"

"Us sez!" Marjorie had mounted the bench, aflame with the fine fire of righteous indignation. She shook her fist. "An' we woan't 'ave none o' it, d'ye 'ear? Ye ain't goin' t' shop us up! We'll 'ave no spies tellin' our secrets!"

Marjorie's rallying cry was followed by a rousing cheer from the length of the table. Several, carried away by the passion of the moment, began to stamp their feet and beat with their spoons on their plates. "No spies! No spies!"

The hallway door banged open and Buffle strode into the room. "Here now!" he cried, clapping his hands sharply. "What's all this noise? Finish your meal and get back to work, the lot of you! For shame! Who do you think you are, anyway? Ruffians and rowdies?" He passed through the room, favoring those nearest him with a dark scowl, went out the other door, and slammed it behind him.

Some may have been ashamed at having been thus caught out by the steward, but neither Winnie nor Marjorie were among them. Winnie fixed her eyes vindictively on Amelia, who by now was red as a flannel petticoat and close to tears. "Spy," she hissed under her breath.

"Spy!" echoed Marjorie.

Amelia went from red to white, put her apron to her eyes, and began to sob softly.

"That's enough," Lawrence gritted, and took her by the

arm. "Come on," he said, getting up and clambering over the bench. "We're leavin'!"

"Happy riddance!" Marjorie exclaimed.

Winnie sat back and took a deep breath. Her good humor had been restored.

In an open pantry in the deserted back hallway, Amelia, still sobbing, allowed herself to be comforted by Lawrence.

"I'm sure they didn't mean nothin' by it," he said, patting her shoulder with awkward solicitude. "They was jes' teasin' us."

"Winnie Wospottle wasn't teasin'," Amelia said, wiping her eyes with the corner of her apron. "She was the one 'oo started it." Amelia felt herself genuinely embarrassed and hurt by what had transpired in the servants' hall. But she was also not above exploiting the situation for all it was worth—and in her mind, it promised to be worth a good deal. She gave another sob and put her apron to her eyes again. " 'Oo cares about 'er ol' secrets, anyway? She kin keep 'em, fer all o' me."

Lawrence, to give him due credit, looked utterly wretched. "She's jes' jealous, is all," he muttered. "She an' me, we uster go 'round together, back in Brighton. We—" He straightened with a look of determination. "But that was *before*," he said emphatically. "A long while before. I washt my 'ands o' 'er then an' I wash my 'ands o' 'er now."

Amelia looked up at him through tear-wet lashes. "It's over, then?" she asked, with a pretty hesitation. "Yer sartin?"

"It's over," Lawrence said firmly. "Ye've got nothin' t' fear." He put his finger under Amelia's chin and tilted it, gazing earnestly into her eyes. "I'm yers, Amelia. All yers, 'eart 'n' soul 'n' body. I wants nobody but ye."

"Oh, Lawrence," Amelia sighed, her own heart near bursting. She could have borne any kind of taunt or teasing from any number of Marjories and Winnies to hear Lawrence speak thus. But she longed to hear more. She pressed her advantage. "I only wish," she began tremblingly. "I mean, dear, 'f we feel like this, why can't we—?"

Lawrence bit his lip. "Ye know 'ow 'tis wi' me, Ame-

lia,'' he said unhappily. "I wants t' get on i' this world, an'
th' young Lord Marsden promises t' help me learn t' mekkanic motorcars. It's not right to—''

"But *I* kin 'elp ye git on!'' Amelia cried, pleading. "I
kin ask Lady Marsden fer a place, don't ye see? I'm sure
Miss Ardleigh'll give me a good char'cter. An' we kin be
married an' I'll work an' we'll save ever' penny t'ward yer
mekkanic shop.'' She twined her slender arms around Lawrence's neck. "Oh, Lawrence, let's!'' she whispered passionately into his chest.

Lawrence's arms came around her and he brought his lips
to hers with fervent longing. Amelia might have achieved
her fondest wish on the spot if it had not been for the interruption.

In the hall outside the open pantry door, there were voices.
Lawrence dropped his arms and stepped back, as Amelia
wiped her mouth and straightened her cap. Peering around
the door frame with some fear that they might have been
overheard, she recognized Meg, the housemaid whose bed
she was sharing for the weekend, and the footman, Marsh,
to whom Meg was promised. The pair had apparently been
quarreling with some heat, for they carried their controversy
down the hallway with them.

"Scupper that,'' Marsh was saying in a low, furious
voice. "Ye shudn't've bin talkin' t' 'im at all, I tell ye, Meg!
'E was tryin' t' weasel secrets out o' ye.''

"But 'e wa'n't no weasel,'' Meg said with tearful breath-
lessness, taking several small, hurrying steps to keep up with
the other's strides. "An' anyway, I was careful. I di'n't say
nothin' about th' letter, er you, er—''

" 'Ush!'' Marsh was fierce. "Nivver mention that name,
d'ye 'ear? 'F anybody finds out 'bout 'im, our goose is
cooked! Now, git on t' yer lunch, an' eat like nothin's th'
matter.''

"Will I see ye tonight?'' Meg whispered, imploring.

"Are ye packed t' go wi' me?''

Her voice grew desperate. "I *can't* go wi' ye, Marsh!
Dad's sick. 'E needs me. 'Ow kin I leave 'im?''

" 'Ow indeed?'' asked Marsh, and stalked off.

For a moment, Amelia heard nothing but Meg's weeping.

She moved to go to her, but Lawrence took her arm.

"No," he said in a hoarse whisper. "She'll think we've bin spyin' on 'em. Snoopin' on their secrets."

Spying? Amelia was suddenly seized with the hysterical desire to laugh.

18

Man's timid heart is bursting with the things he must not say,
For the Woman that God gave him isn't his to give away;
But when hunter meets with husbands, each confirms the
   other's tale—
The female of the species is more deadly than the male.

—RUDYARD KIPLING
"Female of the Species"

The criminal classes are so close to us that even the policeman
can see them.

—OSCAR WILDE
*A few maxims for the instruction
of the over-educated.*

U pon her return to Easton Lodge a little past one in the
afternoon, Daisy went directly to her suite of rooms,
where she stripped and bathed quickly, suffused with the
despairing sense that she could never scrub off the dirt and
odor of the workhouse—or, like Lady Macbeth, the blood
that she had all day felt on her hands. She changed into a
luncheon dress of stiff garnet silk and sat to have her hair
rearranged, all the while listening for the luncheon bell,
which would not ring until Bertie and Brooke came in from
that unspeakable business at the Folly.
  On any other day, Daisy would have been beside herself

at the thought of delaying luncheon for nearly an hour. That concern paled, however, in comparison with the other horror which every hour grew greater. She stared blindly at her reflection in the mirror as her maid added a few fresh garnet-colored chrysanthemums to her hair. But all she saw was a pair of apprehensive eyes, the pupils grown large and dark, and pale lips that would tremble in spite of all her efforts to still them. She had been so foolish, so desperately, dreadfully *reckless*, and now it would all come out. Not in public, of course, for Bertie would act swiftly to protect her, as he had done when Charlie Beresford's wife made such a howling to-do over her correspondence with Charlie. But Bertie could do nothing if it got into the newspapers. Oh, dear God, the newspapers, she thought, with a shudder. They would be on her like leeches!

The luncheon bell sounded and Daisy opened a jar of color and shakily rouged her pale lips and cheeks. Then she stood and picked up her handkerchief, resolute. She must compose her face in a careless smile, walk downstairs as if she had not a care in the world, and chat with her guests— all the while trying to think out what to do.

Should she go to Brooke, confess what she had done, and throw herself on his mercy? Perhaps he would consent to take her away somewhere until the commotion died down— to Mexico, perhaps. He was always running off to Mexico to see about his mines. Or perhaps she should appeal first to Bertie. She frowned, trying to think things through in something like a logical fashion. Perhaps she should take matters into her own hands, and do what had to be done without confiding in anyone else. When she was sure that at least some of the damage had been repaired, she could speak to Bertie, or to Brooke, or to both of them. Mexico was always an option, of course.

She went to the door, glancing over her shoulder, as she always did each time she left this room, for one last look in the cheval glass. The image there was perfection itself: that of a woman at the very peak and pinnacle of her beauty, a woman without peer in the entire realm. She smiled, and the woman in the glass returned the smile famous for its caressing sweetness and voluptuousness, the smile that enchanted so many men. In praise of that smile, Oscar Wilde had once written a graceful sentiment on the back of her theater program. The first line went something like, "Daisy's sweet smile commands my passion." Poor Oscar. Neither his art nor his place in society nor his powerful friends had protected him from outraged morality and the fury of the law. She shuddered. How pitiable a future in prison must be.

Once again the despair engulfed her, and she was reminded of Oscar's horrid little book, *The Picture of Dorian Gray*. How could she appear so lovely and serene and pure, while within be so torn and tormented by what she had done, what she wanted to do, what she had failed to do? She felt herself a woman of great dreams and high hopes, not for herself, but for her causes, for all the poor, helpless people she hoped to help. And yet she continually betrayed those dreams by her deadly carelessness. It was as if she had been given the heart to do wonderful things, but her judgment was unequal to her heart, and her fortune and social position had cursed her. And now this awful business with Reggie— Oh, God, was there no end to the troubles she created for herself?

A little later the twenty guests were seated at tables for four arranged in one corner of the drawing room, screened off from the rest of the room by a row of potted palms. The group was subdued. Of course, they already knew what had happened, but when Bertie stood beside his chair, tapped magisterially on his water goblet with a spoon, and announced that Reggie Wallace had been shot dead, little cries of pretended astonishment rippled around the room.

"Murdered? Reggie?" cried Felicia Metcalf, her gloved hand going to her mouth, her eyes wide.

"Wallace?" Malcolm Rochdale exclaimed. "Preposterous! The man can't be dead. He was hale and hearty at dinner last night. Quite his usual self."

"Don't be tiresome, Malcolm," Verena Rochdale retorted acidly. "Nobody remains hale and hearty with a bullet in his head." She reached into her reticule, took out a bottle of salts, and handed it to Felicia. "Didn't you hear what Bertie said? Reggie didn't just turn up his toes and die. Somebody *shot* him!"

A vision of Reggie lying dead flashed through Daisy's

mind. The thought made her sick and giddy, and she reached unsteadily for her champagne glass. But it wasn't his death she had to fear, she reminded herself. It was what he had left behind that concerned her.

Malvina Knightly, her bosom full of hothouse roses, let out a loud wail. "What an unspeakably horrible thing!" she cried. "One simply *cannot* trust the servants these days. They are a criminal class. We shall all be murdered in our beds!"

"Now, now, Malvina," her husband Milford murmured, and patted her hand, his diamond rings flashing. "You have nothing to fear, my dear. Whoever did in Reggie is certainly not interested in *you*."

"Milford is right, Malvina," said old Sir Thomas Cobb, with a look that was meant to express sadness. Sir Thomas was Reggie's father-in-law. But there had never been any love lost between them, Daisy knew, especially after Reggie's wife died. In fact, old Sir Thomas had accused him more than once of murdering her. "But one mustn't be too quick to accuse the servants," Sir Thomas added. "If you ask me, it's the Anarchists who did it. Talk of criminals! They have it in for anybody who has property."

Sir Friedrich Temple, who had sat silently until now, spoke up. "Whatever the motive for Reggie's murder, we can be sure that Bertie has the situation well in hand," he said. "I had the privilege of being with him when he was organizing things, and I can report that he has taken several important steps to insure our safety."

Bertie looked gratified. "Thank you for your confidence, Freddy. Of course, it goes without saying that we are all terribly saddened by—"

Bertie's voice became a buzzing in her ears, and Daisy reached for her champagne glass again. The bewilderment, the shock these people were expressing—it was all quite ridiculous, of course. Every person in the room had heard of Reggie's death within moments after his body was found. But pretense was so much a part of their lives that it came without effort, without thought, even. They pretended that their marriages were satisfactory, their money sufficient, their friends congenial, their love affairs stimulating. Lies, all of it! Beneath those shrouds of pretense, their marriages decayed, their friends deceived them, and their love affairs made a mockery of the word. Even now, as she looked around the room, she could not name three who were what they seemed. The glittering jewels were paste, the expressions of marital contentment were false, the fat purses supplied by the moneylenders—

Daisy caught Samuel Isaacson's sharply knowing glance and turned away, only to encounter the glance of her husband, like a slap on her cheek. Reading accusation in his look, and anger, she shivered. Her maid had reported that Brooke had stationed himself over the body until Bertie arrived. What had he seen? What did he know?

"—a terribly tragic event, of course," Bertie was saying in a melancholy tone, "and we shall all certainly miss dear old Reggie. He was a splendid sportsman and a loyal friend." He paused and cleared his throat. "But I daresay that you have already glimpsed the difficulty. There are many who, if they learned of Reggie's unexpected and calamitous departure—coming only a day after the death of the stableboy—would not hesitate to use it to drape our names in scandal. This matter must be kept among ourselves."

"Scandal!" Celia Rochdale exclaimed. She licked her pretty lips, her eyes bright. "Oh, dear!"

"It's all right, Celia," Eleanor Farley said comfortingly. "You're far too young to worry about scandal. No one could possibly believe that you had anything to do with—"

"One is *never* too young to concern oneself with scandal," Verena Rochdale said.

"But what about the police?" Lillian Forsythe asked. "When they come, the press won't be far behind."

The police! Daisy stiffened. That was something she had not considered. If the police discovered—

"Not to worry, Lillian." Brooke was speaking to Lillian, but Daisy felt that his remark was directed to her. "Bertie has taken complete charge of this affair. Matters are well in hand."

There was a buzz of excited response around the room. Taken charge of the affair? What could that mean? Daisy searched her husband's expressionless face, but found no clue.

Bertie nodded gravely. "Brooke is quite right, Lillian. You are not to worry about the police. Desirable as it might be to officially exonerate each of us from suspicion—"

"Exonerate *us*?" Felicia jerked upright in her chair, Verena's salts in her hand. "Why, that's ridiculous! Pardon me for contradicting you, sir, but no one can possibly suspect *us* of shooting Reggie."

"Or of bashing a stableboy on the head," Lillian put in, lifting her chin. "Utter nonsense!"

"Exactly," Bertie said soothingly. "The problem is, however, that although an official investigation would certainly allay any public suspicion that one of us in a moment of lunacy lost his or her head and committed murder, we cannot permit it. Ergo, no police."

There was a spontaneous burst of applause. Daisy suddenly felt limp, like a marionette whose strings had gone loose, and a feeling of gratitude swept through her. Dear Bertie! He already knew, without her appealing to him, how much she needed his protection!

"But at the same time," Bertie was continuing, "we cannot permit Reggie's murder to go unresolved. We must find the guilty party. To accomplish that, I have personally commissioned an investigation, in which I intend to play a substantial role."

Daisy heard Knightly's sudden chuckle. "Do you, Bertie? By Jove, what a capital idea! A murder investigation—what fun! Only *you* would have thought of it." He pursed his lips. "I wonder—what would you think of a small wager on the outcome?"

"A wager?" Felicia cried, half-hysterically. "You can speak of betting, when dear Reggie lies dead? What kind of man are you, Milford Knightly? Have you no *soul*?"

"I should think it in doubtful taste, myself," Malvina Knightly agreed, with a sliding glance at her husband.

"Oh, don't be such a prude, Malvina," Knightly returned. "There's no reason why we can't have a bit of fun out of this dreadful affair. Why, Reggie himself would be the first to lay odds. He wouldn't want us sitting around, drawing long faces and moaning about how sad we are.''

Thomas Cobb was scowling. ''I don't understand the bit about commissioning an investigation. What is all that about, Bertie?''

''It is about murder, Thomas,'' the Prince said sagely. ''And while I agree with Milford that we might indeed have a bit of seemly sport, our inquiry will be conducted on the most professional basis. Of that I assure you.''

''Professional basis?'' Daisy asked. Now that she was assured that the police would not be involved, she felt much better. ''But if not by the authorities, then by whom, Bertie?''

''By two of our own, my dear Daisy,'' the Prince said. ''By Charles Sheridan, with whom many of you are acquainted, and his associate, Miss Kate Ardleigh.''

There was a profound silence. ''Miss . . . Ardleigh?'' Lillian asked, her voice rising incredulously. ''You must be joking, sir!''

''Not at all,'' Bertie said, smiling and rubbing his hands. ''Charles Sheridan, for those of you who don't know, is a world-class scientist, whose credentials in the modern investigation of crime have already become well established. He assures me that Miss Ardleigh—Kate—is an asset to his work, and that the two have worked together successfully in the past. And I, of course, shall personally supervise the inquiry, and monitor its every phase.''

''Bravo, Bertie!'' said Milford Knightly. His wife glared at him.

The Prince ignored the remark. ''One of my first tasks has been to order an autopsy of our deceased comrade, who now resides in the game larder.''

''The game larder?'' Felicia Metcalf reached for the smelling salts again.

''I have also dispatched Kirk-Smythe to guard Reggie's room.'' His Highness paused and looked about him. ''Now, do you have any questions?''

''Guard Reggie's room?'' Daisy repeated faintly. But that would make it difficult to—

''Righto,'' Bertie said. ''Might be valuable evidence there, you know.''

Sir Thomas did not appear to be pleased. "What's all this about the modern investigation of crime?" he asked petulantly. "What the deuce is modern in police work?"

Bertie waved his hand carelessly. "Oh, looking for things with magnifying glasses and microscopes. Taking pictures of them with cameras. Finding marks on bullets and such like. Did you know that an expert can look at a bullet and recognize the gun from which it was fired?"

Lillian Forsythe gave a little gasp of surprise, and Malcolm Rochdale frowned. "Marks on bullets?" he asked. "Sounds like jiggery-pokery to me."

"Not at all, Malcolm," the Prince said. "Not at all. I myself have not yet mastered these forensic techniques, of course, but I assure you that Charles Sheridan has. That is precisely why I have asked him to undertake this criminal investigation."

"I still don't understand what a microscope has to do with a man who took a bullet through the head," Sir Thomas said, sounding confused.

"Charles will explain it all to us," Bertie said. "He's out and about just now, interrogating a possible witness to the boy's death. Later, of course, he will want to question the gentlemen."

"Question the . . . gentlemen?" Sir Thomas asked, frowning. "You mean, *us*?"

"Quite so," Bertie said. "How else is he to learn where we were last night."

"Exactly, Thomas," said Lillian Forsythe. "He must confirm that you could not have been at Daisy's Folly, lying in wait for Reggie."

"Charles is not with us," the Prince went on, "but Miss Ardleigh is here." He smiled warmly. "Stand up, my dear. Ladies and gentlemen, may I present to you Miss Kate Ardleigh, our female investigator. After luncheon, she will hold court in the morning room, where she will ask each of the ladies to confirm her whereabouts last night."

"*Our* whereabouts?" Lillian asked in a choked voice.

"Exactly, Lillian," Sir Thomas mocked. "She must confirm that you could not have been at Daisy's Folly, lying in wait for Reggie. The female of the species, you know."

"But a *servant* did it," Felicia insisted wildly. "Why must we submit ourselves to . . . to . . ." She choked.

"Splendid question, Felicia!" Bertie said approvingly. "Why must we submit? The answer is quite simple. Without our collective effort it will be impossible to identify *which* of the servants is responsible." He glanced around the room. "And until this is done, we cannot enjoy our weekend with any easiness or pleasure—as Reggie would undoubtedly have us do. So I encourage you to answer forthrightly any and all questions Kate and Charles may put to you." He rubbed his hands together, beaming. "Now, if there are no more questions, shall we carry on with luncheon? I understand that we are about to be served a most delectable ptarmigan pie."

With an anticipatory smile, Bertie sat down.

As Kate suffered through the stiff, uncomfortable meal and the following futile interrogation of the lady guests, she thought time and again of the Prince's luncheon performance—a strange and wonderful exhibition of . . .

Of what? The more Kate thought about what had happened, the more confident she was of what she had witnessed—and the less certain she was of the motives that lay behind it.

The Prince's performance had been pure comic opera, there was no question about that. With a few nonchalant words, a light chuckle here, a dismissive gesture there, he had reduced Reginald Wallace's death to something that Gilbert and Sullivan might have contrived, and trivialized the investigation by suggesting that the assembled company had nothing to fear from it. By the time he had finished, every guest must have believed that His Highness's primary intention was to dispose of the unpleasant matter as swiftly and efficiently as they were to put away the ptarmigan pie (a Royal favorite which everyone else thoroughly detested), by revealing that one of the servants was the guilty party.

Kate went to the door and told the footman waiting outside to assemble the upstairs maids so that she could interview them. Then she went to stand by the window, looking out on the garden, still thinking about the Prince's motive.

Was he simply getting past a sticky place by making light of it? That was possible, of course, for his tact and *savoir faire* were often praised, and he was admired for his social diplomacy.

But she could not overlook the possibility that the Prince might have intended to disarm the guilty person. A murderer who felt overconfident might be more likely to commit a revealing mistake. Or the Prince might know who had committed the murder and was intent on protecting him—or her. Kate had observed Daisy's shaking hands and distraught manner and had seen the look the Countess had given the Prince when he announced that there would be no police investigation. Her face had been swept by an expression of gratitude and relief so intense, so overpowering that Kate had felt its force halfway across the room.

And if Kate had seen or heard anything of importance in the hours since she had accepted assignment to this investigation, she reflected as she turned to greet the first of the servants, it was that look.

19

Charles found the Prince at a desk in the library, working on papers he had taken from a leather portfolio. He looked up from his writing and said, "I'll be with you in a moment, Charles."

As he was waiting, Charles looked around. The library was one of Easton's most beautiful rooms, high-ceilinged and elegant, with Persian carpets on the floors and agreeably placed windows and walnut shelves along the walls, under an ornately carved plaster frieze. The shelves were filled with several thousand books bound in scarlet morocco to match the scarlet draperies. Some several hundred, Charles knew, were volumes of theology, obtained by one of Daisy's pious ancestors in exchange for several manors on the estate. Above the shelves hung gilt-framed oils of Maynard ancestors and prints of various sporting and military scenes. Reading tables, map cases, leather chairs, and commodious sofas were arranged throughout the large, light room, and on the tables were arranged decorative objects: celadon bowls, Faberge cigarette-boxes, jade carvings from the Orient. It was a place where guests might gather to read, write, or enjoy a quiet game of cribbage or bridge.

The Prince threw down his pen and stepped around the desk. "Ah, Charles. I am sorry you had to miss luncheon.

We not only had an excellent ptarmigan pie, but a most delicious raspberry fool. Have you made any progress?''

"Perhaps," Charles said cautiously.

"Well, then," the Prince said, "let me hear about it." He seated himself on a nearby sofa and motioned Charles to the chair opposite. "Tell me what you have found," he said, taking out a cigar.

Charles sat down. "It is beginning to seem that there *is* a connection between Wallace's murder and the death of Your Highness's groom. Wallace was seen leaving the stable at approximately the same time as the boy died.''

The Prince lighted his cigar. "Your informant is reliable?"

"I believe so. He is deaf, and communicating with him is difficult. But he seems to have keen powers of observation, and I can think of no good reason why he should fabricate a false story.''

"So Wallace was shot because someone—a servant, no doubt—thought he killed poor Harry, eh?" The Prince drew deeply on his cigar, blowing out a cloud of pungent blue smoke. "A cogent theory, I must say. Reggie was murdered for the sake of revenge.''

"It's one theory," Charles said, wary. "I'm not sure I subscribe to it, however." In fact, revenge was such a weak motive that he couldn't imagine why the Prince would give any credence to it. The boy was a stranger at Easton, and new to the Prince's retinue. What servant would care enough to risk his own life for the sake of revenge?

"Of course," the Prince said thoughtfully, "the theory does not require us to assume that Reggie actually murdered the lad. He wasn't the sort to cosh a stableboy, particularly *my* stableboy, for no reason. All we have to assume is that someone *thought* he killed the youngster. This person—distraught with grief, no doubt, and tormented by the thought of the poor boy's sorrowing mother—acquired a gun, stalked his target until he was alone in a deserted place, and—" The Prince raised his plump hand, pointed his cigar at Charles as if it were a gun, and said gravely, "Blam."

Charles cleared his throat. "I fear," he said, "that there is other evidence to be considered." He reached into his pocket and took out the handkerchief that Kate had pointed out to him at the scene of the murder. He handed it to the Prince.

"What's this? A woman's handkerchief?" The Prince examined the dainty, lace-edged thing. "Hold on," he said, half to himself. "Here are some initials, worked into a design in the corner. Looks like—" He stopped.

"It looks like an *F* and a *W* intertwined," Charles said softly. "Frances Warwick. It's Daisy's handkerchief."

The Prince handed the handkerchief to Charles and turned to tap the ash from his cigar, concealing his face. "Where did you get it?"

"In a flower bed, a dozen paces from Wallace's body."

"It proves nothing," the Prince said brusquely. He heaved himself off the sofa. "Daisy lives here, you know. And women lose their handkerchiefs in the most damned awkward places." His chuckle was forced. "I've had to come up with a few quick explanations in my time, believe me, Sheridan. Alexandra may be hard of hearing, but there's nothing wrong with her eyes. She can spot an unfamiliar handkerchief at thirty paces—even under the bed."

Charles stood also. He took out the note and extended it, with genuine regret, to the Prince. "Before you conclude that the handkerchief has nothing to do with the crime, I think you must read this, sir."

The Prince's eyes flickered. "No," he said, taking several large puffs on his cigar.

Charles sighed, thinking that denial served no good purpose. "Then I shall have to read it aloud."

"Oh, very well, then," the Prince said heavily.

Charles unfolded the note. " 'Meet me at the Folly,' " he read aloud, " 'after everyone has gone to bed.' It is written on Daisy's stationery," he added. "I believe it to be her hand."

The Prince turned toward the window. He was silent for a moment. "Where was it found?" he asked gruffly. "By whom?"

"On Wallace's person. Miss Ardleigh saw it very soon after the body was discovered. She confiscated it so that no one would be tempted to remove it."

The Prince turned, his shoulders hunched. "No one else has read it but the two of you, and myself?"

"To my knowledge, only you and I, sir. Miss Ardleigh gave it to me unread."

"Good girl." A smile ghosted across the Prince's fleshy mouth and then vanished. He drew himself up, stern. "You can't think that Daisy killed the poor wretch."

"I'm afraid it is a possibility we must consider, sir. After all, whatever it was that Wallace wanted to talk with you about last night seemed to involve Daisy."

The Prince shook his head in manifest disbelief. "But that's preposterous, man! What motive could she have?"

"Blackmail, perhaps. She and Wallace—"

The Prince snorted scornfully. "Their affair was common knowledge. One can't be blackmailed over something that everyone knows, for pity's sake. In any event, it was over long ago." His mouth tightened, and Charles wondered how sure he was of his assertion. Albert Edward might be heir to the throne, but that did not mean that he was confident in his prowess as a man.

The silence stretched on for a moment. "Perhaps she was in debt to him," Charles said finally. "I have heard it frequently reported—have read it in the newspapers, as a matter of fact—that the Warwicks are increasingly short of funds. It is even said that they plan to sell part of this estate."

"She may be in debt, but not to Wallace." The Prince gestured sharply. "If you insist on barking up that tree, go talk to Isaacson."

"Ah," Charles said. "You're suggesting that Isaacson loaned—"

"I'm not suggesting anything, damn it," the Prince said testily. "Just talk to him, that's all. Find out what he has to say." He looked away. "Anyway, a person of pedigree doesn't kill for money."

"But such a person might kill for reputation," Charles persisted, "and that is the word Wallace used in my hearing last night. For many, a reputation is even more important than the family estate."

"Rubbish." The Prince straightened his shoulders, seeming to arrive at some sort of determination. "I must tell you that the lady in question might have made an appointment with Wallace, but she did not keep it.''

''How can you be sure?''

''Dash it all, man,'' the Prince burst out angrily, ''do I have to say it outright? Daisy couldn't have killed Reggie. I was with her the entire night, from shortly after we retired until almost breakfast time. She did not leave the room, even for an instant.''

Charles regarded him thoughtfully. If the Prince could un-equivocally confirm Daisy's whereabouts, why had he not said so at once? ''The whole night?'' he asked gently. ''You are able to swear to that, sir, under oath?''

The Prince suddenly leaned forward, balancing on the balls of his feet, thrusting his head forward with an angry bullishness. ''You dare to contradict me?'' he asked in a steely voice.

Charles stood his ground. ''It is a question I am compelled by your own commission to ask.'' The Prince's belligerent evasion had already given him his answer. But that aside, it was not likely that the matter would go as far as a courtroom. The Royal alibi—impeachable or not—would suit the pur-poses of the law even if it failed to answer to the demands of truth.

The Prince spoke with an elaborate patience. ''If you are still too dense to comprehend the obvious, Sheridan, let me analyze this case for you. Wallace killed the stableboy, for some reason unknown to us, then realized he had been seen and identified. He shot himself to avoid being accused.'' He thrust his cigar into Charles's face. ''Daisy may have planned to meet him—in fact, he might even have killed himself there and at that time because he believed she would shortly dis-cover his body. But she did not go to the Folly because she was with me, and that's all there is to it. *Do you under-stand?*'' The last three words were punctuated with jabs of the princely cigar.

''I must respectfully disagree,'' Charles said, refusing to be intimidated. ''I expect the autopsy to reveal that Wallace could not have committed suicide. The surgeon arrived a short time ago and is at work now.'' He paused. ''And there is the handkerchief and the note, both of which point directly to Daisy. It might be argued that she crept out of the room while you slept and went to meet Wallace—and to murder him.''

The Prince stood unsmiling, saying nothing. The pulse at his temple had begun to beat visibly and his thick lips had tightened. When he spoke at last, his voice was heavy. ''Are there no other possibilities?''

''Yes,'' Charles said, feeling a wave of compassion for the man. There was no mistaking the depth of his feeling. ''There is a quite obvious one, actually.''

''What is it, man? Stop beating about the bush!''

Charles measured his words, conscious of all they implied. ''Someone may have attempted to make it appear that Daisy is guilty.''

The great eyes were starting out of the head and the pulsing vein pounded as if it would burst. ''But why, man, *why*? What under the sun could be the reason?''

''You have no idea?''

''Of course not,'' the Prince exclaimed. ''Why should I?''

''Because, sir,'' Charles said, ''*you* may be the reason.''

There was a lengthy silence. When the Prince spoke at last, it was only to say, ''Ah,'' in a long, sad syllable. After a moment, he added, ''You will concentrate on that angle, I assume.'' He closed the subject with a slight, dismissive movement of his plump hand. ''Where are you off to now?''

''We have only an hour before tea. I need to speak to the surgeon and see whether he has drawn any conclusions. I should also have a look at Wallace's room. And I must speak with Miss Ardleigh, to learn what she has discovered from her interviews.''

''Of course. Please extend my compliments to your charming associate, whose competence and discretion I am only beginning to appreciate.'' The Prince gave Charles a slantwise look. ''Do I perceive a connection between the two of you that extends beyond the professional?''

''You do, sir,'' Charles said. He smiled for the first time since he had come into the room. ''Kate has agreed to become my wife.''

The Prince hooked his fingers in his waistcoat pockets and heaved an exaggerated sigh. ''So another American woman is about to invade one of our staid old families, eh? You can't be content with one of our English girls?''

''I have always believed that if I could make a marriage with a kindred spirit, her nationality would be irrelevant.''

The Prince made an expansive gesture. ''Well, I must say I like the originality of these American women. They bring a little fresh air into society. They are livelier and less hampered by etiquette, are they not? And I do believe that they are not as squeamish as their English sisters, and better able to take care of themselves.''

''Kate is decidedly unsqueamish,'' Charles said, ''and most certainly able to take care of herself. In fact, she would protest the very idea of my taking care of her.''

''What a prize,'' said the Prince admiringly. ''For heaven's sake, old chap, marry the lady forthwith. However, by way of caution I should probably report a remark of Lady Neville's on the occasion of Jenny Jerome's marriage to Randy Churchill.''

''Oh?''

''Yes.'' The Prince chuckled. '' 'I like the Americans very well,' Lady Neville said, 'but there are two things I wish they would keep to themselves. Their girls and their tinned lobster.' '' He extended his hand. ''I do congratulate you, Charles. She is a lovely woman.''

''Thank you, sir,'' Charles said.

''Now, then,'' the Prince said, returning to the desk. ''There are two more bits of business. At luncheon, I suggested to the company that you might tell them something about modern methods of crime detection. Several seemed quite interested in the topic. What would you say to giving us a short lecture after dinner this evening, before the fireworks are set off?''

Charles nodded reluctantly. He had no difficulty speaking to the subject, but he should have to be careful that what he said did not alert someone in the audience as to his methods and intentions. ''And the second bit of business?''

''When you go to Wallace's room, send Kirk-Smythe down here—as soon as you're done with him, that is.'' The Prince picked up a sheaf of papers. ''There are several telegrams to be sent off. I shall leave them here for him. And oh, yes, would you mention to him that I am about to exhaust my supply of cigars?''

20

It has long been an axiom of mine that the little things are infinitely the most important.

—SIR ARTHUR CONAN DOYLE
"A Case of Identity"

I t was an hour before tea when Kate dismissed the last of the upstairs maids, shuffled her notes, and sat back in her chair in the morning room, filled with weary frustration. The interviews had to be done, of course; it was necessary to question anyone who might have information about the movements of the guests the night before. And she *had* looked forward to it. In fact, when Charles had told her that she was to interrogate the women, Beryl Bardwell had given a joyful *hurrah*—internally, of course. She would be doing real detective work at last, work that would provide her a glimpse into authentic investigative procedures and would serve as a rich mine of valuable information for her future fictions. More than that, she would be able to see into the criminal mind, even into (she thought with a tremble of excited and half-fearful anticipation) the very heart of darkness.

But as far as Kate could discern, this afternoon's interrogations had yielded only little things—odds and ends of information of trivial significance. Instead of looking into the heart of genuine evil, she had been given glimpses into the gray soul of boredom and dispirited ennui, which fostered petty misconduct, moral dissipation, and promiscuous behaviors not criminal in themselves and prosecutable chiefly in the divorce courts. However, Kate reminded herself, the fear of public exposure was real and powerful enough to motivate all sorts of criminal actions. It was entirely possible that Reginald Wallace had been killed because he knew some secret thing—a small, secret thing, perhaps, but potentially embarrassing to someone who could not afford to be embarrassed. What had he known? Who had a secret to hide?

As it turned out, however, all of the women seemed to have secrets to hide, and it proved almost impossible to obtain an honest answer to the question, "What did you do after everyone else retired?" Kate had not imagined that the female guests would be so expert in dissembling, or that answers would have to be got by taking so roundabout a path, challenging the respondent, if necessary, to the point of tears or near hysteria.

By this circuitous and painful means, she learned that Celia Rochdale, against the express prohibition of her mother, had met Andrew Kirk-Smythe for a late-night tryst at the Folly. Collapsing in sobs, the frightened girl swore that the lovers had neither seen nor heard anything suspicious during the two hours they had spent there. She could not swear, however, that they had not been seen, either at the Folly or coming or going. Indeed, upon her return to her room an hour or so after midnight, Celia herself had caught sight of Lady Metcalf, wearing her robe and clutching a decanter of wine, groping her way down the hall from the direction of the west wing, where the men's sleeping rooms were located.

"I'm sure she didn't see me, though," she added tearfully. "If she had, she would have told Mama this morning. As you must not," she implored Kate once again. "Mama would immediately marry me to that wretched Baron Smartly, and I have given my heart to Andrew!"

Kate promised and made a note to suggest to Charles that Kirk-Smythe be interrogated. It was possible that Wallace had gotten onto the lovers and threatened to reveal their liaison to Lady Rochdale, who was obviously bent on keeping her daughter virginal until the day of her marriage to a lord—a marriage that would amplify the family fortune. Confronted by a blackmailer, Kirk-Smythe might have chosen to commit murder, rather than risk his sweetheart's reputation.

Felicia Metcalf was more resistant to Kate's questions, but after offering several different renditions of her narrative, she broke into a fit of noisy weeping and produced what she swore was the final, truthful version. The night before, after retiring, she had arrayed herself in a seductive negligee and sat by the fire, emptying a decanter of Madeira while she waited in vain for Reginald Wallace. After several hours, she finally fell into her bed alone, having concluded that her faithless friend had retired with someone else.

"I felt it was Lillian Forsythe," she said bleakly. "Some people simply cannot resist an opportunity for deceit."

To judge from the heavy bags under her eyes, Lady Felicia was still suffering from her physical and emotional excesses. She was also suffering, or so she claimed, from a desperate remorse. For instead of having spent the night in the arms of Lillian Forsythe, Wallace had been lying murdered on the cold ground in the garden of Daisy's Folly.

"And I doubted his faithfulness!" Lady Felicia moaned, rolling her eyes. "Oh, if only I had gone in search of him, or raised an alarm. I might have saved him!"—a speculation which inspired another round of fresh weeping.

But Lady Felicia's theatrical grief had something of the ersatz about it. More importantly, Kate was in possession of a key contradictory fact: that Celia Rochdale had seen Lady Metcalf about one a.m. returning from the west wing. Confronted with this intelligence, the lady produced yet another version of her narrative. Around three quarters past twelve, having consumed her decanter of wine, she had taken her candle and made her way to Wallace's room. The empty room confirmed her suspicion that her lover was in Lillian Forsythe's bed. She snatched up his decanter and carried it back to her room, where she attempted to quench the fires of her jealousy with yet more Madeira. She had drunk herself into a stupor about three a.m.

Whether this new version was the truth or only another embroidery, Kate could not be sure. Beryl Bardwell, however, proposed an alternative, and quite plausible, theory. When Wallace did not appear, Lady Felicia might have gone to the Folly, where (she supposed) he was dallying with Lady Lillian. Encountering him on the path, she charged him with betraying her, took out a gun, and shot him dead. Kate made a note to discuss the matter with Charles.

As for Lady Lillian herself, she had no tears to shed over Reginald Wallace. "Felicia has it all wrong, as usual," she said coolly. Then she added, with some smugness, "I spent the night with Friedrich Temple—and if you don't believe me, you can ask him."

According to Lady Lillian, Temple had suggested the dalliance, their first, during the last waltz of the evening, just before the company had assembled to pick up their candlesticks and troop off to bed. Lady Lillian was nothing loath, albeit rather taken aback by such a precipitous proposal from a man who had hitherto been a bit above such friskiness. The liaison had apparently been to the liking of both, for Temple remained with her until her maid appeared to open the curtains and bring in the tea tray.

"I trust, Miss Ardleigh," Lady Lillian added in a chilly tone, "that my confidences will go no further than this room. I have told you these things only because His Highness directed us to be forthright."

Kate suspected that Lady Lillian was less interested in honesty than in flaunting the fact that she had not gone to bed alone—especially after Sir Charles had rejected her. But her liaison with Sir Friedrich came as something of a surprise to Kate, who had herself received his attentions. In lieu of questioning Sir Friedrich, she queried Lady Lillian's maid Adelma. The girl substantiated her mistress's story, reporting that yes, a tall gentleman with sandy hair and beard had been in madame's room as she arrived with the tea tray. She had been a bit startled by his presence, she confessed, since madame's lovers were usually sent packing before the maids were about.

The other interviews were no less interesting. Malvina Knightly testified to having spent the night in the company of her husband Milford, a fact borne out by her lady's maid, who had seen the couple to bed with cups of hot chocolate and awakened them with a tray of tea and toast around eight. In response to Kate's question about whether the Knightlys shared the same bedroom at home, the maid reported tartly that they did not. Kate smiled, speculating that a weekend in the country might have awakened the couple's romantic ardor.

Eleanor Farley reported that she had gone to sleep immediately upon retiring and slept the night through, with the exception of two inconvenient visits to the water closet at the end of the hall, near her room. On the first of those visits, at about twelve-thirty, she recalled a brief and somewhat embarrassing encounter with Samuel Isaacson, wearing a brown silk dressing gown and slippers and tapping at the door of Verena Rochdale's room.

"To tell the truth," Eleanor giggled, "I couldn't decide which of them would have the worst of it. Samuel Isaacson is so *old*, and Verena Rochdale is such a prude."

Lady Rochdale, for her part, asserted in a tone of high dudgeon that she had slept entirely and indisputably alone, her husband having occupied another room some distance down the hall, and that if Mr. Isaacson had attempted to enter her room (mistaking it for his own, no doubt) she knew nothing of it. But there was an apprehension in Lady Rochdale's tone that made Kate wonder if the woman was telling the truth. The upstairs maids were more forthcoming in their replies to Kate's questions, but they had been asleep in the servants' wing of the house, quite distant from the guests' bedrooms, and could only confirm the hours at which their mistresses retired and rose.

Finally, the only lady remaining to be questioned was the Countess herself. Kate was about to go in search of Charles to ask if she should undertake the interview when there was a tap on the door and he came in. Her heart lifted with pleasure and she went to him eagerly, hands out, but stopped when she saw that he was accompanied. The man with him was tall and slightly stooped, in his late thirties, clean-shaven except for brown muttonchop whiskers, and pale, as if he spent most of his time indoors. He walked with a noticeable limp, Kate saw, a kind of quick, crabwise scuttle, his right leg being shorter than the left. His name was John Miles, and he and Charles were obviously well acquainted. He was the surgeon from Chelmsford who had been summoned to perform the autopsy.

Kate extended her hand when Charles introduced them.

"I am glad to meet you, Doctor Miles," she said. "I hope the autopsy has yielded some useful information."

Miles's eyes widened and he turned to Charles with undisguised disbelief. "Oh, come now, Charlie. You don't mean to say that this *woman* is your associate?"

"And soon to be my wife," Charles said, and put his arm around Kate's shoulders. "You'll find her, as I have, a remarkable woman, with uncommon interests."

"Well, I'll be damned," the doctor muttered in an astonished voice, fixing Kate with a penetrating stare. She was not sure whether she should feel affronted or complimented.

"You certainly will be," Charles said, "if you go about regularly insulting your friends' wives-to-be." He smiled at Kate. "Pay no attention to this rogue, Kate. He knows so few singular women that he does not know how to respond when he meets one. Were your interviews productive?"

"I have certainly heard enough lies," Kate said, rueful. "The ladies seemed remarkably unwilling to part with their secrets, and the servants appear to have none." She gave the surgeon an inquiring look. "Was anything learned from the autopsy?"

"John is about to tell us," Charles said. He pulled out a chair at the table and Kate took it. Charles took another, and motioned to the surgeon. "Sit down, John, and give us the gory details."

"I doubt Miss Ardleigh will want to hear," Dr. Miles said, seating himself.

"You have nothing to fear in that regard," Charles said. "Kate is no doubt curious." He took her hand. "Say on, John."

The surgeon gave Kate a doubtful look, but obeyed. "Very well, then. From the damage to the cranial region—specifically, the two frontal bones and the frontal lobe of the brain—I have concluded that the path of the bullet was almost perfectly horizontal."

Kate was listening attentively. "Then he *was* sitting down when the bullet struck him," she said thoughtfully, "and the assailant was standing."

The surgeon gave her a searching look. "I believe you are correct, Miss—"

"Kate, please."

"Kate, then." He shifted in his chair. "You are correct. The victim was six feet two inches tall. Had he been standing, and his assailant standing, the missile would most likely have taken an upward trajectory."

"If he were seated, however," Charles said, "he should have pitched forward and fallen facedown. Yet he was found faceup. His killer must have turned him over. I wonder why."

"Perhaps to be certain that he was dead," the surgeon remarked.

"Or to be certain that the note in his pocket should be noticed immediately," Kate said. "It was loosely folded and inserted into the pocket with a good bit of paper protruding—hardly the way a gentleman would have safeguarded an appointment for an assignation."

Charles nodded, and she knew he had made note of her point. "I take it that we can discount the probability of suicide," he said to the surgeon.

"It would have been most awkward for the victim to have held the weapon horizontally in front of his forehead, with the barrel perfectly level," Miles replied. "In my experience, suicides shoot themselves in the temple or behind the ear, with the muzzle held against the head."

"When I examined the body," Charles said, "I noticed powder burns to the forehead, suggesting that the weapon was discharged at a distance of six inches or less, but not in contact with the skin."

"Agreed again."

"You recovered the projectile?"

The doctor produced a small glass vial. Charles uncorked it and shook out a lead pellet about the shape and size of his small fingernail. He examined it, then gave it to Kate. It was heavier than she had expected, with a slightly roughened, silvery-gray surface. The base was concave and the nose, originally round, was now somewhat flattened. She shivered, thinking that the thing had just been plucked out of Wallace's brain, and placed it back into Charles's extended hand.

"Soft lead," Charles said thoughtfully, turning it over in his fingers. "Perhaps a hundred grains, probably thirty-two caliber. Fired from a derringer or a small revolver.'' He turned to the surgeon as if for confirmation.

"You're the expert, Charlie,'' the doctor said with a shrug. "But yes, I would agree. A derringer or revolver.''

"Why did it not . . . go all the way through?'' Kate asked.

"Because the handgun in question fires a low-weight, low-velocity bullet,'' Charles replied. "It lacked sufficient momentum to penetrate the occipital bone.'' He reached into an inner pocket of his jacket and took out a small leather kit. From it he extracted a short knurled rod with a needle fixed to one end and began to inscribe a *W* upon the base of the bullet.

"What the devil are you doing?'' Miles demanded.

"I am marking the fatal missile with the victim's initial so as to prevent its being confused with any other.''

"But we have no other,'' Kate said.

"Not yet.'' Charles reached into another pocket and took out a small hand lens. "If, however, we come upon a weapon similar to the one that discharged this bullet, we will fire it and compare the test bullet against this one. The more significant similarities we find, the more confident we can be that we have discovered the murder weapon.''

John Miles brightened. "Of course!'' he exclaimed. "As Professor Lacassagne did a few years ago in Lyons. Now, *that* was a brilliant piece of forensic detecting!''

"Almost,'' Charles replied. "Good enough to convince the court, at any rate. I fear, however, that the fact that a weapon has fired the fatal bullet does not, in and of itself, tell us who fired it.'' He turned the bullet under the lens. "Six grooves,'' he murmured, "with a right-hand twist.'' He pointed with the needle. "And this groove is noticeably deeper than the others.''

"If I remember what you said this morning,'' Kate said, "that means that every other bullet fired from the murder weapon will have six grooves with a right-hand twist, one of which is deeper than the others. And oh, yes, it will be thirty-two caliber.''

"Precisely,'' Charles said, giving Kate the smile of a teacher who has just heard the recitation of a star pupil. "I would wager that these characteristics differentiate the weapon that fired this bullet from ninety-five to ninety-nine percent of similar weapons.''

Kate shook her head wonderingly. ''It's the tiniest details that make the difference, isn't it?''

The surgeon whistled. ''Well, I can see that criminals won't have much of a chance from now on. With information like this, the police will—''

Charles laughed curtly. ''The police are ill-equipped and ill-trained to gather information like this. Judges and juries don't know what to do with it, either. Of course, the impact of such testimony can loosen a guilty tongue, and the criminal may confess if he is confronted with facts which he knows to be true. But it will be a great many years before criminals are regularly convicted on the basis of scientific proof of guilt.''

''I daresay you're right, Charlie,'' the surgeon said. ''The juries I have encountered have very little regard for scientific testimony.''

Kate laughed. ''If Conan Doyle only knew about these new techniques, Sherlock Holmes might not have to go through such protracted contortions of logic.''

Charles replaced the bullet in the vial and pocketed it. ''Perhaps Beryl Bardwell should educate him.''

''Beryl Bardwell?'' Miles asked, looking mystified.

''A mutual friend with an informed interest in such matters,'' Charles said, and Kate smiled.

21

That Edward [the Prince of Wales] loved Frances [Daisy] is beyond question. The open recklessness with which he championed her cause was enough to prove the intensity of his infatuation. . . . But his letters show more than infatuation: they show the depths of a growing devotion.

—THEO LANG
The Darling Daisy Affair

Chatsworth

My Darling Daisy,

We have an enormous but pleasant party here, though everything reminds me so much of the happy days we spent here two years ago! . . .

We have had some very pleasant shooting today, many rabbits and some high pheasants.

We go to Town on Saturday till Monday, and on to Sandringham on 13th.

God bless my own adored little Daisy wife!

For ever yours,
Your only love,
Bertie

Charles saw Miles to the hallway, then returned to stand beside Kate's chair. He smiled down at her and touched the thick russet hair piled on her head, untidy now, after an afternoon's work. Ink smudged her cheek and there was a matching stain on her index finger, testimony to the penned notes in front of her.

Charles's glance lingered. He thought that she made an earnest, pretty detective and would make an even lovelier wife. He followed with his eye the curve of her shoulders, the rounded swell of her breasts under the stuff of her dress, the soft waist he felt quite sure was uncorseted. Then, guiltily aware that he was trespassing in dangerous territory and uncomfortably warm with the desire that suddenly coursed through him, he pulled his attention back to the matter at hand. He sat down on the other side of the table, carefully keeping his eyes on her face.

"May I hear the results of your inquiry?" he asked.

"It will be a short recital," Kate said, and reported what she had learned, adding her surmises at the end. "Of the women," she concluded, "only Malvina Knightly and Lillian Forsythe can provide corroborated accounts of their whereabouts for the entire night. I am assuming that their statements will be borne out by their companions, as they are by the maids. The other women have no alibis. They all had the opportunity to kill Wallace, but of them, only Felicia Metcalf seems to have had a motive. Jealousy is a powerful passion. It could well have driven her to murder. And she *did* lie about going to Wallace's room."

Teasingly, he took her hand. "You speak with authority. Is jealousy a passion you have experienced?"

She shook her head. "No, Charles. Believe me, please. I have never loved before I loved you." Her face was grave, her hazel eyes truthful, and he flushed, half-ashamed of his banter and marveling once again at her honesty and directness. Most women, schooled in the duplicitous artifice that seemed native to the sex, would have allowed themselves to be reluctantly coaxed to a coy admission of former lovers.

Then her lips curled in a smile, humorously teasing in its turn. "Of course," she added, "jealousy is Beryl Bardwell's stock in trade. To take away jealousy as a motive for her various murders would be like stealing crimson from an artist's palette.''

He laughed too, delightedly. ''Very well, then. Let us assume, on the irrefutable authority of Beryl Bardwell, that Lady Metcalf's jealousy could have driven her to shoot Wallace.''

Kate reclaimed her hand, becoming serious. ''Actually, Charles, it would not have been easy for *any* lady to shoot the man, at least as we have reconstructed the crime.''

''Indeed?'' He was surprised. ''You don't think a woman emotionally capable of such a criminal act?''

''Of course I do,'' Kate said firmly. ''The female of the species can be even more deadly than the male, given sufficient provocation. But we have established, have we not, that Wallace was seated when he was shot? I observed at luncheon yesterday that whatever else he was, the man was unquestionably a gentleman. I doubt that he would have remained sitting in the presence of a lady. Of *any* lady,'' she repeated, ''especially one that he had disappointed. A consciousness of guilt would have brought him to his feet immediately.''

Charles stared at her, dumbfounded. ''Of course!'' he exclaimed, wondering why he had not thought of this small but significant bit of information. ''I myself know how impossible it is to sit in the presence of a standing lady. The body simply assumes the orthodox attitude, with or without the mind's consent. So,'' he added, ''it is a man we are looking for.'' Thinking of Daisy, he felt inordinately relieved.

''I should think so,'' Kate said, ''but I don't believe we can rule out the possibility that a woman—particularly one with whom he was on friendly terms—might have bidden him to sit down. In any event, it is something we must consider.''

Charles nodded, feeling a swiftly increasing respect for Kate's keen intelligence and reflecting, in a kind of mute celebration, that he could not have been more blessed in his choice of a wife if he had searched the length and breadth of England.

Kate was continuing. ''Verena Rochdale might have had the opportunity, although you must ask Isaacson whether he was with her last night, as Ellie suggests. But Verena appears to have known Wallace only in society. I could uncover no relationship between them and no motive that might have compelled her to kill him. And speaking of Ellie, I fear it is impossible for me to believe that she had anything to do with the man's death. If you think otherwise, you must speak with her and draw your own conclusions.''

''And the servants?''

''I learned nothing from them that either amplified or contradicted their mistresses' stories.'' Kate glanced at Charles and added, ''I have not yet talked to Lady Warwick. I thought that you might wish to join that conversation.''

''Perhaps it would be best if we saw her together,'' Charles replied. ''Before then, we should have a look at Wallace's room, and on the way, I will tell you what I learned from the farrier. But first—'' He took her hand once again. It lay in his, small and inexpressibly precious, though it was ink-stained. ''You've had no second thoughts, Kate?''

''About our marriage?'' Her glance was direct and clear, nothing reserved. ''None. Have you?''

''I am surer now than ever before,'' he said, standing. He pulled her to her feet and into his arms, kissing her with a sudden burst of passion that nearly unnerved him, and, he feared, must have frightened her. Overtaken by a rush of desire to possess her that he hardly knew how to quell, he stepped back and dropped his hands to his sides.

''How soon can we be married?'' he asked, thinking that even a few days' delay was too long.

She looked down, then up at him again. ''I fear I do not know what is customary, Charles. What would your family expect?''

He frowned, remembering Robert's wedding in St. Paul's Cathedral, a protracted, ponderous affair which had required the attentions of a battalion of cloth makers, seamstresses, flower merchants, bakers, caterers, and coachmen, who had been remunerated through the sale of thousands of acres belonging to his sister-in-law's father. He remembered the months of negotiations over the marriage settlement, the contentious arguments between the fathers of the groom and the bride, the prolonged debates over terms and allowances.

"What my family expects is of no relevance to us," he said firmly. "My brother's marriage was the social event of the year, attended by half a dozen minor Royals."

"Your family could hardly spare the time or effort just now to be involved with an elaborate wedding," Kate said thoughtfully. "They might even wish us to wait until after the year's mourning is done with."

"Wait? Not if I have anything to say about it!"

Kate touched her finger to his face, tracing the line of his brow. "A year is much too long, I think," she said softly.

Charles put his arms around her once again. "Then perhaps we could induce Barfield to marry us without ceremony," he said, his lips against her fragrant hair. "Next week, perhaps." Barfield Talbot, with whom Charles was well acquainted, was the vicar of the parish where Bishop's Keep was located. "I will speak to him myself as soon as the weekend is over." He snapped his fingers. "No, by heaven! I shall straightaway send off a telegram!"

Kate's eyes grew large. "Charles! I hardly think—"

"A fortnight?" He shook his head urgently. "No longer than that, surely. No longer, Kate, please!"

"Let us speak more on this later, Charles," she said. "You have an urgent commission to resolve matters here. When you have satisfied the Prince, we can settle the details of our wedding." She stood on tiptoe to kiss him lightly. "I promise you, my dear, it will not be long."

Charles took her hand and kissed it, feeling that he loved her far more than he could say. "Well, then," he said, with a deep sigh, "the sooner we are done, the sooner we can begin our happiness. So let us get on with this murderous business and have it over! Shall we go to Wallace's room?"

Kate nodded. "Have you spoken to his manservant yet?"

"His manservant? No, it hadn't occurred to me."

"Well, then," Kate said, "why don't we ring for the house steward and ask him to send Wallace's servant to the room? We can interview him there."

"Of course," Charles said, wondering once more why he had not thought of that.

* * * *

Wallace's bedroom was on the second floor, Kate discovered
as she accompanied Charles up the central staircase. They
went into the west wing and down a long hallway, where
Charles pointed out the room where he himself slept. Rooms
for single men were designed for sleeping and dressing, it
appeared, and were smaller, less elegant, and more spartan
than the ladies' rooms.

As they approached Wallace's room, they saw Kirk-
Smythe, stationed outside the door, speaking with a young
girl, a laundry maid, it appeared from her basket. Kirk-
Smythe's arms were folded and he was shaking his head
adamantly.

"Sorry, miss," he said. "No one comes into this room
until the investigation is finished. Orders of His Highness."

The girl gulped. "But 'tis my job t' git th' sheets fer th'
washin'!" she replied desperately. " 'F I doan't, Mrs. Wospottle'll sack me! She counts *ever'thing*, down t' th' last
pillercase!"

"It's all right, Kirk-Smythe," Charles said. "Hello,
Meg," he said.

The girl jerked around. "Sir?" she asked apprehensively,
then appeared to recognize Charles. "Sir!" she exclaimed,
seeming—oddly, Kate thought—even more frightened. From
the name, Kate recognized her as the farrier's daughter, of
whom Charles had spoken on their way upstairs.

"It's not likely that Lord Wallace's bed was slept in last
night, Meg," Charles said in a kindly tone. "And if it were,
it won't be slept in tonight. The laundering can wait."

The girl's chin trembled. "But that woan't— That woan't
satisfy Mrs. Wospottle," she said, half-choked. "She'll still
be wantin' 'em done."

Mrs. Wospottle, Kate thought, seemed a bit unreasonable.
And it was odd that the upstairs maid who was responsible
for the rooms on this corridor had not already remade the
bed. But Charles was smiling at the girl in a kindly way.

"Well, then," he said, "you may go into the room and
get the sheets, if you must."

Kirk-Smythe took out a key, unlocked the door, and the
girl slipped inside as if a wolf were snapping at her heels.
"Am I to wait?" he asked.

Charles shook his head. "The Prince asked me to send you to the library, where some telegrams are to be dispatched. I was also asked to tell you that His Highness is about to exhaust his supply of cigars."

Kirk-Smythe seemed to linger. "About last night, Sheridan—" He shifted uncomfortably and his eyes went to Kate, a red flush creeping along his jaw. "His Highness being otherwise occupied, you see, I was given leave to pursue my own interests. A certain young lady and I . . ." He hesitated, his mouth twitching. "That is to say—"

"Celia has already spoken to me about your meeting last night," Kate said gently, "and I have relayed her account to Sir Charles."

"Then you know what transpired." The young man was visibly relieved. "Celia's a lovely girl and I mean to marry her, if she will have me. In fact, I plan to ask His Highness to intercede on my behalf." His face darkened. "But Lady Rochdale is a damned termagant, if you don't mind my saying so. If she knew that her daughter and I—"

"Lady Rochdale will know nothing from us," Charles said. "Did you see or hear anyone in the vicinity of the Folly last night?"

Kirk-Smythe shook his head.

"As the Prince's guard, I assume that you carry a gun."

Kirk-Smythe lifted his trouser leg, reached into his boot, and pulled out a small, deadly-looking derringer. He handed it to Charles. "I have had it on my person since His Highness and I arrived at Easton," he said.

Charles turned the gun over in his hand, opening the breech and examining the cartridge in the chamber. "A forty-one caliber," he remarked.

"Correct. Has the fatal bullet been recovered?"

Charles returned the gun. "Yes. It was fired from a smaller weapon, thirty-two caliber, most likely."

"Ah," Kirk-Smythe said, and slipped it back into his boot. He straightened and handed the room key to Charles. "I should see to those telegrams now." With a half-bow to Kate and a muttered "Ma'am," he went quickly toward the stairs.

Charles pushed the door open and Kate followed him into

the room, where the girl was stripping the bottom sheet from the bed to add to the pile on the floor. The room was high-ceilinged and dark, with a dark green wool rug on the floor and heavy green damask draperies over the window. Kate went to them and pulled them open to allow light into the room. Turning, she saw a bed against one wall, a large, barrel-fronted mahogany dresser against another, and a fireplace with a white-painted mantel-shelf let into a third. A small writing table sat beside the window, and with it a carved wooden chair. A more comfortable upholstered chair in green, with a small oak footstool, was placed beside the fireplace.

"What are we searching for?" she asked.

"I don't know," Charles admitted, looking around. "Something, anything that might provide a clue to the motive for Wallace's murder." He went to the dresser and began to pull out the drawers.

There was a soft knock at the door, and Kate went to it. A frock-coated manservant was standing stiffly outside. "I am Richards, ma'am. Sir Reginald's valet." He glanced at the open drawer in which Charles had been searching. "You are the gentleman commissioned by His Highness to investigate Sir Reginald's murder?"

"I am Charles Sheridan, and this is my assistant, Miss Ardleigh." He stepped aside to allow the girl to leave the room with her basket of sheets. "Please accept our condolences on the death of your master, Richards."

Richards inclined his head and the starchiness went out of him. "Thank you, sir. If there is anything I can do, you have but to ask. Poor Sir Reginald—" He swallowed. "Well, sir, it's a dreadful shame, that's all I can say. Appalling, is what it is."

"It is indeed a great pity," Charles agreed sympathetically, as Kate went to the writing table. Upon it was a clock, a green blotter, an inkwell, a collection of pens, and a leather portfolio filled with clean sheets of heavy vellum, embossed with the Easton seal. She raised the blotter, which appeared to be clean. There was nothing under it, and nothing in the drawer.

"I wonder," Charles was saying, "whether you know of

anyone who might have borne ill will toward Sir Reginald?''

The man's face hardened. '' 'Smatter of fact, sir,'' he said, "I do.''

Kate turned, surprised, and Charles asked, "Who?''

"Sir Thomas, sir,'' Richards said, with much feeling.

"Thomas Cobb?'' Charles asked, his eyebrows going up.

"Sir Thomas is—was—Sir Reginald's wife's father, sir. There has been bad blood between them since Lady Wallace died. Sir Thomas, you see, believed—oh, quite wrongly, I assure you—that his daughter was murdered.''

"Murdered!'' Kate exclaimed.

"Yes, madam.'' Richards's lips thinned. "By Sir Reginald.''

Charles mulled this over. "I see,'' he said presently. "Have you ever heard Sir Thomas threaten Sir Reginald?''

Richards became earnest. "Oh, several times, sir. They quarreled often, and heatedly. Yesterday, as a matter of fact, just here. Sir Thomas's room is down the hall, you see, and he stopped on his way to dinner.''

Of course, Kate thought. That explained why Sir Thomas, who had been seated beside her at dinner, had spent the entire meal glowering across the table at Sir Reginald. Had the unmistakable animosity between the two men blossomed into something much deadlier?

"How did Sir Thomas suppose his daughter's death to have taken place?'' Charles asked.

"Lady Wallace was injured when she and Sir Reginald were out riding, sir.''

"Ah, yes,'' Charles murmured. "I recall something about a fence.''

"Indeed, sir,'' Richards said. "Her horse refused a fence and she was thrown against a tree. She survived for several days, unable to speak. Sir Thomas was most distraught. He charged that . . . well, that Sir Reginald had struck his daughter.''

"And the supposed motive?''

Richards dropped his chin into his high starched collar. "At the time, Sir Reginald was . . . on friendly terms with Lady Warwick.''

Kate shivered. Under the circumstances, it was perhaps

not surprising that Sir Thomas had accused his son-in-law, or that he glared at him across the dinner table. More surprising, actually, was that the two men had agreed to come to the same house party. Was something to be made of that fact?

She was glancing around the room, wondering where to search next, when her attention was caught by a folded paper on the floor beside the bed. She went to pick it up.

Charles was going on with his questioning. "Setting Sir Thomas aside, Richards, are you aware of anyone else who might have wished your master harm?"

Richards pushed his lips in and out. "One does not wish to speak ill of a lady," he said carefully, "but Lady Metcalf . . . that is to say . . ." He stopped, looking uncomfortable.

Kate stepped forward. "She was infatuated with your master, was she not?" she asked. "Perhaps embarrassingly so?"

"Yes, thank you, madam," Richards said. "That is exactly the case, I fear. Lady Metcalf made Sir Reginald's life a misery. She lives only three miles away, you see. She is always coming to call, and even invites herself to dinner. And when he tried to suggest to her—oh, in a most gentlemanly way!—that he wished to be let alone, she fell into an extraordinary fit, in front of the servants." He shook his head, clucking reproachfully. "She was a great humiliation to him, and eventually, he was forced to advise her of his feelings. I am sorry to say so, but the lady might have wished to avenge herself. A woman scorned—"

"Thank you," Charles said. "Can you think of anyone else?"

Richards seemed to be about to speak, then closed his mouth.

"If you have thought of anyone," Charles said, "anyone at all, I should be most grateful for your opinion."

Richards sighed. "I do hate to say it, sir."

"I am sure, Richards. These things are never pleasant. Who is it you have in mind?"

"Lord Warwick, sir."

Kate was not surprised to hear it. Love affairs seemed to be taken lightly by the Marlborough set, but there must have been some strain between Lord Warwick and his wife's former lover. She fell into a bemused wonderment, thinking in what a complicated *ménage* of relationships the Warwicks lived. Lady Warwick; her husband; her former lover, Wallace; her present lover, the Prince of Wales. It would be remarkable if Lord Warwick did not have a lover, too, she thought suddenly. If so, who was she? Lady Lillian, perhaps?

"I see," Charles was saying. "Did Lord Warwick and Sir Reginald have words, Richards?"

"Yesterday, sir. Lord Warwick seems to have believed that Sir Reginald had possession of a letter belonging to Lady Warwick. Oh, but he was wrong, sir!" he interjected. "Sir Reginald would not have lowered himself to steal a lady's letter!"

"Perhaps it came into his possession by some other means," Charles said. "Can you report any particulars of the conversation?"

"I'm afraid not, sir. Lord Warwick was quite unspecific in his charges, except to say that he feared that the Warwick name would be damaged, and Sir Reginald denied knowing anything of the letter. I must say, sir," he added, "that Sir Reginald bore himself like the gentleman he was, even under Lord Warwick's intemperate attack."

"Well, then. Is there anything else?"

Richards thought for a moment, then shook his head. "No, sir."

"Thank you, then, Richards. I believe that will be all."

When the man had left the room, Kate held out the folded paper. "I found this on the floor, beside the bed, Charles. It must have fallen from the sheets when the maid pulled them off."

Charles took it from her, unfolded the paper, and began to read. " 'My Darling Daisy, We have an enormous but pleasant party here, though everything reminds me so much of the happy days we spent here two years ago! . . . ' "

22

Be fair or foul, or rain or shine,
The joys I have possessed, in spite of fate, are mine.
Not heaven itself upon the past has power;
But what has been, has been, and I have had my hour.

—JOHN DRYDEN
The Countess of Warwick's favorite poem

After luncheon was over, Daisy pleaded letters to write and declined an invitation to participate in an impromptu croquet tournament with several of the guests. She went up to her second-floor suite, where she sat in the yellow velvet chair beside her window, listening to the loud ticking of the jewel-encrusted gold clock Bertie had given her and trying to prepare herself for what she now realized she could not avoid: a conversation with Charles, to whom she would have to confess some part of the truth.

Daisy recognized herself as a schemer—a gifted schemer, at that—whose impulsive actions often required her to redeem herself through clever stratagems. But scheme and strategize as she might, she could find no way around Charles. Damn Bertie, anyway! If the man were not so prone to theatrical gesture, there would have been no guard posted at the door of Reggie's room. She could have recovered that dreadful letter and saved herself and Bertie—and patient, complaisant Brooke, whose chief concern was always and forever the precious Warwick name—untold embarrassment, perhaps even public humiliation.

That was impossible now, of course. Daisy had known Charles for many years. He had invariably impressed her, and even awed her upon occasion, by his intellect, his thoroughness, and his determination. If Bertie's foolish note were hidden in Reggie's room, Charles would certainly find it.

After sitting for a time lost in thought, Daisy rose from the chair and began nervously to pace back and forth, the clock on her dressing table a loud metronome marking time to her movements. Of course, there was a slim chance that the letter would not come immediately to light. Reggie knew his way around Easton Lodge. He might have hidden it anywhere—in a map case in the library, or in one of the thousands of books, or even at the Folly. And Charles could have no clear idea what he was searching for. He might overlook the letter among Reggie's papers, assuming there were any. Or, having found it, he might intentionally pass over it out of a gentleman's sense of propriety and decorum or a respect for the monarchy. Yes, Charles, who came of the Somersworth Sheridans, understood how important it was to maintain appearances, protect reputations, preserve the monarchy. And it was no exaggeration to fear that the monarchy could be threatened by the Crown Prince's indiscretions. The Queen said so herself, often and loudly enough that Daisy had come to think that it was the Royal mother's complaints that prompted the Royal son's flagrant misbehavior.

Daisy turned to the window and pulled back the Belgium lace curtains that underhung the yellow damask drapes. She looked out toward the edge of the park, where the grounds staff had finished setting out the fireworks for tonight's display and was now raking the clipped grass. The difficulty was that she could not count on Charles's being alone when he searched Reggie's room. More likely, he would ask Kate Ardleigh to help him. Daisy did not know the American woman well, but she suspected that Kate would not be fettered by the same sense of social propriety that might restrain Charles. Still and all, the woman seemed prudent, and not likely to speak should Charles bid her to be silent. Even if they should find the letter, it would be safe in their hands, as safe as might be, under the circumstances. She was confident that she could persuade them to return it to her, and if not to her, then to Bertie—unless perhaps they thought it suggested a motive for Reggie's murder.

At the thought, Daisy took in her breath sharply. The missing letter was awful enough, but it was easy to explain in comparison to that note she had written to Reggie, which had almost certainly been on his person at the time of his death. And there was the missing pistol.

Oh, God, that wretched pistol! Should she assume that it had simply been taken by one of the servants and would never again come to light? Such a thing was entirely possible, of course. Much minor thievery occurred in an establishment of this size, especially when it was invaded during weekend house parties by armies of strange servants who often loitered about with too little to do. And the gun was a pretty thing, made by the Prince's favorite gunsmith. It would make a nice souvenir. She could almost convince herself that its loss, while coincidental, was unrelated to Reggie's death and hence unimportant.

But something told her that this was a forlorn hope. No, reporting the theft of the gun to Charles was probably the shrewder move, in case the weapon came to light and proved to be the instrument of Reggie's death. One would think it impossible to trace a bullet to the gun that fired it—but Bertie had spoken at lunch of scientific methods, of microscopes and marks on bullets and the like. For all she knew, Charles might be able to link the fatal bullet to her gun. At the thought, Daisy was seized in a grip of cold, clutching fear so powerful that it made her knees weak, and she sank into the chair once again.

After a long while, she glanced at Bertie's clock on the dressing table, the face of which was enigmatically inscribed with a line from her favorite poem, "I have had my hour." Those words always heartened her, reminding her that she had led a charmed life. She had inherited one of the greatest fortunes in England, married one of the kingdom's handsomest and most titled lords, and gathered in her embrace the Empire's most powerful man. Yes, whatever dilemmas the future held, whatever hazards and dangers, she had had glories enough.

She looked at the clock again. It would soon be time to

dress for tea. She would go to Reggie's room now. If she could not retrieve the letter herself, perhaps the search was over and she could discover what had been found.

Daisy's timing could not have been more perfect. As she reached the west-wing corridor that led to Reggie's room, Charles was just shutting the door. Kate was with him, and they were talking earnestly, their heads close together, their hands touching.

Daisy watched them, momentarily struck by a painful envy. She had had many lovers, but they had brought her only an empty passion that left her surfeited yet unsatisfied. She hoped that Charles would ask Kate to marry him after all, and that the American would say yes. Under other circumstances, she would have taken great pleasure in fostering their relationship, as she had done with so many others. But the expressions on their faces as they saw her brought her back to her reason for being there and gave her the answer to at least one of her questions. They had found the letter or the note, or both. She would have to brazen it out.

Charles gave her a small smile. "We have uncovered certain evidence that we must talk with you about, Daisy."

"Of course," Daisy replied with the smile that always put people at their ease. In her usual fashion, she took charge of the situation, gesturing toward the closed door.

"Shall we speak in Reggie's room?" Without waiting for an answer, she opened the door and swept in, noticing that the linens were missing from the bed. Perhaps that's where the discovery had been made. It would be like Reggie to simply slide Bertie's letter under his pillow!

She seated herself in the largest and most comfortable chair, waited for Kate to adjust the draperies and Charles to bring forward two more chairs, smoothed her skirts, and smiled.

"This . . . *evidence* you have uncovered," she said carelessly, intending to imply by her tone that it was barely significant enough to warrant her attention. "Does it perhaps include a note from me to Lord Wallace and a letter from His Royal Highness to me—a letter of a rather personal nature?"

The expression on Charles's face—a kind of relief, mixed

with concern—told her that she had guessed correctly, and that her candor had achieved the effect she desired.

"You knew that Wallace had the letter?" he asked.

"I thought it quite likely. It went missing on Thursday, the day of his arrival. At first, I hoped I had merely misplaced it, but after an exhaustive search I began to fear it was stolen."

"Did Wallace tell you that he had possession of it?"

"Not in so many words," she said. "But there was something in his manner that told me clearly enough. Reggie and I were once . . . quite well acquainted. I knew him very well. He was withholding something of importance from me, and he felt guilty about it."

"Felt guilty?" The room was so quiet that she could hear the ticking of the clock on the writing table.

"Yes." Daisy lifted her shoulders and let them drop in a small, casual shrug. "He still loved me, I believe, and did not wish to harm me."

"Then why," Kate asked in a puzzled tone, "would he have taken the letter? What did he mean to do with it, or to gain from it?"

"I have asked myself that same question," Daisy admitted. "I believe he hoped to entice me to return to him. It was a vain hope," she added lightly, "but he might have deceived himself."

"So you wanted to talk with him to confirm your suspicions and perhaps induce him to return the letter," Charles said.

"Yes," Daisy replied. "I wrote a note and slipped it to him during the dancing, asking him to meet me at the Folly."

"Did you meet?"

"No," Daisy said. She looked down at her hands, turning the emerald ring the Prince had given her. "I was—"

"His Highness has said that the two of you were together," Charles said evenly. "Is it true?"

Daisy nodded, feeling a great wave of gratitude. Nothing compelled Bertie to do this. Once again, he was protecting her!

"Were you in the vicinity of the Folly last night?"

"I was there yesterday at luncheon. After that, no." She

looked up and let her glance rest full on Charles. "How soon can you return His Highness's letter to me? Surely you can see that it has nothing to do with this unfortunate murder," she hurried on. "And I am certainly innocent. Quite apart from lacking opportunity, I would never have left my note on Reggie's body. And had I known before we left for Chelmsford this morning that he was dead, I would surely have recovered Bertie's letter." She frowned slightly. "I daresay the murderer knew nothing of the letter, either. Otherwise, it would not have been left where you found it. It would have been a most remarkable and useful trophy."

Kate cleared her throat. "Unless it was intended to implicate you and the Prince in Wallace's murder," she said.

Daisy felt her heart thudding against her ribs. "The . . . Prince?" she whispered.

Charles was somber. "The fact that your mutual motives are protected by a mutual alibi might be seen in some quarters as rather too convenient."

Daisy was jolted by a sudden fear as strong as a powerful electrical shock. The pistol!

Charles was watching her closely. "You've thought of something."

"Something else is missing from my room," Daisy said shakily. "From the same drawer that contained the letter."

"A gun?" Kate asked.

"A small pistol. A present to me from His Highness."

Charles leaned forward. "It disappeared at the same time as the letter?"

Daisy shook her head. "I saw it in my drawer when I searched on Thursday evening for the letter, and again on Friday. I discovered it missing only this morning, before we left for Chelmsford."

"But the person who stole the letter knew it was there," Kate said.

"Yes, I suppose so," Daisy replied. "The letter was in the top drawer of a leather box filled with recent correspondence. The gun was in the second drawer."

"Can you describe the weapon?" Charles asked.

"It is a pretty little thing," Daisy said, "a silver-plated

revolver, with mother-of-pearl handles, inlaid with my initials.''

"A thirty-two caliber weapon?''

Daisy nodded, fear knotting her stomach.

"The autopsy surgeon recovered the fatal bullet," Charles said. "It is a thirty-two caliber.''

Her hand went to her mouth. "Oh, God," she whispered.

"Where were you early yesterday morning?" Charles asked.

"Yesterday morning? Friday?" Friday seemed an eternity ago. "I . . . I think I slept rather late. Yes, that's right. My maid came in to wake me and I sent her away so that I could sleep for another hour. Then I dressed and came down for a late breakfast, where I met Kate." Kate gave a confirming nod.

"And your husband?" Charles persisted.

"Brooke? Up and about, I suppose. He is an early riser.'' She frowned, not at all sure where this was going and frightened by the harder edge she could hear in Charles's voice. "Why are you asking about Friday? And what does Brooke have to do with any of this?''

"Charles is asking about Friday because that's when the boy was killed," Kate said softly.

Daisy's eyes went from one to the other. "And you think that I . . . or that Brooke—" Her throat tightened. "That's ridiculous! The boy's death was entirely accidental. None of my guests, and certainly not my husband, had anything to do with it!''

"Wallace was seen leaving the stable about the time of the boy's death," Charles said. "He may have witnessed it, or even been involved in it." His glance seemed chilly, unfriendly. "You can't tell us where Lord Warwick was at the time?''

She shook her head wordlessly. Brooke was not a man customarily given to violence, but she had once seen him strike a groom who had been abusing a horse, so severely injuring the man that he lay close to death for some days. Was it possible that he had lost his temper and struck the boy, and that Reggie had witnessed the deed?

But there was more. Brooke had been in her bedroom on

Thursday. She had come in from a conference with the housekeeper to find him there, uninvited and unexpected, standing beside the desk where her letter case sat, in plain sight. He could have taken the letter.

But why would he? Brooke had recently begun to object to her entertaining Bertie because their intimacy attracted so much public attention and the Royal visits were so hideously expensive. But that gave him no motive for taking Bertie's letter and hiding it in Reggie's room. Unless, of course, he intended to implicate her, and perhaps Bertie as well, in Reggie's murder.

At the thought, Daisy shivered violently. "No!" she whispered. Brooke would never do such a thing! To embroil her in this mess would be to entangle himself and tarnish the Warwick name. Brooke's sense of decorum and propriety, his concern for the family reputation, would never allow that.

But even as Daisy thought of this, she thought of something else. Brooke knew better than anyone the lengths to which Bertie would go to champion her. He would know that even if the Prince were confronted with the clearest, most incontrovertible proof that she was guilty of murder, he would never permit her to be brought up on charges, let along face trial. Brooke would know that Bertie would cover up her guilt just as he had hushed so many previous scandals, even that unspeakable business about his own son Eddy and the East End brothels. He would know that the only punishment Daisy would ever suffer would be her total and unalterable alienation from the Prince's affection.

Her heart skipped a beat, then another, and her hands felt suddenly icy. To separate her and Bertie forever, to put an end to the corrosive gossip and reduce the ruinous expenses of Royal entertainment—*that* was an outcome Brooke would consider worth his effort. That was an end that might justify any means—even murder.

Charles was looking at her strangely. "Is there something else you want to tell us?"

Bewildered and confused, feeling as if the world she had always controlled had suddenly broken loose from her grasp, Daisy struggled for command.

"No . . . no, I think that is all," she said, in a high, brittle voice. As if to rescue her, the clock whirred, then began to strike the hour. She rose, steadying herself. "My goodness, how late it is! We must dress for tea."

"Thank you, Daisy," Charles said quietly. "We may have other questions later."

She made one more attempt. "The letter? I would *so* much like to have it back, you know. I am sure you realize the damage it could do in the wrong hands."

"We must keep it for now," Charles said. "But don't worry. It will be carefully guarded."

Daisy tossed her head. "Oh, very well, then," she said.

Without another word, she lifted her skirts and went before them out of the room and down the corridor, her head high, her back ramrod straight, playing the part she had been born and bred to play. She was Lady Frances, the greatest heiress in England. She was the Countess of Warwick, wife of England's handsomest lord. She was Daisy, lover of the Prince of Wales.

But in her heart there was a terrible hopelessness, for she knew, beyond the shadow of a doubt, that it was over. The Prince cared for her, but he was no fool. He would go on to a less hazardous love affair, to a woman of fewer charms, perhaps, but also fewer liabilities. She would have nothing left, only the minor celebrity that inevitably attended a former mistress of the future king, only the indiscreet letters and the expensive gifts, only her memories.

She had had her hour, and it was over.

23

By indirections find directions out.

—WILLIAM SHAKESPEARE
Hamlet

At teatime, Charles went to the drawing room, which was furnished in Louis XIV style, with frescoed walls and *objets d'art* placed in every niche. The guests were assembled in conversational clusters, several women decoratively arranged on adjoining sofas, a group of men gathered around the Prince at the fireplace talking about racing, others sitting in a corner, discussing Harcourt's reform of the death duties. Without calling attention to himself, Charles quietly detached Sir Thomas Cobb from the death duties group and led him to a curtained alcove at the far end of the room. He would have preferred to have begun his questioning with Lord Warwick, who was in Charles's mind the more logical suspect. But Brooke was talking with the Prince and it would be uncivil to interrupt their conversation.

"You want to speak with me about Reginald's murder, I take it," the old man said. He had a saber scar across one cheek, and his thick, jutting eyebrows, gray beard, and tanned face gave him the look of a grizzled old pirate.

"Just so," Charles replied, thinking that Cobb looked older and more haggard than he had just yesterday. The man's steel-gray eyes were red with fatigue and his forehead was deeply furrowed. "I must speak with everyone." He motioned toward one of the two leather chairs in the alcove and waited until the older man had seated himself before he sat down.

"Ah, but in my case," Cobb said, "you have a particular reason to speak with me." A dry smile cracked his old face. "I do not doubt you have talked with Reginald's man Richards."

"I have." Charles leaned back in his chair, elbows on the upholstered arms, his fingers tented in front of his mouth.

Cobb took a silver cigar case out of his coat pocket and extracted a cigar. Making a ceremony of rolling and sniffing it, then of lighting it, he said at last, "Well, I won't dissemble, Sheridan, or make your task any more unpleasant than it already is. I was not overly fond of my daughter's husband. Not to mince words, I wished him dead and in hell." He pulled his bristling brows together. "But, by George, I did not kill him!"

From the other end of the room came the tinkle of Daisy's light laughter, and a hearty echo from the Prince, the men at the fireplace having joined the women on the sofa. A footman approached with two teacups on a tray, set them on the table, and filled them from a silver pot. Cobb frowned. "Brandy," he said gruffly. The footman nodded and disappeared.

Charles added sugar, stirred, and sipped his tea. "According to Richards, you and Wallace have been at odds for some time."

Cobb pulled heavily on his cigar. "The man killed my daughter Margaret." His face grew dark. "I won't trouble you with my reasons for believing so, but simply assure you that my conclusion is unequivocally and unquestionably correct. The wound was inflicted by a blunt instrument, and not suffered in a fall. Ask the Countess. She knows."

Charles was not surprised that Daisy had withheld that information from him (if it were indeed true). She was privy to so many secrets that she had probably forgotten the greater part of them. "How can you be sure?" he asked.

The footman reappeared with Cobb's brandy in a large snifter. "That, Sheridan, is none of your affair. In any event, I consider Lady Warwick complicitous in the matter. She was Reginald's paramour at the time of my daughter's murder, poor innocent.'' He rolled the brandy in the glass, sniffed it, and sipped. ''She is as responsible as he. The devil of it is that I can do nothing about it.''

''The police—''

''The local constable, whose family have long been Wallace retainers, investigated and found nothing amiss.'' The old man's eyes were bleak and his voice dripped with an acid bitterness. ''The coroner's jury—twelve good men and true to their landlord, Wallace—brought in a verdict of accidental death.''

''Then—''

Cobb finished the brandy and set the snifter on the table. ''I am a realist, Sheridan. Certain things in life can be altered, certain cannot, and it is the better part of wisdom to know the difference. I decided long ago that I could do nothing to bring either of Margaret's killers to justice. It is my burden to live with—and theirs. But it gave me no small pleasure to remind Reginald frequently and pointedly of his culpability.''

Wallace might have found it easier to stand trial for his wife's death than to be sentenced to the venomous harangues of her angry father, Charles thought. The old man must believe himself to be wronged past enduring. Why then was he here at Easton?

''Given your animosity toward Lady Warwick, I wonder at your willingness to be a guest at her home—especially when the guest list included Wallace.'' Perhaps a more interesting question, though, had to do with Wallace's inclusion on the guest list. One of the Warwicks had invited him. Lord Brooke or the Countess? And why?

The other shrugged. ''I am here out of respect for the fourth earl of Warwick, Lord Brooke's father, with whom I had the privilege to be closely acquainted. I most emphatically do *not* admire the way young Brooke allows his wife to manage his life for him, nor do I approve of the fact that both of them seem intent on frittering away the Maynard and Warwick fortunes on foolish entertainments. For the sake of Brooke's father, however, I cultivate the son's company, and—for the sake of his father—he tolerates mine. Once each year he invites me to one of these lunatic house parties

and once each year I set aside common sense and come."
His mouth twisted in an ugly grimace. "These follies, however, do not amuse me. I am chagrined at the sight of the
Queen's heir making a vulgar fool of himself—and risking
the monarchy, as well—over a damned foolish woman. How
can anyone imagine him competent to rule the Empire when
he cannot even rule his own reckless passions?" He snorted.
"The Queen would die of mortification if she understood the
full extent of her son's folly."

Cobb was leaving something out, Charles thought. Retal-
iation was a more likely explanation for his presence than a
sentimental affection for an old friend's son. If Daisy felt
even a shred of guilt for her affair with Wallace and the
subsequent death of Wallace's wife, seeing the old man bee-
tling his brows at her across the tea table must make her
damned uncomfortable. And if Cobb had given up all hope
of achieving justice through the courts for his daughter's
death, to what other extremes might he be moved? Might he
have killed Wallace and attempted to implicate Daisy? Cen-
sorious as he was of the Prince's behavior, might he even
have attempted to implicate him, as well?

Charles drained the sweet dregs of his tea and put down
the cup. "Is there anyone who can corroborate your whereabouts last night?"

The old man croaked out a laugh. "Hardly! It has never
been my practice to hop from bed to bed at these weekends.
I retired to my room at the close of the evening and there I
stayed until shortly after sunrise, when I rose and went for
a long walk. After all this pretense and, posturing, there is
nothing like a quick march over field and furrow to restore
a man's sense of equilibrium."

"Did your quick march take you in the direction of the
Folly?"

"As a matter of fact, I went the other way." Cobb puffed
reflectively on his cigar, the smoke rising in a blue haze
around his head. "Is there anything else?"

"I wonder," Charles said, "whether you brought a gun
with you—a personal sidearm, that is."

"Why the devil would I bring a sidearm?" Cobb retorted
testily. "Should one care to shoot, one can readily equip

oneself from the gun room.'' He made as if to rise.

Charles raised his hand. ''One thing more, if you don't mind. You knew Wallace quite well—at least you did at one time. Would you care to hazard a guess as to the identity of his killer?''

''I'll give you two,'' Cobb growled, and stood. ''One is Lady Warwick.''

''Her motive?''

''She owed him money, of course, and he was beginning to be tiresome about it. And if he were dead, she could stop feeling guilty about Margaret's death.''

''I see,'' Charles said. But if Wallace were demanding repayment of a debt, why had he been invited to Easton, unless—? Unless Daisy, or Brooke, planned to kill him. ''How much money?''

''Ten thousand pounds, more or less. He told me he intended to exact payment this weekend.'' The old man gave a quick, hard laugh. ''One almost pities the poor fellow, actually. Getting money out of that woman must be like wringing whiskey out of a rock.''

Charles studied Sir Thomas. It appeared that he knew nothing about the Prince's letter. Had he stolen it and planted it in Wallace's room, he would certainly have claimed that Wallace was using it to coerce Daisy into repaying the debt. That the old man had mentioned nothing about the letter seemed to Charles to exonerate him from the murder—unless he was being deliberately subtle.

''That's one guess,'' Charles said. ''What's the other?''

A smile flickered. ''Anarchists, Sheridan. Anarchists.''

A few moments later, the chair opposite Charles was occupied by Felicia Metcalf. Her hair was laced with a black ribbon, and she had arranged a heavily fringed black silk shawl around the shoulders of her lavender tea gown—tokens, Charles concluded, of mourning for Wallace. But if there were other signs of her grief, they were lost in the grand majesty of her offended dignity.

''I said everything I had to say to Miss Ardleigh.'' Felicia's tone was glacial. ''Since she has surely reported my answers to you, Charles, I cannot think why I must respond to still *more* questions.''

Charles refused to take offense. ''I apologize for the intrusion into your privacy, Felicia,'' he said softly. ''It really is most unforgivable of me, at a time when you are so heavily weighed with grief. Please believe that I would not trouble you if the Prince had not commanded me.'' He paused. ''Miss Ardleigh tells me that you and Reggie were close friends.''

Some of the ice began to thaw. ''We were,'' she said sadly. A lacy handkerchief appeared and was dabbed quickly to the eyes. ''Quite close.''

''Intimate, I believe,'' Charles said with sympathy.

The sigh was heavy. ''I cannot deny it.'' A blush rose to the cheeks that Charles suspected had already been reddened with a rub of *papier poudre*.

''Then perhaps you can help me to understand this appalling business.'' Charles made a helpless gesture. ''I confess to being entirely at sea, without a clue, as it were. Who do you think might have wished poor Reggie dead?''

Lady Metcalf, appeased, sat forward. ''I have been giving a great deal of thought to that myself,'' she said briskly. ''At first—did Miss Ardleigh tell you?—I believed that Reggie and Lillian Forsythe had gone off together. When I learned he was dead, I entertained the possibility that Lillian herself might have killed him.'' She simpered. ''In a moment of pique, of course, when she learned that while Reggie might briefly respond to another's physical charms, his heart belonged to me. But now I am given to understand that Lillian and Sir Friedrich spent the night together. She could have had nothing to do with it.''

''I must agree with you, Felicia.'' Charles leaned closer. ''I wonder,'' he said, ''whether Reggie mentioned anything to you about a certain . . . letter in his possession.''

She pulled in her breath. ''A letter?''

''He said something of it to you?''

For a long moment she did not answer. Then she cried, in a low, broken tone, so unlike her affected speech that it startled Charles, ''Oh, what a foolish, foolish man! I begged him to be careful. I warned him not to meddle with Daisy, no matter how much money she owed him. And I *especially* told him not to discuss it with Brooke.''

Charles gave her the same stern look he would have given to a miscreant child. ''I see, Felicia, that you have been concealing something of great importance. You must make a clean breast of it.''

She went stiff. There was no mistaking the very real fear in her eyes. Mutely, she shook her head.

He rose from his chair. ''Then I shall be forced to ask His Highness to step over here, and you can tell him that you know nothing that might help us resolve this matter.''

She gnawed her lip. ''I'm not sure there's anything to tell,'' she said at last.

He sat down again. ''I shall be the judge of that.''

With a reluctant sigh, she yielded. ''I only know that it had something to do with a letter of Daisy's. Reggie meant to speak of it with Brooke.'' She swallowed hard. ''There. That's all I know.'' She looked up at him, her eyes wide. ''Truly it is, Charles.''

''What sort of a letter?'' he asked.

''Why, one of their old love letters, I suppose. Daisy and Reggie, I mean.'' She made a disgusted face. ''When they were lovers, they used to write daily.''

Charles spoke carefully, conscious of the importance of his question. ''Exactly what did you think Reggie meant to say to Brooke?''

Fear shadowed her eyes. ''Must I?'' she whispered.

''You must,'' he said emphatically.

Her voice was low and hesitant. ''I thought . . . I imagined that he planned to offer the letter to Brooke in return for repayment of Daisy's debt to him. She owed him—close to ten thousand pounds.'' She held out her hand in appeal. ''He didn't *say* that, Charles. It is only what I *thought*. I could be dreadfully wrong. In fact, I am sure that I am wrong! Reggie would not have stooped to blackmail. And Brooke could not have—'' She drew a ragged breath. ''No Warwick could have—''

''Could have what?'' he prompted.

She swallowed hard. ''Have killed him,'' she whispered. Her eyes were wide. ''Oh, please, Charles! You must not tell

Brooke that I have any knowledge . . . that I might suspect . . . that it might even have crossed my mind for a moment—''

He touched her hand. The Warwicks were among the most powerful families in England. If Brooke or Daisy learned of Felicia's accusation, guarded as it was, they would view it as slander. She would never be invited to another social event—the kiss of death to anyone in her circumstances.

"I trust you will not discuss this business with anyone else," he said. But he did not need her assurance. The terror in her eyes told him that she would not dare to speak a word.

The third person to occupy the chair opposite was Francis Brooke, Lord Warwick. He slouched comfortably in it, his long legs stretched out before him, turning the fine waxed tips of his dark Kaiser mustache as he gazed the length of the ballroom. He was a strikingly handsome, clean-shaven man with dark eyes and brows and firm, chiseled features, his crisply curled hair clipped short, his manner marked by the unconscious arrogance of one whose family had lived in a castle for hundreds of years. Warwick Castle, Brooke's ancestral home, was more than a castle, of course; it was an historical monument whose restoration was made possible by his marriage to Daisy, who had been the wealthiest heiress of her era.

Where had all that money gone in only fifteen years? Charles wondered. Had the Warwicks spent it on their properties—Easton Lodge, Warwick Castle, the London house, the estate in Scotland? Or had it been lavished on expensive entertainments, particularly those involving the Prince?

"Damned fine gathering," Lord Warwick said in a bored, drawling voice. He signaled to the footman to refill the whiskey glass he had brought with him.

"Agreed," Charles said, although he privately thought that he would much prefer to be off with Kate in the wild, far away from blackmail and murder.

There was an extended silence as both men regarded the company at the far end of the room, the women splendid in their lavish tea gowns, the men handsome in their dark coats and patterned waistcoats. Daisy and the Prince were tête-àtête on a red velvet love seat, and Eleanor Farley, at the grand piano, was accompanying Lillian Forsythe and Friedrich Temple in a German *lieder*. It was a picture of privilege.

After a moment, Warwick roused himself. "Bertie tells me that you are coming along famously with your investigations," he said, and downed his whiskey in one gulp. "Discovered anything of interest?"

"Nothing very firm," Charles said. "It does appear, however, that Wallace may have known something about the death of His Highness's stableboy. Reggie was seen leaving the stable around the time of the lad's death."

"I say," Lord Warwick said with mild regret. He sighed. "Somehow, one always felt that there was something . . . oh, not quite the thing in Reggie." He paused, watching the Prince rise and extend a hand to Daisy, who stood and walked with him to the French doors that opened into the conservatory. For a moment they paused, he looking down at her, she laughing up at him, a poised, elegant couple. Then they disappeared into the mysterious green recesses of the conservatory. The door closed behind them.

"Not quite the thing?" Charles asked.

Lord Warwick seemed to pull himself back from a great distance. "I don't mean that he was . . ." He frowned. "No, nothing of that sort. I simply mean that one was not confident in his . . ." He gave up the effort. "Oh, you know what I mean."

"I understand," Charles said delicately, "that he and Lady Warwick were once quite friendly."

Warwick turned his glance on Charles and became, with an effort, blandly affable. "Oh, quite," he said. "Yes, quite." He cleared his throat. "I expect they saw quite a bit of one another, once, you know."

"I also understand that Lady Warwick may have been in his debt."

"Now, now, old chap," Warwick said, wagging his forefinger with a sudden, roguish smile, "one mustn't believe everything one is told." He went back to twirling the ends of his mustache, his eyes on the French doors. "I b'lieve, however, that she was. In debt, I mean." He coughed. "To Reggie, that is. Lady Warwick has her own private fortune," he added, with the air of a man who feels he is clarifying a murky point. "She may call on me from time to time for advice, but one does not wish to intrude unless one is asked, you know." He chuckled without mirth. "One does not volunteer."

"Did Reggie speak to you recently about that debt?"

"To me?" Warwick was not looking at him. "Oh, no, not to me. Perhaps, though, Lady Warwick spoke to him about it." He made a vague gesture. "Yes, I feel quite certain she did. Or at least, she meant to." There was a long pause, and then Warwick said, half to himself, "I s'pose now there will be a great deal of confusion. One deals with the heirs, of course, and with solicitors, which rather delays things." He brightened and signaled to the footman again. When his glass was full, he held it up in salute. "Which rather delays things," he repeated triumphantly, as if it were a toast, and dispatched the drink in one gulp.

The man's speech was becoming blurred, and Charles felt that he should ask the important questions while Warwick was still capable of answering them. "The autopsy surgeon retrieved the fatal bullet," he said. "It was fired from a thirty-two caliber gun."

"Most unfortunate," Lord Warwick said, his face mournful. "Alas, poor Reggie, I knew him." He smiled, pleased with himself. "Shakespeare, you know." His smile faded. "My wife," he added obliquely, "knew him rather better."

"There is a thirty-two caliber gun missing from Lady Warwick's bedroom."

"Daisy's misplaced another gun?" He focused his eyes on Charles with some effort. "Really, she must be spoken to about her carelessness."

"Lady Warwick has misplaced more than one gun?"

"My darling Daisy wife would misplace the crown jewels, Sheridan. She has grand ideas for saving the world, but a perfect want of responsibility. The crown jewels," Warwick repeated. His eyes went to the French doors again. "I s'pose that's ironic," he said with an elephantine sadness. "Do you think that's ironic, Sheridan?"

"Did you know that her gun was gone?"

Warwick shook his head from side to side. "Sorry, old

chap. I'm not helping very much, am I?'' He started to get up and sat back again, abruptly.

''Did you know that a letter was missing from her room?''

''A letter, too? Can't say that I did.'' He stared at Charles with such effort that his eyes almost crossed. ''Darling Daisy's quite careless about things. But don't worry, old chap. It'll turn up. Up schmup,'' he said cheerfully, raising his empty glass. ''Up schlup.''

''One more question,'' Charles said. ''Where were you last night?''

''Las' night?'' Warwick pulled his earlobe. ''Las' night? Let's see, now. Where—?'' He snapped his fingers, suddenly remembering. ''*I'll* tell you where I was las' night, Sheridan!'' he exclaimed gleefully. ''I was drunk las' night, tha's where I was!''

With abrupt suddenness, his head fell to one side and he began to snore.

24

The lad came to the door at night,
  When lovers crown their vows,
And whistled soft and out of sight
  In shadow of the boughs.

"I shall not vex you with my face
  Henceforth, my love, for aye;
So take me in your arms a space
  Before the east is grey.

"When I from hence away am past
  I shall not find a bride,
And you shall be the first and last
  I ever lay beside."

—A. E. HOUSMAN
A Shropshire Lad

Back home at Bishop's Keep, Amelia's responsibilities as lady's maid to Miss Ardleigh (in which, truth be told, she took a great pleasure) were only part of her duties. Since the Bishop's Keep household was small, Amelia helped the parlor maid dust and sweep the main rooms, assisted the butler with the silver, and from time to time laid tea in the servants' hall and helped the little kitchen maid with the washing up.

But here in the grander surroundings of Easton Lodge,

Amelia's duties were confined to serving Miss Ardleigh's
personal needs—sponging and pressing her dresses and ribbons, laying out her undergarments and outer garments, helping her dress, and arranging her hair. These duties, she had
discovered, were light in comparison to those of other lady's
maids, for Miss Ardleigh's wardrobe was not elaborate and
she wore her hair simply. Thus, Amelia found herself with
time on her hands and the freedom to use it as she chose.
As long as she kept to herself and did not interfere with
others' work, she was free to look around the great house,
to be amazed at its size, dazzled by its magnificence, and
dumbfounded at the thought of the price that must be paid
for such grandeur—a sum that seemed to her (who had only
once in her life seen a five-pound note) to be equal to all the
gold in the Exchequer.

Of course, Amelia's freedom of access, like that of most
servants of her time, was severely restricted. She was not
permitted to enter the main wing of the house, so she could
not marvel at the sixteen Siena columns that lined the massive entrance hall, supporting its arched and paneled roof, or
gape at the veritable zoo of Lord Warwick's hunting trophies
that lined its walls and were spread on its floors and displayed in its corners: the heads of antelope and oryx and
sambur and stags, of lions and tigers and panthers; the skins
of zebra and leopard and polar bear; the horns of rhinoceri;
the stuffed bodies of pheasants, even the stuffed head and
shoulders of a magnificent giraffe. (Hunting in East Africa,
Lord Warwick and his friend Colonel Patterson had shot four
giraffes. "A little cold-blooded," he admitted in his memoirs, which Amelia herself would read in after-years, "but
we had had a long chase, and we didn't stop to think that
one trophy apiece of such harmless and beautiful beasts
should have sufficed us.")

If Amelia was not permitted to marvel at Lord Warwick's
trophy hall, neither could she wonder at the grandeur of his
wife's gold and white Louis XIV drawing room, or the library with its wealth of richly bound poetry and classical
literature (shelved together with the cheap paper detective
novels in which Lady Warwick took a passionate interest).
Nor was she allowed to wander, mouth open in awed amaze-

ment, up the broad stone staircase to the state bedrooms, where elaborate beds spread with cashmere coverlets and hung with silk canopies embossed with ancestral arms waited in stiff formality for their Royal occupants.

Amelia could not intrude into these areas of the house because they were reserved to the use of the family and their guests. In these latter Victorian times, for the most part, servants were required to remain behind the green baize doors that separated the domain of the master and mistress from that of the employee. An intricate system of uncarpeted and unlit back stairs and back corridors ensured that hot water and fresh linens could be carried to the bedrooms, dinner could be conveyed to the dining room, and morning and evening trays could be transported to those in need of a little something to wake them or put them to sleep—all quite invisibly, of course.

This separation of the classes and the reduction of the servants to invisibility was sometimes carried to extremes of apartheid. The Duke of Portland regularly sacked any housemaid he encountered in the corridors. Lord Monfred, according to his butler, never spoke to an indoor servant except to give an order, and his maids had to turn and face the wall when a family member or guest approached. In 1888, a writer in the *Fortnightly Review* observed, "Life above stairs is as entirely severed from life below stairs as is the life of one house from another." And while the Countess of Warwick was not inordinately strict about such matters, servants at Easton Lodge were not to be seen; they were, in fact, deemed (and deemed themselves) invisible.

So when Amelia went for a walk, as she did shortly after tea on this Saturday afternoon, it was in the region belowstairs, in the servants' wing of Easton Lodge. For the sake of the servants' efficiency, this first-floor and basement area was divided (as it was in most grand houses) into three distinct regions, each of which was under the command of one of the three upper servants: the male house steward, Buffle; and the female cook, Mrs. Bagshot, and housekeeper, the elderly Mrs. Lynnford. For the sake of the servants' morality, a great concern to late-Victorian employers, these daytime working areas (and the nighttime sleeping attics as well) were carefully segregated by sex, the menservants being confined to one region, the women to another. While their betters might enjoy sexual high jinks in the sumptuous bedrooms of the Folly and the main hall, such pleasures were strictly forbidden to the servants, whose virtue was additionally enforced by morning and evening prayers and by compulsory chapel.

Buffle's region encompassed the plate scullery, the steward's pantry, the strong room, the wine and beer cellars, and the small rooms where the footmen and valets brushed clothes and shoes, cleaned and filled the lamps and trimmed the wicks, and sharpened knives. Although Lawrence did a great deal of lounging about in the steward's room and Amelia would have loved to join him there, she could not enter this male zone, nor would she have felt comfortable there. Amelia's mother may have taken in washing to supplement her husband's weekly ten shillings, but she had raised her daughter to know the difference between a man's place and a woman's.

The housekeeper's domain included Mrs. Lynnford's own comfortable parlor (also used as an office, to conduct the purchase of supplies), the stillroom, the servants' hall, and a separate storeroom filled with cleaning provisions and equipment and lined with china cupboards and linen presses. Amelia had felt emboldened to peek into these and was then so impressed by the magnificence of the contents that she shut them up speedily, lest she inadvertently soil or break something. Mrs. Lynnford was also responsible for the preparation of tea, and used the stillroom for this purpose. Amelia was familiar with this room, since it was there that she prepared the night and morning tea trays she carried to Miss Ardleigh's bedroom. When she was free, she occasionally dropped in to see whether a biscuit had been left lying about, or a small cake. She was usually disappointed, however, for the estimable Mrs. Lynnford was a careful woman and wise in the ways of servants, and locked up the tea provisions between times.

The cook, Mrs. Bagshot, ruled over the kitchen, sculleries, the game larder, fish larder, pantry, ice and coal rooms, and (since much game was taken on the estate and had to be cleaned and prepared for eating) a separate building for salting and smoking. She also had her own spacious parlor, where she kept the kitchen's accounts and met with the tradesmen who supplied her small kingdom. Mrs. Bagshot was justifiably proud of her kitchen, which was equipped with the latest innovations in roasting ranges, stewing stoves, boiling stoves, turnspits, hot plates, and hot closets, but she was also a kind soul who was rather pleased than otherwise at Amelia's goggle-eyed wonderment at these technological miracles. (They were not that miraculous, since each stove consumed almost three hundred pounds of very real coal each week, which had to be carried in by the sculleries, mostly young girls, and returned one tenth that weight in ash, which the sculleries had then to carry out.) The kindly Mrs. Bagshot had invited Amelia to sit on a stool in the corner and observe the hurly-burly of food preparation.

In most grand houses, the laundry was a fourth belowstairs domain, ruled over by the laundress (whose stature was almost but not quite as high as the other three Uppers) and set somewhat apart. This segregation was owing both to the history and to the nature of the laundering process. In previous decades, when the household was much smaller, Easton's laundry had been sent out to a laundress in Little Easton; when, for the sake of greater efficiency, a laundry was installed, the laundress was more independent than the other servants. Further, laundering produced a great deal of steam and smell and had to be adjacent to a drying-ground. The laundry, then, was usually located on the outskirts of the main servants' area, readily accessible to the gardeners, grooms, coachmen, and footmen. The strict segregation of the sexes which took place in the other household regions was therefore difficult to maintain. If the servants played hanky-panky tricks, it was in the laundry that the games typically took place.

Amelia enjoyed her tour of the kitchen, but she could expect no such invitation into the laundry. It was the dominion of Winnie Wospottle, Lawrence's old lover and Amelia's avowed enemy. But Amelia's bedmate Meg worked there, and since on this Saturday afternoon, Mrs. Wospottle was still at tea with the other upper servants in Mrs. Lynnford's parlor, Amelia went to talk to Meg. The last time she had seen her new friend was in the corridor outside the servants' hall after lunch, where Amelia had overheard the argument between Meg and her footman-lover Marsh, Marsh urgent for the two of them to go off together somewhere, Meg reluctant to leave on account of her sick father. Remembering Meg's distress, and wondering where in the world the two could possibly be going, Amelia was anxious to talk with her. She could not give away the fact that she and Lawrence had overheard the quarrel, though. Meg might think they had been spying.

In fact, as Amelia came around the corner of the corridor and made to enter the main laundry room, she was nearly bowled over by Marsh, who was on his way out of the laundry room door, his eyes slitted, his face pulled together in a frown that was even darker than usual. She flattened herself against the wall as he brushed past, wondering what had made him so furious.

The laundry was a large, windowless room with a low ceiling, plaster walls, and stone floors. Buckets, washboilers, and scrub boards were neatly stacked in the corners, and the whitewashed walls were lined with wooden and stone sinks, drying racks, and shelves for laundry supplies: bars of soap (to be shaved into the hot water), bluing, and starch. In the middle of the floor stood several wooden hand-turned washing machines, with wooden wringers attached. But while two other laundry maids were up to their elbows in hot water at the sinks, there was no Meg.

With a little hesitation, Amelia went into the adjacent ironing room, where she found her friend at work at a wooden ironing table, ironing sheets. The iron Meg was using was a heavy affair weighing at least eight pounds, which had been heated on a stove in one corner on which sat two other irons, similarly heating. Owing to that stove and a large coal-fired hot-water boiler in another corner, the room was very hot.

Meg looked up from her work, her eyes red-rimmed and puffy. She bit her lip. "H'lo, Amelia," she said in a low voice.

"Y've been cryin'," Amelia said. "Was it Marsh?"

"Ye better not stay," Meg said, setting her iron on the stove to heat. "Mrs. Wospottle doan't like ye."

"Winnie Wospottle is 'avin' 'er tea in Mrs. Lynnford's parlor wi' th' rest o' th' Uppers," Amelia said. She frowned. "Is't Marsh yer cryin' fer? I saw 'im leave. Nearly knocked me down, 'e did."

Meg shook her head dumbly, then nodded, then shook it again and burst into tears. Without another word, Amelia gathered her friend into her arms, and the two young women stood in a mutual embrace. After a minute, Amelia fished in the pocket of her apron for a handkerchief.

"Remember wot ye said t' me?" she said, drying the tears from Meg's cheeks. "Wotever 'tis, 'tain't bad 'nough t' carry on so." She paused. "An' d'ye remember wot else ye said? Ye ought t' do wot th' upstairs ladies do an' 'ave lots o' men, so when ye fall out wi' one, there's another one waitin'." She smiled. "*That's* wot ye said."

But this small comfort produced only fresh weeping. Amelia stroked Meg's curly brown hair, and when she was calmer, led her to a scrubbed pine table stacked with embroidered and lace-edged linens, all carefully ironed, and sat her down on the bench.

"Now, tell," she commanded.

Meg wiped her nose on her rough cotton sleeve and shook her head. "I daren't," she whispered.

"It'll make ye feel better," Amelia said. She touched Meg's cheek. "Truly 'twill."

Meg sighed heavily. " 'E's leavin', Marsh is."

"Ooh, Meggie, that's too bad," Amelia said sympathetically. And although she already knew the answer, she added, "Are ye goin' wi' 'im?"

Meg shook her head sadly. "I've got t' look after my dad. He ain't well."

"Where's Marsh goin'?"

"T' Lunnon." Meg gulped at the thought. "An' after that, Paris, 'e says."

"Paris?" Amelia asked, as surprised as if Meg had announced that her lover was flying off to the moon.

Meg nodded. She leaned forward, lowering her voice to a whisper. " 'E's a Anarchist, ye see."

"Wot's a An . . . Anarchist?" Amelia asked.

"E's somebody 'oo wants t' change things, t' make it so that people like us 'as somethin', 'stead o' nothin'." Her face shone with pride. "But ye can't tell nobody, Amelia. T' most folks, a Anarchist's a very bad thing."

"Why?"

"Marsh says it's 'cause th' rich are afeared," Meg replied. "They'd 'ave t' give up wot they got t' th' pore people."

Amelia thought that many people might indeed be afraid—the people upstairs, for instance. She wondered whether, if Marsh and the Anarchists achieved their goals, the Queen might be forced to give up her throne. If she did, would some poor man get it instead of the Prince, or would there be no king at all, as in America, where the people ruled themselves? It was an idea at once terribly frightening and deeply exciting. She gave up that line of thought and turned to another.

" 'F I was ye, Meggie, 'an I loved a man," she said stoutly, thinking of Lawrence, "I'd go wi' 'im, dad er no dad. Ye only love onct an' that's a fac'."

Meg hung her head, and the tears began again to trickle down her cheeks. " 'E's changed 'is mind," she said sadly. " 'E doan't want me t' go after all." She blew her nose on a scrap of cotton. "An' 'f I go, I'll niver git t' come back."

"Why not?" Amelia asked, taking her hand. "Yer not a slave, Meggie. Nobody kin tell ye wot t' do. Why can't ye go away an' come back agin?"

Meg's expression was so totally despairing that Amelia's soft heart was wrung. " 'Cause," she said hopelessly, "I stole somethin'. Marsh tol' me t' do't, an' I did."

Having been in service since she was thirteen, Amelia was not shocked at this revelation. Every servant in her acquaintance had taken something from his or her employer at one time or another, and some repeated their thieving on a regular basis. The stolen item might be as trivial as coffee or tea or a pillowcase, or something more substantial—a piece of plate, sometimes even a piece of jewelry. She frowned, thinking of the magnificent jewelry that must be lying in the bedrooms upstairs. The footmen were not supposed to be on those floors, nor the laundry maids, but the back stairs afforded a ready access, and it would be easy enough to slip in and slip out unseen.

"This thing ye took," she said apprehensively, "is it worth a lot of money?"

"Money?" Meg repeated, her pretty brow furrowed. "Well, no. I doan't s'pose it was worth a lot o' money, not like jewels er somethin'."

Amelia smiled, relieved. "Well, then," she said cheerfully, "I can't see as ye've anythin' t' worry over, Meggie. Wotever 'twas ye took can't mean much t' ye. All ye 'ave t' do is put it back."

Meg did not smile. "I can't put it back," she said. Her voice was shaking. Her small hand, in Amelia's, was as cold as December. "Marsh tol' me to, 'cause 'e was afeared, so I tried. But I lost it, an' Marsh says we're in awful trouble." She bit her lip. " 'E says now as 'e doan't *want* me t' go wi' 'im! 'E says it's too dang'rous where 'e's goin', wi' bombs an' all. An' now I'm afeared 'e'll go off t' Lunnon an' take a new luv an' forgit all 'bout me. An' I'll niver see 'im agin!"

And the sobs, which had somewhat abated, returned with greater force than ever, leaving Amelia feeling utterly helpless in the face of Meg's tumultuous grief.

25

Things in contingency are never more than probable.

—WILLIAM WENTWORTH, 1635

So many strange contingencies are improbable in the highest degree.

—CHARLES DARWIN, 1859

For Charles, the evening dragged dismally. His teatime conversations had left him with the realization that the criminal or criminals were hidden in a forest of mysterious motives and purposes and would not be easily flushed out. Worse, he had reason to fear that there might be more murder before the weekend was over. Why else had the killer retained the weapon, instead of leaving it as one more incriminating piece of evidence at the death scene? Because Charles could not be sure of the target, it was difficult to know when to act and what to do.

But Charles was nothing if not determined. He soldiered on. There was the usual formal dinner to be got through (he was seated at the far end of the table, much too far away from Kate, stunning in a sea-green gown that set off her russet hair and emphasized the curve of her breasts, the imagination of which made Charles grow uncomfortably warm). Dinner was followed by the usual withdrawal of the ladies so that the men could enjoy their port, cigars, and conversation, during which gathering the group kept assiduously from the subject of murder and offered Charles nothing to feed any of his several theories about the crimes.

Having adjourned, the men joined the ladies in the drawing room, where the Prince, with a great deal of hyperbole, introduced Charles as the "scientific detective extraordinaire" who was well on the way to solving "poor Reggie's dreadful murder"—a vast overstatement, in Charles's estimation, of both his qualifications and his current accomplishments.

Charles spoke for thirty minutes on the subject of scientific methods of crime detection. He was keenly interested in the subject and usually enjoyed extempore speaking. But tonight he found himself weary from the afternoon of interviews and disheartened by the thought that he had still more suspects to question. He also felt that he had to carefully guard his remarks, out of concern that the perpetrator might be in the audience. For this reason he avoided the subject of hair and fiber evidence and fingerprints, which, while novel and not yet accepted, even by Scotland Yard, promised to be the most reliable means of individual identification ever devised. He conjectured that if another crime were planned, the criminal, hearing of these forensic techniques, might take precautions against leaving such traces. For the most part, he talked about recent advances in toxicology, reminding his audience of the 1882 trial of George Henry Lamson, when Dr. Thomas Stevenson's testimony on poisonous alkaloids helped to convict the defendant of murder, and the more recent and notorious American trial of a man suspected of poisoning his wife with morphine. He also talked about Professor Lacassagne's recent work on the identification of bullets, and about the methods of tying a fatal bullet to a particular weapon. But he was depressed by the thought that not even the identification of the deadly weapon would unravel the two murders the Prince had commissioned him to solve. The attribution of the bullet to the weapon that fired it could not prove whose finger had pulled the trigger. And since he tended to discount Lady Warwick as a prime suspect, feeling that she herself was one of the criminal's targets, identification of the gun (should it indeed prove to be hers) would lead nowhere. Nor was there any other physical evidence that could be scientifically manipulated to yield the identity of the killer. The guilty person would have to be discovered by some other means, and Charles, scientist that he was, found this realization discouraging. As a consequence, his talk was less lively than usual. Indeed, he thought, it was tepid and rather boring.

But when he finished speaking and sat down, he was surprised at the robust round of applause he received. He was even more surprised when the Prince approached him, trailed by Sir Friedrich and Milford Knightly, each of whom, in turn, shook his hand and congratulated him on a sterling presentation.

"Extraordinary lecture, Charles," the Prince said heartily. "A most fascinating topic, first-rate, really. You make all this detecting business sound jolly good sport."

"Indeed," said Sir Friedrich, with the first enthusiasm Charles had seen him display. "It's a wonder that any criminal quarry escapes, with such miracle hounds in hot pursuit."

"A splendid stalk you've described," Milford Knightly said admiringly. "Good show, Sheridan."

"Thank you." Charles felt his answer to be feeble, but it was difficult to respond intelligently to men who believed that the pursuit of a murderer was jolly good sport.

The Prince stroked his beard, his large eyes gleaming. "I must say, you've given me something to think about. I never imagined that there could be so many fascinating ways to bring criminals to earth. Tell me more, why don't you, about this business of comparing bullets. How is it actually done?"

Charles repeated part of what he had said earlier, and added, "What is needed, of course, is greater analytic precision. Bullets could be compared using two microscopes side by side, and superimposing the images by means of prisms or mirrors. Microphotographs could then be taken which would clearly demonstrate a match."

"What a novel idea!" exclaimed the Prince. "Why don't you assemble such an apparatus? Surely every police department in the nation would find it extraordinarily useful."

"I fear not, sir. The expense of the equipment and the cost of the skilled operator would be difficult for most police districts to justify. In London, it might be used frequently, but in a smaller town perhaps only once in a decade. The only solution, I think, is to develop a centralized forensic laboratory to which police departments throughout the country could submit evidence.''

The Prince snapped the Royal fingers. "Exactly my thought!" he exclaimed energetically. "And who better to head up such an effort than you, Sheridan? I'll mention it to the Home Secretary next week and see whether funds can be found to support it."

Milford Knightly was frowning. "But what about Scotland Yard, Bertie? Isn't that what they're supposed to be doing?"

"Scotland Yard," the Prince said contemptuously, "is mired in metropolitan politics and graft. Look at their performance on the Ripper business, for instance. All sorts of announcements and schemes, and never a solution." He shook his head, warming to his subject. "No, what's needed is an independent laboratory with the most modern equipment. One that is completely separate from any of the police districts. One that can't be manipulated by special interests."

Charles felt himself dejected again, remembering the story he had heard from a certain Inspector Abberline not long before: that the Prince himself had suppressed Scotland Yard's investigation of the Ripper killings because it had come too close to the Palace. To Crown Prince Eddy, and to the Prince's friend Randolph Churchill, whom Abberline claimed had masterminded the killings. Charles doubted that any crime laboratory could be completely autonomous or independent, or that the Palace would not use such an instrument to its advantage whenever necessary. And as for the idea that he might be in charge—well, that was out of the question, given his brother's illness and his approaching marriage. Still, it was not a good idea to argue with the Prince, especially when he needed the Royal cooperation on the matter at hand.

"Agreed, Your Highness," he said noncommittally.

"It's this blasted investigation that's getting you down," the Prince said. He clapped Charles on the shoulder. "Come on, old man, chin up! With all that science at your fingertips, I'm sure you'll get a grip on things."

"I fear I already have rather more of a grip than I would like, sir," Charles said ruefully. He glanced at the others. "I wonder if we might have a private word."

"Of course." The Prince turned to Temple and Knightly. "You chaps go along and tell Lady Warwick to shoot off the first Roman candle in fifteen minutes." As soon as they were out of earshot, the Prince turned. "What's all this, Charles? You are abysmally gloomy. You are casting a pall over our revels."

Perhaps the pall was deservedly cast, Charles thought, since they were reveling in the shadow of murder. But he only reported without comment the seach of Wallace's room, the discovery of the Prince's letter, and the subsequent conversation with Daisy. As he spoke, the Prince turned grave. As Charles might have predicted, his first concern was for the letter.

"My letter," he said shortly. "You have it?"

Charles nodded. "I am keeping it safe, sir. I will return it to you shortly."

"Not to me," the Prince said, turning down his mouth. "The letter belongs to the lady to whom it was sent—although I do think she must learn to be less careless with her possessions." There was a guttural annoyance in his voice and his face had gone hard. "First her handkerchief, then her letter. Who knows what the devil she will lose next?" Charles was about to tell him about the missing pistol when he added, "I have already assured you that Daisy could not have been involved in this crime because she was with me. I take it you have discovered nothing that would contradict my statement."

Charles agreed gravely that he had learned nothing to the contrary. "Your corroboration aside," he said, "I believe it is highly improbable that Lady Warwick is guilty. As she herself pointed out, if she had shot Wallace, she would have removed her note from his person and then gone immediately to his room to retrieve the letter. What's more, both the note and the letter were far too easy to discover. I believe that someone intended them to be found, and through their discovery, meant to implicate her." He paused. "I have begun to wonder if the crime itself was not committed in order that she might be accused. In fact, I can think of only one logical objection to that theory.''

The Prince was incredulous. "You're saying that Wallace was murdered solely to cast blame on Daisy?"

"I am suggesting the possibility," Charles said. "The pistol you gave the Countess—which is of the same caliber as the murder weapon—is missing from her room. If it were found and confirmed as the fatal gun, a jury might be persuaded to convict her."

The Prince's heavy face took on a bullish expression. "You can leave off worrying about a jury. Why, even if she were exonerated, the scandal would be titanic. It would swamp the monarchy and destroy the Warwicks. I cannot allow that to happen!" He narrowed his eyes. "Whom do you suspect?" When Charles hesitated, he added angrily, "Come, man, out with it! You must have suspects! You've been at this at least eight hours. What have you been doing? Twiddling your thumbs?"

Charles sighed. The Prince was accustomed to getting what he wanted with a snap of his fingers. He could hardly be blamed for his impatience, or for his failure to understand the tedious, time-consuming work of investigation. "I have seriously considered Lady Metcalf, Sir Thomas Cobb, and Lord Warwick. The first two appear to have a motive for killing Wallace, but for various reasons I have discounted them as improbable. I plan to interview several others, also, although they have solid alibis for the entire night, and I doubt that anything will be learned from questioning them."

"And you think that Lord Warwick would scheme to send his wife to the dock?" the Prince asked sarcastically. "Don't be absurd, Sheridan! Brooke, as much as I, would want the entire matter hushed up."

"If you will excuse me, sir," Charles said evenly, "I believe that Lord Warwick could be confident that the matter *would* be hushed up. He, better than anyone, would know that Your Highness would never permit Lady Warwick to be charged with murder. He might also entertain the hope that, should you be called upon to champion his wife to that perilous extent, you might feel compelled to end your relationship with her."

The Prince stared at him, comprehension dawning on his face. "By Jove, Sheridan," he whispered after a moment, "I believe you've got it right! Warwick is a fine fellow, one of the best, but he's not altogether tolerant. I hate to say so about a gentleman of his exemplary breeding, but he can be damned difficult when he sets his mind to it. If you don't believe me, ask Daisy. Poor girl, she's borne the brunt of his displeasure."

Charles did not speak the thought that came immediately to his mind: that some would consider Lord Warwick justified in being "difficult" about the Prince's cavalier appropriation of his wife.

"I am not arguing that Lord Warwick is guilty," he said, "I am only raising the possibility. In any event, it is not my most pressing concern at the moment. It is the missing pistol that I am most worried about."

"The pistol? The one I gave Daisy?"

"Yes. It is quite likely to be the murder weapon. As I said a moment ago, I can think of at least one objection to the theory that the murder was part of a plot to implicate her ladyship, and that is the fact that the gun was not discovered at the crime scene."

"I see," said the Prince thoughtfully. "If the killer had wanted it to appear that Daisy had shot Wallace, he would have used her gun and left it beside the body, as if she had carelessly dropped it. The nail in her coffin, as it were."

"As it were," Charles agreed dryly. "The absence of the gun suggests two possibilities. First, that someone else—not the murderer—picked up the gun before Miss Ardleigh and Sir Friedrich discovered Wallace's body. Second, that it was retained with the intention of—"

"Of using it again!" the Prince exclaimed. He clasped his hands behind his back and began to pace back and forth.

"Yes," Charles said soberly.

"You think someone might try to kill me?"

"I am considering the possibility of a conspiracy, and in that theory, there are two possible targets: Your Highness and Lady Warwick."

"Daisy?" The Prince was startled. "But why?"

"May I speak frankly, sir?" Charles asked. He did not

fear the Prince's wrath, but he had to have his confidence.

"Assuredly," the Prince said.

"Lady Warwick holds what most believe to be aberrant political views, Your Highness, and there are many among the aristocracy who have a deathly fear of Socialism. It is widely suspected that, as your intimate, this untrustworthy woman is the recipient of political secrets."

The Prince had been frequently charged, in the press and elsewhere, with irresponsible pillow talk, to the extent that the Queen had refused him access to the Red Boxes in which she received State documents and had forbidden all of her ministers to discuss sensitive political matters with him. "What's more," Charles added, "you did visit a workhouse this morning, at her insistence. Some might see that as a clear indication that she has already seduced you to her side of the ideological fence, so to speak."

The Prince stopped in mid-stride. "Assassination of the Heir Apparent for showing an interest in his less privileged subjects? This is not the first time I have viewed such terrible situations, you know. A decade or so ago, I went dressed as a workingman about the East End with Charles Carrington, having a look at slum conditions."

"As you say, sir," Charles replied, "you went incognito, with the knowledge only of those who supported your efforts. This morning's trip is an entirely different matter, given Lady Warwick's political leanings."

He shook his head. "Your idea still seems extreme. Entirely irrational."

"Extreme, yes, impossible, no. And conspiracies usually spring from an irrational conception. I think we must make provision for every contingency, however improbable it might appear. Would you not agree, sir?"

"Oh, I suppose. What do you propose?"

"To arrange for your security," Charles replied. "You are admirably proficient with the shotgun, a weapon which is highly effective for self-defense at close range. And if memory serves, the Countess shoots reasonably straight."

The Prince stopped pacing and straightened his shoulders. "Defend myself? By Jove, I most certainly could!" He frowned at Charles. "I don't suppose you're suggesting that

Daisy and I spend the night guarding each other, after all you've said about our connection.''

Charles shook his head. "What I propose is that each of you withdraw a shotgun from the gun room, retire to your individual quarters with a trusted individual, and lock the door and windows. As your guard, I suggest your personal valet. Only one of you need remain awake. If anyone attempts to force an entry, you will have sufficient time to respond.''

"And who do you propose to assign to her ladyship?'' The Prince pushed out his Hanoverian lip. "If you're going to suggest Sir Friedrich, I shall have to object. After what I heard about his brash approach to Lillian last night, I hardly think he would be a good choice. And it won't be Lord Warwick, either. In my mind, he is still the prime suspect.'' He pulled his brows together. "In fact, I daresay he is far more likely to have killed Wallace than some irrational Anarchist.''

"I shouldn't think, sir,'' Charles said wearily, "that this is an Anarchist plot. In fact, I was about to suggest that Miss Ardleigh stay with Lady Warwick. She has uncommon courage and can be trusted implicitly, both of which are paramount conditions. She must act not only as Daisy's guard, but her wardress.''

"Of course,'' the Prince said, satisfied. "Miss Ardleigh will provide Daisy with an unimpeachable alibi. But what about Kirk-Smythe? Why can't I have him? Guarding my body is his business.''

"With your permission, sir, Kirk-Smythe will work with me. We will serve as a roving patrol, a mobile police force, as it were, able to respond instantly should anything untoward occur.''

"Kirk-Smythe is a good man,'' the Prince agreed, "thoroughly experienced in military maneuvers. But what of yourself, Charles? I shouldn't think this sort of thing is quite up your line. Will you be all right?''

Charles smiled. "I think so. I've been in worse situations.''

"Oh, right. So I have heard.'' The Prince turned to look

toward the doors that opened onto the veranda, where the guests were gathering to observe the fireworks display. "But that was quite some time ago. I had almost forgotten."

"So had I, sir," Charles said. "So had I."

26

I like high life, I like its manners, its splendours, the beings
which move in its enchanted spheres.

—CHARLOTTE BRONTË

Destiny always has a sad side to it. For instance, I who was always longing to be free, have chained my life. I shall never be
alone, never. I shall be surrounded by the etiquette of court,
whose principal victim I shall be.

—EMPRESS EUGÉNIA,
wife of Louis Napoleon of France

The fireworks were a splendid display, arching into the
heavens in extravagant traceries of brightly colored
light. For Kate, the sight awakened a deep nostalgia. She had
grown up with Independence Day fireworks celebrations, and
she had not seen such a presentation since she left New York
almost two years before. So much had happened since then—
her inheritance of Bishop's Keep, the publication of more
and more of Beryl Bardwell's work, and soon her marriage
to a man she deeply loved and respected. She couldn't help
feeling like the char girl in the fairy tale who woke up one
day to discover herself transformed into a beautiful princess, able to do and have anything she chose. As she held
Charles's hand and murmured with the others at the golden
showers of sparks, she felt giddy with wondering delight.
But when Charles told her what he had learned during his

teatime conversations and confided the plan for the evening to her, she sobered quickly enough.

"There may be some danger," Charles said in a low voice, under the sound of the explosions that rattled the windows and shook the furniture. "But Daisy needs to be watched, and you're the only person I can trust. Kirk-Smythe and I will be nearby, in case you need us. Will you do it?"

"Of course," Kate said, and was rewarded by a swift kiss and a lingering touch. "But *what* do I do?"

"Just use your head," Charles said. He squeezed her hand and was gone.

When the fireworks were over, Lady Warwick proposed dancing, but the Prince replied with a massive yawn that it had been an exceedingly long day and he for one was too tired even to play bridge. His Highness having put an end to the evening, the others had perforce to agree. Although it was only a little after eleven, the company gathered their candles at the foot of the main staircase and trooped dutifully off to bed, or to whatever other pleasures they had arranged for themselves.

Kate waited a few minutes to be sure that the hallway was clear, then took her candle and went to Daisy's room, where she found her and her lady's maid in the midst of preparing for bed. A shotgun was leaning incongruously against a chest of drawers, on top of which was displayed a lavish bouquet of hothouse gladiolas and fern.

"I've never held one of those," Kate said, glancing at the gun, "but I suppose you know how to use it."

"Oh, quite," Daisy said, as the maid finished brushing her hair. She dismissed her with a gesture and turned back to Kate. "There's a tea tray on that table, Kate. Do help yourself."

"Thank you," Kate said, poured a cup of tea, and put several small cakes on a plate. She saw that the bed had been turned down, revealing lavish lace-edged silken sheets. On a bedside table was a bowl of heavily scented roses. The yellow damask draperies were pulled shut and a bright fire burned in the grate. The only sounds were the hissing of the gas lamps on the wall, which shed a golden glow over the room, and the ticking of an elaborate gold clock on the writing table, with the curious inscription, "I have had my hour."

Wearing a gold satin dressing gown, Daisy pulled a yellow velvet chair closer to the fire and sat down. "I'm dreadfully sorry that you must sacrifice a night's sleep just to keep a watch over me. But I must confess to wanting to talk with you in private. Charles has told me that—" She stopped, as if she weren't sure how much she should say.

If Charles hadn't already told her, he soon would, Kate thought. She sat down in the opposite chair and put her cup and plate on the small carved table beside it.

"Charles has asked me to marry him," she said, "and I have said yes. Neither of us want an elaborate wedding, and his family is rather distracted just now with the illness of his brother. We hope to be married quickly, without fuss, in the local parish church."

"Oh, my dear!" Daisy exclaimed, and clapped her hands. "I am delighted for both of you! Charles has always seemed to me to be a rare man, and you—" She put her head on one side, her gaze thoughtful. "Jenny Churchill is the only American woman I have known intimately. You are rather like her, you know."

"But Lady Churchill comes from a wealthy family," Kate protested. "I am an orphan, and Irish, and the aunt and uncle who raised me—he is a policeman in New York City—were very poor. I grew up in a family of six children, and had to make my own way in the world. I worked as a governess and . . ." She stopped herself before she mentioned Beryl Bardwell. "And have done other things," she finished lamely. "I don't see how Lady Churchill and I can be compared."

"That may be," Daisy said, "but you and Jenny are both beautiful. Even more, you are both extraordinarily spirited and independent. I have always admired women who assert their freedom to do as they choose, no matter who says otherwise." Regret flickered in her eyes. "That is a sort of freedom I have never enjoyed."

Kate, who had been about to protest the idea that she was beautiful (her face was better described, she thought, as "strong-featured"), now found herself protesting the idea that Daisy was confined by anything.

"But how can you say that you're not free?" she asked in amazement. "You, of all women—"

"Because I am the mistress of the Prince of Wales?" Daisy's laugh was gently mocking. "Do you think I *chose* that distinction?"

"Well, yes, I suppose I did," Kate admitted. "Didn't you?"

Daisy pulled her dressing gown closer around her, her face half in firelight, half in shadow. "I admit to a certain scheming for Royal attention," she said slowly, "but at the time, it was Bertie's help I needed, not his romantic attentions. I was involved in a rather messy disagreement with Lady Beresford over a letter I had written to her husband, and Bertie was the only one who could intervene to save me from scandal." She looked pained at the recollection. "But that's beside the point. The truth is that once His Royal Highness has decided he wants a particular woman, it is utterly impossible for her to refuse him, however *she* may feel."

"Oh," Kate said, suddenly seeing through the romantic veil she and Beryl Bardwell had thrown over the affair.

"And once he has preferred a woman," Daisy went on, "she is his alone—except, of course, that her husband may also enjoy her. But in many ways, the Prince is like a spoiled child, extraordinarily demanding of time and attention and fearful of spending an evening without some amusement. If there is a gap of even one hour in his engagement book, he looks at it with a sinking heart." Her sigh held a bitter irony. "I should have had a great deal more freedom if His Highness had preferred someone else."

"You don't love him, then?" Kate asked. "Pardon me if the question is presumptuous," she added hurriedly, but Daisy did not seem to mind.

"I am rather fond of him," Daisy said, "and he is foolishly affectionate toward me. He is infatuated, I suppose, which is not at all the same thing as love." She waved her hand as if she were dismissing the idea. "It is so hard to say what love is, don't you find?"

"Well . . ." Kate said. For her, love was an emotion not

easily confused with any other. But perhaps that was because she had loved only one man in her life—Charles. What's more, she had naively imagined that Daisy and the Prince must love one another deeply and romantically, else why take so many risks? Why engage in an affair, if not for love? Was it simply for the sake of passion? Or was one partner using the other for his—or her—own ends? Why indeed? The question required a great deal more thought.

"It is not just the time and the attention the Prince requires that makes my life difficult." Daisy shifted in her chair, her pretty mouth tightening. "It is the extraordinary expenditure of money. To be painfully honest, Kate, the expense of entertaining Royalty is beyond imagination. The weekend's entertainment—I could have fed all the poor in the workhouse for six months with what I've spent. And every time Bertie comes to visit, as he does quite often, his rooms must be redecorated and new entertainments prepared."

"It must be quite costly," Kate murmured, thinking that the price of a princely lover was much higher than she had imagined.

Daisy continued, almost as if she were talking to herself. "Brooke and I have already spent the whole of next year's income, and we owe almost seventy-five thousand pounds, with little expectation of repaying. Reggie held one of my notes," she added reflectively. "Perhaps, now that he is dead, I shan't have to pay it. If that is true, Brooke will be very relieved. He is so anxious about money these days. If he could find some way to put an end to our dreadful expenditures, I'm sure he would seize it."

Kate hoped that Daisy realized that she had not solicited this confidence about the Warwicks' financial situation and would not come to regret speaking so openly. But everything Daisy said, especially her admission of the Warwicks' extraordinary debt, pointed to Lord Warwick's guilt. What if he had killed Wallace and implicated his wife in order to convince the Prince to find another mistress? Of course, the money Daisy owed Wallace would have provided an additional motive. Kate made a mental note to tell Charles what she had learned.

There was a long silence, broken only by the loud ticking of the clock on the writing table. After a time, Daisy spoke again. "Another great difficulty," she said sadly, "is that having been preferred by Bertie, I find myself cut off from all other friends. There is no one to whom I may speak, no one whom I trust enough to unburden myself." There was an unutterable sadness on her face. "Not even my poor husband, who long ago lost all love for me. Not that I blame him, of course. The Warwicks are a conservative family. They have been much embarrassed by the notoriety that attends my situation."

Kate, hardly knowing what to say, remarked, "I suppose many of your friends are jealous."

Daisy nodded. "They're convinced that I have power, and they're continually begging me to obtain Royal favors for them. Felicia Metcalf, for instance, wants a knighthood for her ne'er-do-well brother. She was furious with me when I told her yesterday that Bertie wouldn't even consider passing his name to the Queen."

Kate was listening attentively. Lady Metcalf had certainly been angry enough to kill Wallace for his imagined perfidy. Had she been furious enough at Daisy to attempt to make her look a murderess? Struck by the double motive, Kate decided it, too, was worth mentioning to Charles.

Now that she had someone to talk to, Daisy did not seem to want to stop. "But the loss of friends and companionship isn't even the worst of it," she said passionately. "There are so many things I wish to do and cannot. You saw my little needlework school, and you have heard me speak of the need to change the Poor Laws and encourage education and clean up the London slums. There are some things I am free to do, of course, but I must limit these activities, for everything I do reflects on the Prince."

"Like this morning's expedition," Kate said quietly.

"Exactly. It was hazardous to take the Prince to the workhouse. There are those at Buckingham Palace, friends of the Queen, who find Socialist uprisings and Anarchist plots behind every such innocent expedition. This makes it dangerous for Bertie to entertain any view, however inoffensive, that has the slightest tinge of liberalism. And Bertie himself suffers from a great ambivalence. He is perpetually torn between his apprehension of what must be done and his desire to conceal from himself that all is not well with the best of all possible worlds. Those who reveal unpleasant things are not liked the better for it." She shook her head. "So you see that my position—which so many naively envy—even denies me the right to express my political views or lend my weight to causes that cry out for my help."

"I do see," Kate said sympathetically, feeling that the last few moments' conversation had altered forever her view of rank and privilege. "But surely you can look forward to a change, can you not? I mean—" She stopped, not quite sure what she meant.

Daisy's dark blue eyes were amused. "If you are asking whether I will be Bertie's mistress forever, the answer is no. I think, in fact, that my hour is about to come to an end. Until now, deserved or not, Bertie has bestowed utter confidence upon his 'adored little Daisy wife.' But when he learns that others have seen his letter—that silly, indiscreet 'Darling Daisy' letter—he will be frightfully embarrassed and angry."

"Not angry at you, surely."

"He will not express his indignation openly," Daisy said. "But it will change things between us. I will be a woman who has put him into a difficult position, and he cannot tolerate that."

"Then you shall be free."

"Ah, yes," Daisy sighed. "Like others of his 'virgin band,' my hour shall be ended, and I shall be released from the Royal demands." She was silent for a long moment, while the clock ticked and the fire crackled. When she spoke again, her voice was quietly desperate. "I shall be free, yes. But whatever else I achieve in my life, I will never be other than the once and former mistress of the Prince."

"But that's not true!" Kate exclaimed. "There's your school, your political interests, your social concerns!"

Daisy shook her head. "I will not be taken seriously. Look at my predecessors—Lillie Langtry, for instance, whose achievements as an actress are quite overlooked. All that is said of her was that she was once an intimate of the Prince, and that it was his influence that ensured her success.''

Kate leaned forward urgently. ''I am sure you can find ways to make your message heard. You could run for political office. Or you could write a book. Publishers are constantly looking for new material. If you have ideas, publishers will be glad to give you the opportunity to express them.'' She smiled a little. ''I myself am a writer, albeit of fictions. I know.''

Daisy gave her an odd look. ''You?''

Kate nodded reluctantly, wishing she had not brought it up. But Daisy had confided so many secrets, it seemed only fair to share hers. ''I am the author of 'The Duchess's Dilemma,' '' she confessed, ''which you read in *Blackwell's Monthly*. I am Beryl Bardwell.''

''You?'' For a moment, Daisy looked at her, dumbfounded. Then she threw her head back and laughed. ''Of course! I should have guessed! You watch us so closely and you see us all so clearly. What a remarkable gift!''

''I fear I have used it badly,'' Kate said ruefully. ''Believe me, I shall make a much greater effort from now on to disguise the characters I borrow from life.'' She paused. ''I wonder whether Lady Rochdale ever received an answer to her telegram.''

''I doubt that she ever sent it,'' Daisy said. She shook her head. ''You have a fine talent, Kate, but I could never write like you. Your stories—''

''My stories are simple stories of the dark side of human emotion,'' Kate said. ''You have a *cause* to speak for, Daisy. You may not see your opportunities now, perhaps, but over the next few years, I am sure you will. You have courage, and that's what's required.''

Daisy sighed and shook her head. ''You make it sound so easy, Kate. *You* are the one with the courage.''

''I don't know about courage,'' Kate said. ''It was really quite simple. I was very poor. I had nothing to risk, nothing to lose, and everything to gain.''

''I have nothing to lose, either,'' Daisy said. ''And I suppose that's what gives one courage.''

27

So 'ere's to you, Fuzzy-Wuzzy, at your 'ome in the Soudan;
You're a pore benighted 'eathen but a first-class fightin' man;
We sloshed you with Martinis, an' it wasn't 'ardly fair;
An' for all the odds agin' you, you broke a British square.

—After RUDYARD KIPLING
"Fuzzy-Wuzzy"

After everyone else had gone to bed, Charles and Andrew Kirk-Smythe repaired to the gun room, where Kirk-Smythe augmented the derringer in his boot with a double-barreled shotgun from the rack. Charles selected a Webley revolver and a box of .476 cartridges. He released the catch at the rear of the frame and rotated the barrel downward, exposing the rear of the cylinder and the star extractor. Deftly, he slipped six bullets into the empty chambers, snapped the action shut, and put the cartridge box in his pocket. Then they separated, Kirk-Smythe going in one direction, Charles in another. For the next five hours, Charles moved stealthily around the great old house, outdoors and in, upstairs and down, listening for whispers or footfalls, watching for signs of movement, keeping a careful eye out for anything unusual or unexpected.

But nothing happened. At four a.m., by prearrangement, he met Kirk-Smythe and they established themselves in chairs in the curtained alcove at the end of the second-floor corridor, lit only by a pale rectangle of window high in the wall at the far end of the hall, where the setting moon cast a silvery gleam. They sat silent for a long time, as the tall, walnut-cased clock at the head of the stairs struck every quarter hour with a jarring metallic clang.

Finally, just before dawn, Charles turned to Kirk-Smythe and said, "It seems as if my apprehensions were unwarranted, Andrew." He felt relieved and foolish at once. It was wise to take precautions, of course, but he might have gone too far.

Kirk-Smythe stretched his long legs out in front of him. His boyish face was tired, his blond hair tousled. "It's very well, sir, if you ask me. I certainly didn't relish a close-quarters, hand-to-hand engagement in one of these corridors. Someone could hear the commotion and pop out of one of those rooms, into the thick of things."

"Right," Charles said, leaning back in the chair and closing his eyes. "This is one time I am glad to have gone off the mark." He opened one eye to find Kirk-Smythe studying him intently. "What is it, Andrew?"

"Sorry, sir," the younger man said, somewhat abashed. He smoothed his small blond mustache. "Didn't mean to stare. But being responsible for His Highness, it's my job to size people up, as the Americans say. I'm not heavily armed so I have to see trouble on the horizon, as it were." He cleared his throat. "Not meaning you, of course. It's just that I can't make you out."

"You can't, eh?" Charles rubbed the back of his neck wearily. "What's there to make out?"

"His Highness's opinion of you, for one thing. His instructions regarding you were quite explicit."

"Oh?"

"Yes, sir. The short of it is, when HRH instructed me to join you for tonight's watch, he placed me under your direct command." Kirk-Smythe was watching him with an earnest, if puzzled, respect. "I must say, sir, His Highness holds you in high regard. If you'll forgive my taking a bit of a liberty, I doubt his esteem was earned with a camera or a magnifying glass. And you aren't regarded as much of a gun. In fact, I don't recall ever hearing of your joining a shoot."

Charles grinned. "You're certainly right there, Andrew. I am not fond of blasting birds out of the sky." He liked the young man, who reminded him of himself a decade or so ago, full of ideals and anxious to get on in the world. He considered for a moment, then added, "I assume that discretion is one of the prerequisites of your position."

"I suppose that's true." Kirk-Smythe's eyes twinkled. "His Highness certainly gives me plenty of practice. The stories I could tell—but I don't, of course. If you're asking whether I can keep a confidence, the answer is yes, sir."

"Well, then." Charles clasped his hands behind his head and relaxed in the chair. "When I was about your age, I was in the Royal Engineers."

"You, sir? I had no idea you were in the military."

Charles nodded. "My brother stood to inherit our father's title and the family estates, and I had to choose a life for myself. I wasn't particularly keen on a military career, but I preferred technical studies, and I wanted a practical education. After Eton I took two years at Woolwich."

"Ah, you're a product of The Shop," Kirk-Smythe said.

Charles smiled. "I enjoyed my technical studies—chemistry, landscape drawing, military surveying—and the French and German have been helpful. Even the mathematics proves useful from time to time. It wasn't a gentleman's education, but it has served my interests well. Since I was in the upper rank of the class, I read engineering in the second year, then went to the School of Engineering at Chatham for two more."

"And after that?"

"I had my pick of postings. I had always wanted to study ancient monuments, so I decided on Egypt. Shortly thereafter I found myself a staff officer in the Sudan, in a God-forsaken desert near Abu Fahr."

Kirk-Smythe's eyes opened wide. "Where the Sudanese broke the square?"

Charles nodded. The square was a standard tactical formation made up of four lines of armed infantry, arranged at right angles to each other, forming a hollow square. At the time of his story, modern rapid-fire breech-loading weapons had made it almost impregnable. Almost.

"I was in command of a small survey team on a map-making mission," Charles said. "We had been out mapping a wadi, when we happened to join up with a foraging expedition which was attached to a regiment bivouacked in the bush nearby. As we neared the camp, we heard the sound of fighting.''

As he spoke, the sights and sounds, so long repressed from his memory, began to come back to him, and he shivered. It was not a story he relished, and he wasn't sure why he had begun. But now that he was into it, he might as well go on.

''We came over the hill to discover that the regiment was under attack by a hoard of Sudanese, a virtual wall of howling humanity, armed with swords and spears and a few modern firearms captured from us.''

''Fuzzies, my commander called them,'' Kirk-Symthe put in. ''He was in the Sudan for a time. He said those heathen had heads like hayricks, the hair sticking out everywhere. But he greatly admired their courage. Played cat and banjo with our forces, he said. Knocked us hollow.''

''They were fighting for Islam,'' Charles said, ''for the same God we believe in, ironically, but whose words are spoken through a different prophet. They had nothing but iron spears and swords, against a foreign invader armed with Martini-Henrys. Yes, they were courageous. They were also first-class fighting men, with nothing to lose.''

Kirk-Smythe gave him a horrified look. ''You're calling *us* a foreign invader? Don't know that I'd quite put it that way, sir. After all, we did defeat them. That says something for the justice of our cause.''

Charles grunted. ''If it had been merely a matter of virtue, our bones would be bleaching somewhere in the Sudan. The question was decided by firepower.'' He gave Kirk-Smythe a sidewise look. ''You've never shot a man, have you, Andrew?''

''No, sir.''

''When you point a gun at a man's head and squeeze the trigger, what he believes and how deeply and why, his values, his desires—all become totally irrelevant. It's a simple matter of mechanics, physics, and biology.'' He settled deeper into his chair. ''Anyway, the regiment had formed into a square and were desperately attempting to hold their own. Captain Blake, who was in command of the foraging expedition, was about to send us down in a diversionary assault when he was struck and killed by a stray bullet—one of our own, most likely. I looked down at the camp and saw that the Sudanese attack had been so savage that the warriors had broken the square, and the troops were engaged in hand-to-hand combat. Something had to be done, so I took command in Blake's place.'' He smiled a little, now, at his own young folly, born of the arrogance of his place in the world, his sense of duty—and the belief that he had nothing to lose. ''We charged down the hill, shrieking at the top of our lungs, and created a diversion that allowed the regiment enough time to regroup and fight off the attack. The next day, our forces routed the Sudanese and established a stronghold at Abu Fahr.''

Kirk-Smythe was shaking his head. ''Hold on a minute. I've heard that tale. But the way it was told to me, it was Captain Blake who led the charge down that hill, knowing that he and his detachment would be slaughtered. He was a hero. He was even awarded a posthumous Victoria Cross.'' He gave Charles a quizzical look. ''He did all that after he was already dead?''

''As far as the world at large is concerned.''

''I don't understand.''

''Of all the men who charged down that hill, I was the only survivor. In the heat of battle, you know, one officer looks rather much like another, and the regimental commander, a Colonel Wentworth, believed at first that Blake had led the assault. Only when they found his body on the hill, and me barely alive at the bottom, did they sort it all out. The next thing I knew, Wentworth was barging around, wanting to make me a bloody hero. He intended to see that I got a promotion and a transfer from the Engineers to his regiment. The damn fool was even starting the paperwork on the Victoria Cross. That's where I drew the line.''

The other was incredulous. ''You refused the V.C.?''

Charles raised his shoulders in a shrug and let them drop. ''After that bloodbath, the V.C. seemed like heroic nonsense. I told Wentworth I didn't want a promotion and that my only real interest was in terminating my military career. Confronted with an uncooperative hero, he substituted a dead one.''

''And you didn't care?''

''It was all the same to me. Blake would have gone down that hill to his death if he hadn't been shot first. So he got the V.C. and I received my discharge.''

''A strange story.'' Kirk-Smythe raised his eyebrows. ''But your valor did not go entirely unrewarded, I should think. Am I to suppose that it had something to do with your eventual knighthood—granted, I believe I heard, for that famous photograph you took of the Queen on her Jubilee?''

''You might,'' Charles said with a small smile. ''The Queen has always been keen where her army is concerned, you know. But still, I was a little surprised when I was summoned to photograph her. I didn't get the whole story until I learned that Wentworth had gone on from Abu Fahr to become the prime minister's aide-de-camp.''

''The Queen is a rare woman,'' Kirk-Smythe said with sentiment. ''God bless her.''

Charles smiled again, reflectively. ''Yes. I suppose it was her way of saying thank you, without having to say why.'' He stretched. ''And now, if you don't mind, I think I'll get some sleep.''

''Good idea, sir. You get a wink or two, and I'll keep watch. The sun will be up in a short while, anyway, and the servants will soon be about.''

A few moments later, Charles was dozing. Studying him, Kirk-Smythe removed a cigar from his coat pocket—not as good as the Prince's cigars, of course, but all he could afford for the time being. He turned it in his fingers regretfully, wishing he could light it. Then he returned to his appraisal of Charles, whose story had answered some of his questions, but raised many others.

An extraordinary man, Kirk-Smythe thought. Really most remarkable.

28

The laundress washes her own smock first.

—*English proverb*

In the third-floor room of the servants' wing where she slept, Winnie Wospottle habitually rose with the sun that streamed through her eastward-facing window and across her narrow bed. Sunday was normally a leisurely day, beginning with staff prayers in the servants' hall, then breakfast with sausages and perhaps even haddock from upstairs and fried apples, followed by the walk across the park to church, after which she and the other upper servants took a half-holiday, Winnie often going to visit her sister Hannah at Little Easton.

It was Hannah, the wife of a cooper, who was responsible for Winnie's leaving Brighton and coming to the Warwicks at Easton Lodge. Hannah, whose cottage was one of the fortunate few with its own well, took in washing in the village. When she learned from a customer that the Lodge laundress had been dismissed (on account of a scandalous affair with an under-gardener), she had written to Winnie and begged her to apply. Winnie had journeyed to Easton, impressed the house steward with her experience, competence, and moral probity, and been granted the post. While she often longed for the gaiety of Brighton and the great gray swell of the Channel, with all of France lying just over the horizon, she was glad to be at Easton, with Hannah so near and the Warwicks quite reasonable of compensation—generous, actually, having given each of the Uppers a quite remarkable five-pound note on Boxing Day. As to moral probity, Winnie had no difficulty assuring Buffle that *her* laundry maids would never be allowed to turn the laundry into a brothel. Where she was concerned, she felt confident that, having once installed herself, she would be free to behave as she liked, more or less. And, more or less, that was the way it had turned out.

Yes, all considered, Sundays were Winnie's favorite day of the week. House-party Sundays were not, however, for all half-holidays were canceled and there was the hot-water boiler to be fired and linens to be washed and dried, even on the Sabbath, the prospect of which did not please her.

Winnie's disposition was not sweetened when she rose from her bed and peered at her image in the small sliver of mirror that hung over her washbasin. Heavy pouches hung under her eyes, relics of the evening's entertainment, and a black temper lurked in her heart. Watching the fireworks display from a corner of the garden last night, she had made one last effort to dislodge Lawrence from the clutches of the grasping young Amelia and had failed. Not even the flirtatious attentions of Lord Rochdale's coachman (a burly, bearded Irishman who wore his hat at a rakish tilt) had eased her frustration.

The sight of her puffy face in the mirror reminded Winnie that she had been supplanted in Lawrence's affections by someone much younger and (truth be told) far prettier than she, and the bitter knowledge caused her to slam her door and sent her stumping heavily down the back stairs.

The hour was still early. The cooks were already at work in the cold and cavernous kitchen, but the corridor that led to the laundry was empty. Winnie noticed, however, that the heavy wooden door that led to the drying-yard was ajar, and she went out of her way to shut it hard, muttering to herself at the infernal carelessness of stableboys and such.

Opening the door to the main laundry, Winnie went in, intending to fire the boiler so that the water would be hot when the laundry maids began the washing. As she entered, she caught the slight but distinct odor of cigar smoke, and scowled. She raised her head and sniffed again.

Yes, cigar smoke, without a doubt, and not the best, at that. A smelly, cheap cigar, such as might be smoked in a stable. Winnie knew cigars, for her father had worked for a Brighton tobacconist and she had early in her life developed a taste for the things—but fine ones, when she could get them. She narrowed her eyes. A cigar meant only one thing: that her laundry had been invaded by some unauthorized person—persons, most likely, male and female. And Winnie, who had by this time wrought herself into a black dudgeon, knew exactly what profligacy had brought them there. Hands on her hips, arms akimbo, she turned to survey the room, hoping to find evidence that would reveal the identities of the guilty parties. When she got her hands on—

That was when she saw him, through the open doorway to the ironing room, which also housed the boiler. Marsh, it was, one of the Easton Lodge footmen. He was seated on a crate at the table in the corner, his head pillowed on one arm on the table, the other dangling. An empty whiskey bottle stood on the table beside him. He was dead drunk.

Winnie checked her angry impulse. She rather liked the black-haired young man, who was the sweetheart of one of her maids and something of a rebel. Since his father died, he had turned surly and resentful, particularly toward Lady Warwick, who had accidentally fired the gun that had injured his father. It was a foolish, even a dangerous attitude and Winnie had told him so, thinking that a word or two from someone who had seen the world might compel the boy to moderate his behavior.

Now that she knew it was Marsh who had made free with her laundry, Winnie was a little less angry. It would be best to let him sleep, at least until breakfast, when a cup of hot coffee would restore him. She went to the boiler, went down on her knees for a vigorous shaking of the grate, then stoked the firebox with coal from the scuttle. When Meg appeared, the girl could carry out the ashtray and bring more coal. The fire blazing merrily, she went out of the room and shut the door on the sleeping Marsh.

Winnie was sorting a mound of soiled towels when Meg came in, settling her cap on her head. Winnie glanced at her, then looked again. Meg's eyes were red and even puffier than Winnie's, and her hair was untidy. She had been weeping.

"I saw Mrs. Lynnford just now," she said in a thin voice.

"She says t' tell ye that th' maids'll use up all th' fresh towels this mornin'. They'll want more."

Winnie pushed the towels aside with a snort. Mrs. Lynnford was an old witch of a woman who thought she was as good as the Queen just because she had her own private parlor.

"Well, Mrs. Lynnford'll just 'ave t' wait 'til these're washed an' dried, won't she?" Winnie growled. "An' 'f th' ol' crow weren't so mean as t' pounds, there'd be a plenty o' towels without 'avin' t' wash on th' Sabbath." She jerked her head toward the closed door. "Yer sweet'eart's i' there, dead t' th' world. I'd see t' 'im, were 'e mine."

"My . . . sweet'eart?" Meg faltered. "But . . . but 'e's gone!"

" 'E's gone, all right," Winnie said. "It's a good thing 'e picked th' laundry t' do 'is drinkin'. I'm not so likely t' git 'im sacked. But ye'd better keep a tighter rein on 'im, my fine girl, er 'e'll lose 'is place sure, an' no character."

Meg was shaking her head. "Drinkin'? Marsh niver touches strong drink."

"It's not touchin' it wot gets a man drunk," Winnie said philosophically, "it's puttin' it down 'is throat. Drunk as a lord 'e be, in the ironin' room."

Meg ran to the ironing room door. Heaping curses on the parsimonious Mrs. Lynnford, Winnie tossed towels into a wicker basket, and turned to sort the sheets. But she was startled by Meg's shriek, and then the sound of hysterical sobbing.

Winnie went to the door. Meg was standing back from the table, her arms wrapped tightly around herself as she swayed back and forth, her eyes riveted on Marsh's unmoving form. Her face was as white as a linen sheet.

"Wot's th' matter wi' yer?" Winnie demanded crossly. "Wot 're ye makin' that noise fer? Ain'tcher ever seen a drunk man?"

" 'E's dead, Mrs. Wospottle," Meg moaned helplessly.

Winnie turned to look. On the scrubbed tabletop beneath Marsh's pillowed head was a puddle of dark blood, nearly dried, which had stained the corner of a scrap of paper on which he had been writing with the stub of a pencil. As

Winnie stepped back, her mouth dropping open in horror, she saw on the floor, where it had fallen from Marsh's dangling fingers, a silver-plated revolver with mother-of-pearl handles.

"Oh, Gawd," she breathed. "Th' pore boy's shot hisself!"

29

Shot? so quick, so clean an ending?
  Oh that was right, lad, that was brave;
Yours was not an ill for mending,
  'Twas best to take it to the grave.

—A. E. HOUSMAN
  "A Shropshire Lad"

Kate received the news of Marsh's suicide from the somber-faced house steward, who had carried the report to Daisy's room on the heels of the maid with the tea tray. Kate, thinking that Buffle's news was something Charles must know immediately, left Daisy and the steward and went in search of him. She found him in his room, stripped to the waist, sluicing his face in his washbasin. He turned, obviously surprised and pleased to see her, and crossed the room in three strides.

"I love you," he said, putting his arms around her. "I love you desperately. When are we going to be married?"

With a thrill of prohibited pleasure, she leaned her cheek against his bare chest. "Immediately after we've told your mother."

He stiffened. "Let's elope and tell her afterward."

"No," she said. She leaned back, looking into his face. "Charles, there has been another death. A footman shot himself in the laundry. He's left some sort of note."

A look of shock, followed by dark anger, crossed Charles's

face. He let go of her. "Wait in the hall while I dress," he commanded brusquely, and Kate obeyed.

There was a crowd of servants gathered around the closed door to the laundry. Kate followed Charles as he shouldered his way through. Inside, she saw a weeping girl sitting on a low stool in the main room, comforted by a buxom woman with red cheeks and tightly furled brown curls peeking out under a white cap. From yesterday's sessions with the servants, Kate recognized Mrs. Wospottle, the laundress. The girl, Kate saw with a start, was Meg, the farrier's daughter, whom she had last seen leaving Wallace's room the afternoon before.

Meg's eyes were swimming with tears. " 'E didn't kill 'isself!" she cried hysterically. She held out her hands, pleading. " 'E didn't kill that man, neither. I swear 'e didn't!"

"What man?" Charles asked.

The laundress gestured toward another door. "There's a note in there, under Marsh's 'ead," she said grimly. "It says m'lady paid 'im t' shoot Lord Wallace."

Kate felt as if she had been struck in the stomach with a closed fist. *Nothing to lose*, Daisy had said. Had she really felt cornered enough to kill?

"Lady Warwick paid a servant to commit murder?" Charles asked with greater calm than Kate would have thought possible.

"No!" wailed the girl. "Leastways, not Marsh!" She began to weep again, wrenching sobs that shook her thin shoulders.

"It's Marsh who's dead, then?" Charles asked Mrs. Wospottle.

"Deader 'n a doornail," the laundress said grimly. She lowered her voice. " 'E was 'er sweet'eart."

"Stay here and find out who discovered the body and when," Charles said to Kate. "I'll have a look in there." He went toward the door.

Kate turned back to Mrs. Wospottle. "Did you find him?"

Mrs. Wospottle's white cap bobbed up and down. "Yes, but I didn't know 'e was dead at first. I thought 'e was drunk.

It wasn't until Meg come that we seen th' note an' th' gun an' made out that 'e shot 'isself. 'E was 'er first luv,'' she added in a low voice, bestowing on Meg another caress. "She's takin' it 'ard."

" 'E *didn't* shoot 'isself!'' wailed Meg. She clasped Kate's hand as if she were being swept into a raging torrent and Kate was her last mooring. " 'E was goin' away to Lunnon to join th' Anarchists. When 'e got a place, 'e was goin' t' send fer me. But they killed 'im first.''

"Th' pore girl's ou o' 'er 'ead wi' grief,'' Mrs. Wospottle said, shaking her head sympathetically. "Marsh drank a 'ole bottle of whiskey an' smoked a cigar afore 'e pulled th' trigger. I s'pose 'e knew there weren't no way out fer 'im. 'E prob'ly reckoned 'e'd get all th' blame fer the gentl'man's death an' wanted t' be sure Lady Warwick got 'er share.'' Her lips tightened and her eyes grew steely. "An' I allus thought th' best o' 'er ladyship. Shows ye 'ow easy they kin fool ye.''

"But 'e didn't do it, I tell ye!'' Meg cried hysterically. "Marsh doan't drink nor 'e doan't smoke. 'E 'ates the filthy stuff. 'E doan't write, neither.''

Kate stared at her, perplexed. "He didn't write, Meg, or he couldn't?''

" 'Tis all one, ain't it?'' Meg hung her head over her knees, her voice muffled. " 'E kin write 'is name an' mine. But 'e left school fer service as soon as ever 'e cud, an' 'e di'n't learn nothin' while 'e was there.'' She raised her head. "Anyway,'' she added with an air of bitter certainty, "Marsh 'ates 'er ladyship. 'E'd niver kill fer 'er, even if she gave 'im fifty pounds. 'E didn't trust 'er, y'see, not after wot she did t' 'is father.''

"What did she do to his father?'' Kate asked.

"She blew off 'is leg,'' Mrs. Wospottle said factually. " 'E was a loader, an' she's a turr'ble bad gun, so 'tis said.''

Kate tenderly brushed the damp tendrils back from Meg's face. "You said 'they' killed him, Meg. Who were you speaking of? Who are 'they'?''

The girl's eyes grew round with a sudden fright, and she shook her head. "I daren't say,'' she whimpered. "They'll kill me, too.''

"They might do that anyway," Kate said with intentional roughness. "You will be safe only if you tell us who killed him and why, so they can be punished for their wrongdoing."

Meg shook her head wildly. "But then 'er ladyship'll find out about th' letter an' I'll lose me place!"

The letter? Of course! "*You* took the letter from Lady Warwick's letter case and put it in Lord Wallace's room?"

"Wot?" Mrs. Wospottle stiffened, horrified. "Ye stole a letter from th' mistress, Meg?"

The girl bit her lip, then nodded, reluctant. "Marsh tol' me t' do't. 'E said we'd git money for't."

"And you took Lady Warwick's gun, too?"

"Th' gun on th' floor in there?" Mrs. Wospottle asked, aghast. " 'Tis m'lady's?"

Meg nodded, the tears coursing down her cheeks. " 'Ow cud I know they'd use it t' kill 'im?"

Kate remembered that she and Charles had found the letter shortly after Meg had taken the sheets from Wallace's room. "And I suppose you tried to get the letter back, too," she said gently.

She nodded. "Marsh decided 'twas wrong, wot we done. 'E was goin' t' give back th' money they gave 'im an' go t' Lunnon straightaway." Her voice rose. "But they killed 'im!"

Kate tipped Meg's face up and spoke softly but firmly. "You must tell us who these people are, Meg. The Prince will protect you."

Mrs. Wospottle leaned forward. "The Prince?" she asked, awed. "Ooh, Meggie, ye've got t' tell. It's almost like the Queen's askin', me girl! 'Tis a R'yal command."

Meg was silent for a moment. "There was two, but Marsh only said one name," she said finally.

Kate stood and held out her hand. "One will do to start with."

Charles opened the door to the ironing room, steeling himself for what he would see there.

Before him, sitting slumped over a wooden table, was the still form of the dark-haired young man he had met in the

farrier's cottage the previous afternoon. Sadly, Charles remembered the sullen cast of the young man's face, his angry
look, the resentment in his voice. Was it his anger that had
brought him to this bitter end? Charles thought of the girl's
tearful protest that her lover had not killed himself. Was it
true? Was this a case of suicide—or of murder?

But there was no time for speculation. Charles went back to
the door of the main laundry room and asked Lawrence, loi-
tering there with the other curious servants, to bring the camera equipment from his bedroom, then returned to the death
scene. He surveyed the room carefully, taking in the coal-fired
boiler in the corner, the drying racks, the ironing table, the
mangle. Nothing seemed out of order, and he could see no
signs of a struggle. He glanced down at the floor to be sure he
would not step on anything of consequence, then approached
the table carefully, noting the empty whiskey bottle, the pencil
and paper, and the attitude of the body—the head pillowed on
the left arm, the right hand dangling, the silver-plated revolver
on the floor beside the right foot.

Marsh's eyes were open and vacant, and the dilation of
the pupils and lack of respiration confirmed that he was quite
dead, as did the coolness of the skin when Charles touched
the hand. A pronounced rigidity in the wrist and elbow confirmed that rigor mortis was well advanced. The entry wound
was located above the hairline in the right temple. It was
certainly consistent with suicide, he thought, but might
equally well have been inflicted by someone standing to the
victim's right. The blood that had puddled on the wooden
tabletop under the head and arm was already dry and crusty.
Marsh had been dead for a number of hours.

Bending over, Charles sniffed, and detected a sharp odor
of whiskey. Then, noticing a large patch of damp on the
sleeve of Marsh's coat, he sniffed there, and discovered the
source of the odor. The whiskey, or some part of it, had been
spilled on the sleeve. He glanced at the bottle, which was
covered with smudgy fingerprints. Did they belong to the
dead man, or to someone else?

Bending still further, he looked at the floor. It was lightly
dusted—probably the coal ash from the boiler—but there
were no discernible footprints. The gun that lay beside the

dead man's right foot, as if it had fallen from his dangling fingers, matched Daisy's description in every detail. Whose finger had pulled the trigger? Whose fingerprints might a closer examination reveal?

Charles straightened, suffused with a sad irony. He had met this young man less than eighteen hours ago; at a guess, he had been dead for six, perhaps even as many as ten of those hours. That would place the time of death before he and Kirk-Smythe had begun their fruitless vigil, perhaps even during the fireworks display, when the explosions would have masked the shot. But the laundry was isolated, here at the end of the corridor, and the walls were thick. Marsh might have been murdered as late as two a.m., when no one was abroad to hear.

There was one other thing: the note, which lay on the tabletop to the right of the victim's head. Taking a hand lens out of his pocket, Charles examined the scrap closely, being careful not to touch it. Pinpoint droplets of blood covered the table surface surrounding the note and yet the paper itself was clean, save for a blood-soaked corner. Charles scanned the few lines, printed in pencil. He was reading them for the third time when he heard a knock at the door.

He straightened and turned, his attention, as he did so, caught by an object on the floor to the right of the door. It was a cigar butt, no more than two inches long. His eyes lighted when he saw it, and he studied it for a moment, thoughtfully. His attention was recalled by a repeated knock, louder, this time.

"Who is it?" he asked.

Kate opened the door. "Lawrence is here with your camera equipment," she said. "And Meg has something important to tell you."

Meg appeared at the door, shuddered violently when she saw Marsh, and turned pale. Mrs. Wospottle put her arms around the girl, and as she did so, her eyes chanced on the cigar.

"There's th' wretched thing," she said, nettled. "I knew I smelled a cigar. Cheap, too."

Charles looked at her. "Do you know cigars?" he asked.

"Know cigars?" Mrs. Wospottle cried. "Fancy I do, at

that. Me father worked fer a tobacconist in Brighton. There wa'n't a cigar i' th' shop I cudn't sniff out wi' me eyes shut.''

"Splendid," Charles said. "We shall hear Meg's tale first. After that, p'rhaps you'll be good enough to enlighten us on the subject of cigars.''

30

Stop, let me have the truth of that!
  Is that all true?

—ROBERT BROWNING
  *"The Gods Thought
  Otherwise"*

The Prince was pacing restlessly in front of the desk in the library, mulling over what Charles had proposed. "I hope your strategy works," he said. "What will we do if it does not yield what you expect?"

"There are one or two other lines of inquiry I can pursue," Charles hedged. He hoped other inquiry would prove unnecessary. "It would be best to obtain a confession if we can, of course. If we do not, Your Highness will be faced with making a difficult and painful judgment on the basis of hearsay testimony and circumstantial evidence."

The Prince pulled a long face. "Are you certain this is the man we should confront first? What of his confederate?"

"I believe this man to be the agent provocateur," Charles said, "and not the actual assassin. For that reason he may be the more likely to confess. Further, we have the girl's word, hearsay though it is. Faced with that—"

"Ah, yes," said the Prince. "The girl's word." He shook his head. "A sad business, very sad. Well, are we ready to begin?"

"I believe so, sir," Charles said, and went to stand behind the corner of the desk. There was a discreet knock on the door.

"Sir Friedrich, Your Highness," the footman announced.

The Prince turned. "Ah, Freddy," he said affably. He straightened his waistcoat and shoved his cigar into his mouth. "Good of you to come so promptly."

Sir Friedrich inclined his head. "I am always at your command, Your Highness." He glanced dismissively at Charles and turned back to the Prince. "What's this about yet another death, Bertie? A suicide, was it?" He made a clucking sound. "Really, this is becoming quite beastly. Perhaps we had all best go back to London, where we are safe."

The Prince smiled thinly. "Indeed, yes. Beastly. But Charles assures me that we are near the bottom of the business. With your help, I believe we shall clear up the last bit."

"With my help?" Sir Friedrich asked, puzzlement written large on his features.

"Just so. I wonder, Freddy, old chap—would you mind taking a bit of dictation?"

The puzzlement became a frown. "With respect, sir, I rather think—"

"Would you mind?" the Prince repeated sharply. He gestured toward the writing table. "The pen and ink await you. Sit down."

Slowly, with obvious reluctance, Sir Friedrich seated himself on a chair at the writing table and picked up the pen Charles had placed there. "What is it you would have me write, Bertie?"

The Prince pursed his lips as if he were fashioning a thought. "Let's see now," he mused, hands behind his back, looking out the window. "How about this? 'Before I die, I wish to confess my complicity—' "

" 'Before I—'?" Sir Friedrich stared, blanching. The pen dropped from his fingers.

The Prince turned from the window. "Am I going too fast for you? Perhaps, then, I should recite the whole text, in order to refresh your memory. 'Before I die, I wish to confess my complicity in the death of Reginald Wallace. Lady Warwick gave me the gun and paid me to do the killing.' " He smiled, showing his teeth. "Shall we begin again? 'Before I die—' "

Temple did not pick up the pen.

"Come, come, man," the Prince said impatiently. "Why so reluctant? We merely want a specimen of your writing."

"For what purpose, if I may be so bold?" Sir Friedrich's voice, however, did not sound bold. It quavered.

"So that we may compare it with the note that was left with the body of the dead footman." The Prince nodded at Charles, who opened the desk drawer and took out the blood-stained note, holding it up by one corner so that it could be seen.

"Ah, yes," the Prince said. "That is the one. A most unfortunate note." He paused, and looked down at Sir Friedrich. "But then," he added regretfully, "I suppose I really don't need to draw this out. You are its author, are you not?"

"Bertie!" Sir Friedrich exclaimed in a horrified tone. "How can you ask such a question? It is beyond comprehension that a man of my breeding would stoop to such a thing."

The Prince was thoughtful. "Quite right," he said. "Beyond comprehension. Then how do you explain the fact that the first letters of the first two words of the suicide note, *Before* and *I*, bear a remarkable similarity to these in the letter you posted to Lord Brooke just last week, which begins with the very same two words? 'Before I depart for Easton . . . ' "

The Prince held out his hand and Charles gave him a folded letter, which he unfolded and made a great show of studying. "Yes," he remarked after a moment, "the two capital letters look extraordinarily alike, even to my unpracticed eye. I daresay an expert in graphology would see more similarities." He glanced up. "You must have been terribly pressed, Freddy. Otherwise you would have tried to disguise your handwriting. But then, you could not copy your victim's hand, could you? The poor boy could scarcely write. The word *complicity* would have been beyond him."

Sir Friedrich made a gulping noise.

"There is also the small matter of the blood," the Prince said. "Charles points out that the table surface under the note was spattered with blood, while the note itself, as you can see, bears bloodstains only in one corner—clearly indicating that the note was placed on the table after the man was shot. Would you not agree?''

Sir Friedrich had turned quite pale, but he said nothing.

The Prince became brisk. ''Well, if you do not feel like writing just now, we shall proceed to the other business. Charles, you have your ink case, do you not?''

''Yes, sir,'' Charles said, and produced a lidded tin box which contained a felt pad saturated with black ink. He was not entirely happy about this demonstration, but His Highness, obviously intrigued by the business of fingerprinting, had insisted.

''Ink?'' Sir Friedrich asked faintly.

''You will find this process most interesting, Freddy,'' the Prince said. ''Charles will take impressions of your inked fingertips, you see, and compare them against impressions left on a whiskey bottle found at the scene of the crime.'' He paused to knock the ash off his cigar into a gilt-edged ashtray. ''I do suppose that you can explain why you and Milford Knightly were drinking with a footman in the laundry?''

''Bertie—'' Temple made an ineffectual gesture, as if to ward off the accusation.

The Prince held up his hand. ''There's more, Freddy. When we have done with the whiskey bottle, we shall compare your fingerprints with those drawn from the murder weapon and from a certain letter.'' The Prince turned to Charles, who opened the desk drawer and produced both. ''*My* letter,'' he added pointedly. ''A private letter, written to Lady Warwick, stolen from her room, and planted in Reggie's bedchamber.''

Sir Friedrich's jaw was working. ''Sir, I—''

''The footman, you see, revealed that you paid him to obtain my letter and Lady Warwick's gun, and later to hide the letter.''

''Revealed?'' Sir Friedrich's face was shocked and white. ''But he is dead! How could he—?''

''Quite so. But unhappily for you, his accomplice—the young woman he coerced into doing the deed for him—is *not* dead. She is prepared to testify to your connivance in this affair.'' His face darkened and he raised his voice, all amiability vanished. "Come, sir!" he thundered. "Do you take me for a fool? Do you continue to deny your complicity in the face of overwhelming physical evidence? Speak, man! I'll have the truth!"

The Royal performance was masterful, Charles thought, and almost made up for the fact that the evidence was not nearly so overwhelming as the Prince implied. To say that the handwriting was similar was a stretch, and as for finger-prints, a match would be obtained only by the greatest good luck. No, what was needed was a confession, and the Prince was the only person powerful enough to obtain it.

There was a knock at the door and an ashen Lord War-wick entered. "I am very sorry to disturb you, Bertie, but it is a matter of great urgency."

"Well?" The Prince was not pleased that his oratory had been interrupted at such a crucial point. "Out with it, Brooke!"

"Milford Knightly has bolted. At your orders, I sent the house steward and two footmen to apprehend him, but he eluded them and made for the stable, where he comman-deered your hunter, which the grooms were exercising."

Sir Friedrich gave a dismayed gasp. Charles, however, could hardly conceal his elation. Flight was as good as a confession.

"Commandeered Paradox, by Jove?" the Prince ex-claimed, slapping his hand flat on the desk top. "We shall hang the fool for a horse thief, if nothing else. You've sent someone after him?"

Lord Warwick nodded. "Kirk-Smythe went in pursuit, the grooms after."

"Tip-top." The Prince gave a gratified grunt. "I'll wager a hundred pounds that we'll have the scoundrel within the half hour. It will be a cold day in hell when Kirk-Smythe can't ride down that loathsome little fellow—if Paradox doesn't dispose of him first."

"I'll just go down and wait, then, Bertie," Lord Warwick said. "When there's news—"

"When there's news," the Prince said authoritatively, "send it here directly."

When Lord Warwick had gone, the Prince turned back to

Sir Friedrich with a Hanoverian scowl. "Now, sir, will you speak? Or shall we twiddle our thumbs until your fellow conspirator is hauled back before us? I warrant you *he* will be quick enough to testify to your guilt."

Charles had been watching Sir Friedrich. The man seemed to have regained his composure, perhaps because he had decided that he had nothing to lose. The only course open to him was defiance.

"Oh, very well," he said crossly. "I have done nothing to be ashamed of. My actions were entirely in the interest of the Crown, and carried out at the instigation of the Crown."

The Prince grew red-faced and his massive chest swelled. "You insult me, sir!" he said icily. "Do you dare to suggest that the blood on your hands is *my* responsibility?"

Sir Friedrich shook his head. "The murders were not my doing," he muttered.

"You accuse Knightly of all three murders?"

"Knightly did not intend to kill the boy," Sir Friedrich said sourly. "The lad inadvertently overheard part of a conversation between Reggie and myself in the stable on Friday morning. Knightly struck him from behind, merely intending to render him unconscious. Unfortunately, he struck too hard. Reggie witnessed the boy's death, then threatened to reveal to you what he had seen, which he might well have done after dinner on Friday night if you had not cut him off."

"Ah," the Prince said sadly, "so Reggie was murdered to insure his silence."

"I would have found another way to keep Wallace quiet," Sir Friedrich said, "but Knightly had borrowed from him to make good a gambling debt, and wanted to be rid of the fellow. Reggie was threatening to expose him as a murderer, a conspirator, *and* a deadbeat." He looked down his nose. "The third man killed, the footman, was an Anarchist. Left alive to carry on his violent ideas, he was a danger to the Crown. Dead, he was no loss to anyone, not even himself."

Charles stepped around the desk. "And what was the nature of the conversation between you and Wallace in the stable?" he asked, drawing the man back to the subject. "What was the purpose of your conspiracy?"

Sir Friedrich threw him a black look but did not answer.

"Let's hear your scheme," the Prince demanded. "Come now, Freddy! I'll have the truth!"

Sir Friedrich looked squarely at the Prince. "Very well. I planned to use your letter to Lady Warwick as a means of compelling you, or her, to end your foolish relationship. That was all I intended. These murders—" He waved his hand. "They were incidental to my purpose. They had nothing to do with me."

"You intended to blackmail us!" The Prince looked thunderstruck.

"Ah," Charles said softly. "And you expected to implicate Lady Warwick in Wallace's murder by using her gun and leaving it at the scene of the crime."

"It was Knightly's scheme to murder him," Sir Friedrich said. "It certainly seemed clever enough at the time." His glance went to the Prince. "I knew, of course, that you would never allow the Countess to be brought to trial."

"But Marsh was also a threat," Charles said thoughtfully, "having procured the letter and the weapon for you." He paused. "I wonder you did not kill him the same night Wallace was murdered."

"*I* was not involved, as you well know, Sheridan." Sir Friedrich's voice was brittle. "I was in Lillian Forsythe's bed."

"That was very clever, too," Charles said. "I don't suppose she suspected that she was merely your alibi."

"But Knightly had an alibi, too, did he not?" asked the Prince.

"If we were to question his wife closely," Charles said, "I imagine we would learn that he left her shortly after they retired and was gone for a half hour or so."

The Prince still looked puzzled. "If the footman was a threat, why *wasn't* he killed on Friday night? And why wasn't the gun left beside Reggie?"

"The gun was not left there because it was needed to kill Marsh," Sir Friedrich said patiently. "After he had written the note accusing Lady Warwick, of course. But Marsh did not appear at Friday night's appointed meeting. It was only the expectation of a large reward that induced him to meet us last night."

The Prince frowned. "And he proved more reluctant than expected to write his own suicide note. So you shot him first and wrote it for him."

"I did no killing," Sir Friedrich insisted. "It was all Knightly's work."

The Prince snorted. "Well, my fine friend, we shall see what he says about *you*."

Sir Friedrich lifted his shoulders in an almost insolent shrug. "As you say, Bertie."

"You make very bold, sir!" the Prince exclaimed, narrowing his eyes. "You dare to—"

"And what if I do?" Sir Friedrich's eyes blazed with a sudden cold scorn. "I tell you, Bertie, I love this kingdom and the Queen. I will not stand idly by while the man who would succeed her makes a laughingstock of all whom the country must reverence, respect, yes, even fear! Your blessed mother herself asked—no, *begged*—me to curb your excesses. She knows that, should you continue unrestrained, allowing your 'darling Daisy' to drag you through one filthy scandal after another, permitting her to turn you toward Socialism, you will be the ruin of the monarchy and the undoing of England as we know it!"

So that was the motive behind the scheme, Charles thought. He had not been far off the mark.

The Prince snorted contemptuously. "My mama is known for her meddling, but I doubt she would countenance murder. *Three* murders, sir, including that of a lad of barely fifteen. You cannot possibly fancy that the Queen would look kindly on such an enterprise. And you cannot escape by blaming Knightly. You are his accomplice."

"Well, then, what of it?" Sir Friedrich demanded. "You cannot try Knightly or me in any court in the land. Weak and profligate as you are in the mind of the people, the public scrutiny of this sordid affair would be your total undoing. Why do you think I have told you all this? The Queen will never let it out."

"You might have hid behind Mama's skirts before you bloodied your hands, Temple," the Prince growled, "but she is no protection to you now that you have connived at murder."

Temple's smile was mocking. "Then try me, Bertie."

"You have had your trial, sir," the Prince said magisterially. "All that remains is the pronouncement of your sentence."

There was a commotion in the courtyard outside, and all three men turned toward the window. A single rider had reined up and dismounted. Through the open draperies, Charles saw that the rider was Kirk-Smythe. A few moments later, he was at the door, breathing hard.

"I am sorry to report, Your Highness, that my mission was a failure."

"Gave you the slip, eh?" the Prince grunted. "Well, Paradox is a fast horse. You're not to be faulted. But we shall have that rascal yet."

Kirk-Smythe shook his head. "I am afraid not, sir. Your hunter refused the wall at the far end of the south meadow, and Knightly was thrown. His head struck a stone. He's dead, sir."

There was a silence. "Poetic justice," said the Prince at last. "That horse has a greater intelligence than most men I know."

Sir Friedrich let out his breath. "It is all over, then."

"No," the Prince said. "It has just begun. For some time, we have needed a commissioner to manage the border issues on the northwest frontier of India. A sticky business, that, Temple. It may require five, perhaps even ten years for you to settle affairs there."

"India!" Sir Friedrich gasped. "But I don't want—"

The Prince pulled himself up to his full height. "What you want is of very little concern to me, my man. Duty calls, and India beckons."

31

The end is what the means have made it.

—JOHN MORLEY
Critical Miscellanies

Monday morning was chill and moist, and the fog was draped in the trees like tulle around a lady's shoulders. Subdued, the guests took their departure in small groups or one by one, until only a few were left. When the Prince was prepared to leave, Kate, Charles, and the Warwicks gathered on the stone steps to say good-bye and wish him a safe journey to Sandringham, whence he was returning.

"And there," he said expansively, "I shall gather Alix and her retinue, and we shall make our way to Scotland for some fine grouse shooting." He raised an imaginary gun to his shoulder, sighted it, and said, "Blam." Kate, who had not seen this unprincely gesture before, hid a smile of amusement.

Lord Warwick bowed from the waist. "We have been deeply honored to have you with us, Your Highness," he said formally. "We hope you will return very soon."

The Prince patted his stout midriff. "I certainly shall, if your chef continues to prepare those quails stuffed with foie gras and garnished with oysters. Birds fit for a king!" He turned to Daisy. "My deepest thanks for your hospitality, Lady Warwick. It has certainly been a most memorable weekend."

Daisy dropped a deep curtsy. "I fear it is one we are not

likely to forget, Sire—though I am certain we should all wish to."

"Ah, yes," the Prince said reflectively. "I think we can count ourselves fortunate to have avoided a scandal." He raised his eyebrows at Lord Warwick. "You know what you are to do, Brookie?"

"I am to inform the coroner—who, by good chance, sir, is close to the family—that Mr. Knightly ran amok and murdered Lord Wallace and a footman, then stole your horse. He died in his attempted escape."

"Excellent. Kirk-Smythe will testify on my behalf, if required. He left early this morning to escort Temple to Portsmouth, where the man will be handed over to the captain of one of the Queen's warships, bound for Bombay. And I shall personally inform Mama of the events of the weekend."

The Prince, Kate thought, seemed well pleased with the way in which the matter had been disposed. He turned to Charles with a vast smile. "Ah, Charles. Once again, I must thank you for your first-rate investigation. If it had not been for you, the scheme would have escaped detection; indeed, it might even have succeeded. All of us are in your debt."

Charles bowed slightly. "It was mostly luck, sir, and Kate's skillful questioning of the laundry maid. If she hadn't persuaded the girl to name Temple, I might still be trying to discover recognizable fingerprints on the whiskey bottle and pistol. And it was great good luck that the laundress was able to identify the brand of Knightly's cigar."

The Prince shook his head. "I always told Milford those cheap cigars of his were abominable," he said. "I never understood why the deuce he fancied the filthy things."

Kate turned to Daisy. "What's to become of Meg?" she asked. "What she did was very wrong, but she is a good girl who was led astray by her love for Marsh. I hope she won't be turned out."

"I think not," Daisy said. "She could have had no idea of the damage her actions might cause. And she has already paid dearly."

"Ah, yes," the Prince said. "Love can make people behave quite foolishly." He became lost in thought for a moment, then roused himself. Turning to Charles, he said,

"Speaking of love, when is the great day? I am sure Alix will join me in wishing to attend."

"Lord Warwick and I would like to come, too, of course," Daisy said.

Kate felt a rush of alarm. If Royalty and aristocracy were to attend the wedding, they would be followed by the press and crowds of the curious, and the ceremony would be turned into a circus. But she need not have been concerned. Charles spoke firmly.

"We plan, sir, to marry very quietly, on account of my brother's situation, you see. As to the date, we have not yet set it." He took Kate's hand and pulled her close to him. "When we leave here, we are going to Somersworth to tell my family the news. Kate refuses to fix a date until Mother has been consulted."

"Commendable, my dear," said the Prince approvingly, "quite commendable. I am sure that the Dowager Baroness will be delighted by her son's choice of a bride. And she will be relieved by the prospect of a continuance of the Somersworth line."

Kate felt a small shiver of cold apprehension. She was not at all sure that Charles's mother would be pleased, and as for the continuance of the Somersworth line, it was something she and Charles had not yet discussed. She supposed there would be children, of course, although Beryl Bardwell was not overjoyed by the thought.

"Now, Charles," the Prince went on, "you must not forget our talk about the national crime laboratory. I am convinced that you are just the man to administer such an undertaking. I realize that it will be some time before your family responsibilities permit it, but we shall speak of the matter again."

"Yes, sir," Charles said, resigned.

The Prince straightened his waistcoat and hung his walking stick over his arm. "Well, I suppose it is time to be off. No need to confound schedules all up and down the line."

Lord Warwick bowed. "Lady Warwick insists on having the honor of driving you to the station, sir. The pony cart is ready in front of the stable."

"Then we shall be off," the Prince said.

As Kate and Charles stood alone together on the steps, waving good-bye to the Prince and Daisy as they trotted down the lane in the pony cart, Kate said, "What do you suppose will happen to their relationship, Charles?"

Charles put his arm around Kate's shoulders. "I should think HRH will shortly convince himself that it is time to find another mistress," he said. "Daisy is a fascinating woman, but she will continue to invite controversy—something he can no longer afford."

The door opened behind them and Bradford stepped out. "Oh, there you are," he said. "I have been looking for you. Poor Ellie is feeling beastly, I am afraid, and has asked me to escort her back to London. I wonder, Charles, old man— would you be so kind as to drive the motorcar back to Marsden Manor? I can send Lawrence along to help out."

"But I am returning with Kate," Charles said. "We were planning to stop at Somersworth to tell Mother about our engagement."

"That's all right, Charles," Kate said eagerly. "I would love to have a ride in the motorcar. Perhaps you can even teach me to drive it!"

Bradford shook his head in mock horror. "I fancied the Dowager Baroness would look askance at your riding a bicycle, Kate. What will she think if you arrive at the tiller of an automobile?"

"I am afraid Mother must make certain concessions," Charles said with a laugh. "The future Lady Somersworth is likely to be quite irrepressible."

HISTORICAL NOTE

The "darling Daisy affair" was the most notorious Royal affair of its day. The Prince of Wales had enjoyed many women before he took Daisy to his bed, and his profligate habits ("this corpulent voluptuary," Rudyard Kipling called him) were well-known throughout the kingdom. Victoria's conviction that his recklessness would incite the poor to destroy the Crown was fed by diatribes against him in the press and in Parliament. "The Prince of Wales must never dishonour the country by becoming King," said one antimonarchist.

The affair began in 1889, when Daisy Brooke, Countess of Warwick, went to Marlborough House to beg the Prince of Wales to intercede with the angry wife of Charles Beresford, Daisy's former lover, who had threatened her with public humiliation over a foolish letter she had written. "Suddenly I saw him looking at me in a way all women understand," Daisy said, and they became lovers. Their relationship continued until sometime in 1896 or 1897. Daisy was a complex woman whose very real desires to do good were constantly overwhelmed by her poor judgment, abominable business sense, and enormous extravagances. It is entirely plausible to imagine, as we have done in this fiction, that the Royal relationship ended because the impulsive Daisy, who was deeply interested in radical political causes, posed too many dangers to the monarchy, and that her efforts to convert the Prince to her ideas were viewed by many at Buckingham Palace as profoundly threatening. Daisy was replaced in 1898 by Alice Keppel, a much more tractable, docile woman who did as she was told. Bertie became king in

1901. The Keppel liaison continued until his death in 1910.

The story of Daisy's affair with Bertie does not end with their sexual liaison, however. In 1914, on the eve of the Great War, Daisy threatened to sell Bertie's letters (including the "adored little Daisy wife" letter we quote in the headnote to Chapter Twenty-One) to an American publisher unless Buckingham Palace paid her a hundred thousand pounds. A year later, her scheme paid off, and she was given sixty-four thousand pounds to hand over the letters. A few, however, made their way to Switzerland, where they came to light in the 1960s, and with them the story of Daisy's blackmail.

The money Daisy received for the letters was not enough to erase her debts, but it wouldn't have mattered anyway, since she never changed her spendthrift ways, foolishly lavishing money on well-meant but often ill-conceived causes. She became an avowed Socialist and ran as a Labor candidate for Parliament in 1923, but she was never accepted by the people she sought to help. Even her efforts to give Easton Lodge to the Trade Union Congress as an international Socialist university were ultimately rejected. The long-suffering Lord Warwick died in 1924, on the verge of bankruptcy, and Daisy's assets by then had dwindled to almost nothing.

"When 'they' write my obituary notice," she wrote in her memoirs, "it should be the record of a woman who feverishly designed many things for the betterment of human lives, while the 'Green Gods' sat smiling at the puny efforts of an imprisoned soul trying to find a way of escape." In the 1930s, she retired to Easton Lodge, where she lived as an eccentric recluse. When thieves ransacked the estate two months prior to her death in 1938, they found little to carry off. In World War II, what remained of the park was turned into a military airfield, and in 1947 the hulk of the lodge was demolished.

Nothing remains of Daisy's Folly.

Bill and Susan Albert
AKA Robin Paige

REFERENCES

For this series, we have consulted numerous primary and secondary sources. The books listed here were most helpful to us.

Blunden, Margaret. *The Countess of Warwick*. London: Cassell & Company, 1967.

Brooke, Frances, Countess of Warwick. *Discretions*. New York: Scribners, 1931.

Brooke, Francis, Earl of Warwick. *Memories of Sixty Years*. London: Cassell & Company, 1917.

Girouard, Mark. *Life in the English Country House*. New Haven: Yale University Press, 1978.

Hough, Richard. *Edward and Alexandra: Their Private & Public Lives*. New York: St. Martin's Press, 1992.

Lang, Theodore. *The Darling Daisy Affair*. New York: Atheneum, 1966.

Montague, Lord, and F. Wilson McComb. *Behind the Wheel: The Magic & Manners of Early Motoring*. London: Paddington Press, 1977.

Thorwald, Jurgen. *The Century of the Detective*. New York: Harcourt Brace, 1965.

ROBIN PAIGE

The Victorian Mystery Series

Read all the adventures of Lord Charles Sheridan and his clever American wife, Kate.

"AN ORIGINAL AND INTELLIGENT SLEUTH...A VIVID RECREATION OF VICTORIAN ENGLAND."
—JEAN HAGAR